REVELATION

THE PROTECTORS #7

SLOANE KENNEDY

CONTENTS

Copyright	v
Revelation	vii
Trademark Acknowledgements	ix
Acknowledgments	xi
Series Reading Order	xiii
Series Crossover Chart	xvii
Trigger Warning	xix
revelation	xxi
Prologue	1
Chapter 1	15
Chapter 2	22
Chapter 3	32
Chapter 4	40
Chapter 5	50
Chapter 6	63
Chapter 7	77
Chapter 8	88
Chapter 9	98
Chapter 10	106
Chapter 11	117
Chapter 12	130
Chapter 13	140
Chapter 14	152
Chapter 15	163
Chapter 16	174
Chapter 17	185
Chapter 18	190
Chapter 19	201
Chapter 20	205
Epilogue	216

Sneak Peek	233
Prologue	235
About the Author	245
Also by Sloane Kennedy	247

Revelation is a work of fiction. Names, characters, businesses, places, events and incidents are either the products of the author's imagination or used in a fictitious manner. Any resemblance to actual persons, living or dead, or actual events is purely coincidental.

Copyright © 2017 by Sloane Kennedy

Published in the United States by Sloane Kennedy
All rights reserved. This book or any portion thereof may not be reproduced or used in any manner whatsoever without the express written permission of the publisher except for the use of brief quotations in a book review.

Cover Images: ©Wander Aguiar

Cover Design: © Jay Aheer, Simply Defined Art

ISBN-13:
978-1544919713

ISBN-10:
1544919719

REVELATION

Sloane Kennedy

TRADEMARK ACKNOWLEDGEMENTS

The author acknowledges the trademarked status and trademark owners of the following trademarks mentioned in this work of fiction:

Tupperware
Facebook

ACKNOWLEDGMENTS

A big thank you to my soul sisters Mari, Claudia and Kylee for being a sounding board for me!

As always, thanks to my betas, Claudia and Kylee.

SERIES READING ORDER

All of my series cross over with one another so I've provided a couple of recommended reading orders for you. If you want to start with the Protectors books, use the first list. If you want to follow the books according to timing, use the second list. Note that you can skip any of the books (including M/F) as each was written to be a standalone story.

Note that some books may not be readily available on all retail sites

Recommended Reading Order *(Use this list if you want to start with "The Protectors" series)*
1. Absolution (m/m/m) (The Protectors, #1)
2. Salvation (m/m) (The Protectors, #2)
3. Retribution (m/m) (The Protectors, #3)
4. Gabriel's Rule (m/f) (The Escort Series, #1)
5. Shane's Fall (m/f) (The Escort Series, #2)
6. Logan's Need (m/m) (The Escort Series, #3)
7. Finding Home (m/m/m) (Finding Series, #1)
8. Finding Trust (m/m) (Finding Series, #2)

9. Loving Vin (m/f) (Barretti Security Series, #1)
10. Redeeming Rafe (m/m) (Barretti Security Series, #2)
11. Saving Ren (m/m/m) (Barretti Security Series, #3)
12. Freeing Zane (m/m) (Barretti Security Series, #4)
13. Finding Peace (m/m) (Finding Series, #3)
14. Finding Forgiveness (m/m) (Finding Series, #4)
15. Forsaken (m/m) (The Protectors, #4)
16. Vengeance (m/m/m) (The Protectors, #5)
17. A Protectors Family Christmas (The Protectors, #5.5)
18. Atonement (m/m) (The Protectors, #6)
19. Revelation (m/m) (The Protectors, #7)
20. Redemption (m/m) (The Protectors, #8)
21. Finding Hope (m/m/m) (Finding Series, #5)
22. Defiance (m/m) (The Protectors #9)

Recommended Reading Order *(Use this list if you want to follow according to timing)*
1. Gabriel's Rule (m/f) (The Escort Series, #1)
2. Shane's Fall (m/f) (The Escort Series, #2)
3. Logan's Need (m/m) (The Escort Series, #3)
4. Finding Home (m/m/m) (Finding Series, #1)
5. Finding Trust (m/m) (Finding Series, #2)
6. Loving Vin (m/f) (Barretti Security Series, #1)
7. Redeeming Rafe (m/m) (Barretti Security Series, #2)
8. Saving Ren (m/m/m) (Barretti Security Series, #3)
9. Freeing Zane (m/m) (Barretti Security Series, #4)
10. Finding Peace (m/m) (Finding Series, #3)
11. Finding Forgiveness (m/m) (Finding Series, #4)
12. Absolution (m/m/m) (The Protectors, #1)
13. Salvation (m/m) (The Protectors, #2)
14. Retribution (m/m) (The Protectors, #3)
15. Forsaken (m/m) (The Protectors, #4)
16. Vengeance (m/m/m) (The Protectors, #5)
17. A Protectors Family Christmas (The Protectors, #5.5)

18. Atonement (m/m) (The Protectors, #6)
19. Revelation (m/m) (The Protectors, #7)
20. Redemption (m/m) (The Protectors, #8)
21. Finding Hope (m/m/m) (Finding Series, #5)
22. Defiance (m/m) (The Protectors #9)

SERIES CROSSOVER CHART

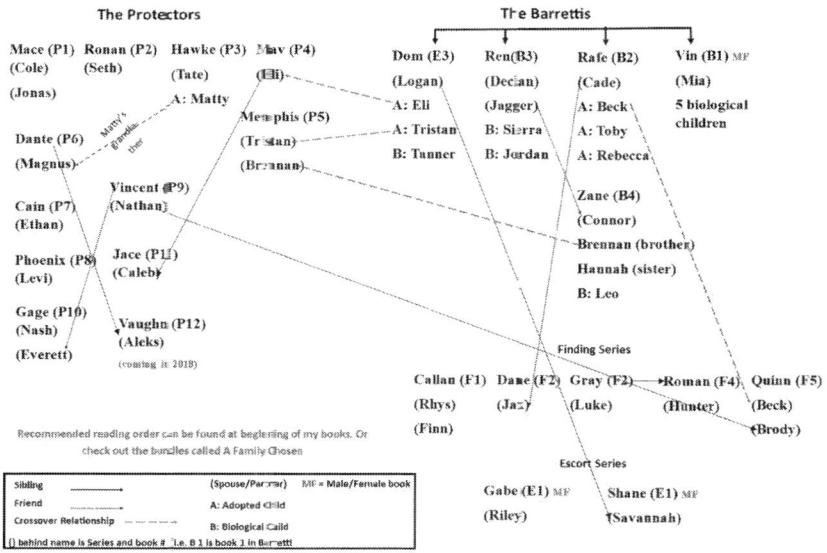

TRIGGER WARNING

Listed below are the trigger warnings for this book. Reading them may cause spoilers:

This book contains references to domestic abuse and sexual assault.

REVELATION

noun rev·e·la·tion \ˌre-və-ˈlā-shən\

A pleasant, often enlightening surprise.

PROLOGUE

CAIN

"Thanks for coming," Ronan said as he nodded at me. I was glad he didn't extend his hand to me. It wasn't that I didn't respect the man – I did...a whole hell of a lot. But touching wasn't my thing and never had been. Luckily, Ronan Grisham and his second-in-command, Memphis Wheland, the two men I dealt with on a regular basis as part of my job, had picked up early on that physical contact was something I liked to steer clear of and they'd respected the boundary.

I nodded and followed Ronan up the stairs of a small, remote house that was located on several acres about thirty miles east of Seattle. The house itself was a run-down piece of shit, but the property was appealing since you could see anyone coming from a ways off and there weren't any immediate neighbors.

The early February air was chilly and damp around us as we each examined our surroundings. There were no vehicles except ours and all the curtains on the front of the house were drawn. I didn't ask what we were doing there because Ronan would tell me when he was good and ready.

Ronan's knock on the front door went unanswered. Since I doubted he'd brought me all the way out here just to visit with whoever lived in the dump, I was about to go back to my truck to get my tools to pick the lock when Ronan reached down and turned the knob. I stiffened when it turned and automatically reached for my gun at the same time Ronan reached for his. He gave me a slight nod and then pushed the door open.

To say the place was a mess was an understatement. I let my eyes adjust to the darkness as I carefully stepped over an overturned side table near the door. Ronan motioned to me and I quickly followed his silent order to clear the house. Debris littered the floor of each room so it took longer than I would have liked to sweep the two rooms near the back of the house while Ronan checked the main living spaces. By the time I met him back in the living room, he was drawing a curtain back to let in some light since the power didn't appear to be working.

Even if the place hadn't been trashed, calling it a dump would have been kind. The furniture was decades old, the thick carpet beneath my feet actually turned out to be a shag carpet that was a disgusting shade of yellow, and the paneled wood walls made the already dreary space darker and even more uninviting, which I wouldn't have thought was even possible. Junk was all over the floor, but it didn't look like actual garbage. More like a mix of clothes, papers and the remnants of some of the cheap wood furniture that had probably once served as a coffee table or set of end tables. The couch was shredded, as was the single armchair in the room. The small eating area outside the kitchen had an overturned table and three broken chairs strewn all over the floor. It looked a lot like someone had broken the chairs over the table. I also saw dents in the wall and guessed that whoever had been smashing the chairs on the table also had taken their aggression out on the walls. There were a few cheap motel style pictures on the floor, their glass overlays shattered.

Ronan and I moved to the kitchen to examine the damage there. Unlike the living room, the stained linoleum floor was covered in garbage and food that had been removed from the open refrigerator. The freezer was open and its contents empty, but I could see a layer of ice still encasing the small space.

Whoever had trashed the place had done it recently – within the last 24 hours at the most, more likely twelve.

"Ronan," I said as I motioned to the edge of one of the countertops. Blood.

The light in the kitchen was poor so we each pulled our phones out and used the flashlights to take a closer look. There was more blood splattered on the backsplash above the sink and several droplets in the sink itself.

I followed Ronan to the two bedrooms. One actually looked untouched, but there was nothing interesting about the room itself. A twin bed with a basic blanket and single pillow and a three-drawer dresser that looked like it was at least thirty years old. Nothing more. No pictures on the walls, no clothes in the closet. The second bedroom was the exact opposite. Whoever had destroyed it had been in a rage. The mattress from the full bed was overturned and shredded on both sides. An endless assortment of clothes covered much of the floor, ripped to pieces along with what looked like the remnants of a torn duffle bag.

Men's clothes.

Ronan leaned down and picked up a light blue piece of fabric that I realized had once been a shirt. But not an ordinary shirt – it was the top from a set of scrubs.

Ronan let out a deep breath.

We continued our examination of the room and found more sprays of blood near the door, along with a larger pool of blood by the closet. Blood was also smeared on the side of the dresser.

The clear evidence of a violent encounter had my insides drawing up tight. How many times had I seen this same scene? How many times had I stood just like I was now – completely and utterly helpless to do anything about it?

"Ronan," I murmured as my eyes fell on something near the bed. I ignored the bloodstains on the mattress and stepped through the debris, grabbing a piece of clothing to pick up the frying pan that had caught my eye. Except it was no ordinary frying pan...it was a heavy cast iron skillet and there was dried blood along one edge of it.

Ronan studied it for a moment and frowned. "Let's talk outside," he said. I put the pan back down as we left the room. Ronan stopped in the living room long enough to close the curtain since we needed to leave the place exactly as we'd found it. On the way out the door, he used the edge of his jacket to wipe his prints from the doorknob.

Ronan's phone rang before he could say anything as we started walking towards our cars. He listened for a few moments before saying, "Send the location to Cain's phone."

I tensed even as a flurry of excitement went through me. It had been a while since I'd seen any kind of real action on the job. The last time had been when I'd gone with Memphis to rough up some guys who'd threatened one of his lovers. But it had been Memphis's show, so watching was pretty much all I'd gotten to do.

Ronan hung up the phone and tucked it into his pocket. His eyes settled on me. "You know I started back at the hospital a couple weeks ago, right?"

I nodded. I'd met Ronan Grisham a few years earlier when he'd offered me a role in his underground vigilante organization. He'd been heading the group at that time, but his recent marriage to a young man he'd known for years had had him rethinking his position as leader and he'd ultimately decided to return to his roots as a trauma surgeon. The newly minted family man who, along with his husband, had taken in three foster kids two months earlier had gone legit, though he still continued to finance the group. He'd handed the reins of the day to day operations over to Memphis.

"I was doing a shift in the ER night before last," Ronan began. "There'd been a fifteen-car pile-up on the freeway that night and we were jammed. All hands-on deck kind of thing. One of the interns sent a patient to radiology without doing a proper exam. The patient ended up going into respiratory failure before they could even get him on the elevator."

"Okay," I said, though I had no clue why he was telling me all of this.

"The guy transporting him called a code and got him back to the

ER. The intern who'd seen the patient panicked when he couldn't tube the guy."

At what I suspected was my confused look, Ronan clarified, "He couldn't get a tube down the guy's throat to help him breathe."

I nodded.

"He needed to do a tracheostomy. That's where you cut an incision into the windpipe and insert the tube that way."

"Okay."

"The intern froze. The nurse who was with him went to find another doctor, but we had three other codes going on at the time. There wasn't anyone to do it." Ronan paused. "By the time I got there after getting my own patient stabilized, the tracheostomy had been done and they'd gotten the guy's vitals stable again. Problem was, it wasn't the intern who performed the procedure." Ronan held my gaze for a moment. "The nurse told me it was the transporter who did it."

It took me a moment to understand what Ronan was saying. A transporter's job was to move patients back and forth between departments – no way in hell that person would have been qualified to perform that kind of medical procedure.

"The transporter – his name was Allen – took off after they got the patient back. I found him in the locker room getting his stuff out of his locker. He tried to deny what he'd done...then he started apologizing. He began jamming his stuff into his bag and then he was gone. I couldn't leave the ER to follow him..."

I nodded. "This is where he lives," I said as I motioned to the house.

Ronan nodded. "I got his address from the hospital's employment records."

I knew what that meant and I was certain he hadn't just waltzed into that department and simply asked them to let him see the records.

"My plan was just to talk to him yesterday when he was scheduled to work again, but he didn't show up for that shift or this morning's. So I figured I'd come here to check it out. Only a qualified medical professional can do that kind of procedure, and from the way he did it, I could tell it wasn't the first time he'd done it."

"So why would someone like that be masquerading as a transporter," I observed.

"I thought maybe he'd had a pulled medical license or something, but there's no record of him having had a medical license in any state under the name he gave HR."

"You think he used a fake name?" I asked.

Ronan nodded. "I had Daisy check his application. None of the information on it checks out...the name and social security number he used belongs to someone who died ten years ago."

"He's on the run," I murmured. "Why not call the cops?" I asked.

Ronan was quiet for a moment. "I agree he's on the run, but not necessarily from the law. Just a feeling," he added. "I met him a few times before that night...he was well-spoken and seemed familiar with the chaos that comes with working in a busy ER. But there was something else about him too. I never sensed he was any kind of threat."

I nodded because I didn't really need to know anymore. Ronan knew his shit. If he felt there was something off about the whole thing, he was probably right. And judging from the scene inside the house, he was a hundred percent on the mark.

My phone beeped and I pulled it out to see a text from Daisy, the girl who handled the IT for the group. I showed Ronan the screen. He nodded.

"I was able to find the form he filled out for his parking pass. He put a valid license plate on it. Daisy tracked the car – it's listed under the guy's alias so he probably paid cash for it at some point when he bought it. It's an older car, but it has a customer assistance feature. Even though it wasn't active..."

"Daisy was still able to hack their system and get his GPS location."

Ronan nodded. "I'd like you to check it out. Feel the guy out. If we need to bring the cops in, we will, but based on this" – Ronan glanced at the house – "I'm more inclined to keep them out of it for a while.

The house is a rental, so I suspect it will be a while before the landlord realizes anything is up."

I nodded in understanding and glanced at the location Daisy had sent me. "He's in the Cascades," I said. "Near Mt. Baker."

Ronan merely said, "Keep me posted and be careful."

I didn't respond as I watched him go to his car. I was both intrigued and leery of the situation. Ronan might think the guy was harmless or in trouble, but I'd seen enough to know that even the most average Joe could be hiding a wealth of evil that no one would have suspected in a million years.

Hell, I had the scars to prove it.

I sighed and tucked my phone in my pocket. I had a long drive ahead of me and no idea what I'd find at the end of the journey.

~

I'd known the weather would be an issue as I made my way farther and farther up into the mountains, but once my truck began sliding back and forth along the narrow, winding snow-covered road leading to the location my GPS was pinging on, I began to regret not putting chains on my tires. Not that they would have done much good, especially since I had nothing to weigh down the empty bed of the truck.

I risked a glance at the GPS screen and saw that I was only a mile from my destination, but with the heavy snow and blowing wind, it may as well have been twenty. I forced my body to relax as a particularly strong gust of wind made the truck swing wildly towards the opposite side of the road. With no guard rail and a sheer drop off, there was only one certain outcome if the truck plunged over the edge, and while I couldn't say I was particularly fearsome of death, I wasn't actively seeking it out.

I slowed the truck as the road began turning away from the cliff's edge and began heading inward. A new sense of focus shimmied through me as I was once again surrounded by dense forest on each side. The wind continued to howl all around me as the snow became blinding and I was forced to drop my speed to just a few miles an hour since the visibility was next to nothing. By the time I entered a clearing and my GPS showed I'd reached the coordinates Daisy had sent me, I was actually feeling somewhat drained. The snow was still heavy as I took in the sight of the small wood cabin in front of me. It was the only building in the sparse clearing, so I could only assume it was privately owned rather than being a part of one of the many resorts that dotted the area. I could see a wisp of smoke trailing up from the chimney. An old, beat-up SUV sat in front of the cabin and I saw that the plates matched the ones Ronan had gotten off the guy's parking pass form which Daisy had included in the text containing the GPS coordinates. Since I knew the occupants of the cabin would have easily seen me coming whether I was on foot or in my truck, I drove up to the cabin and parked next to the SUV. I grabbed my phone from the cup holder and tucked it into my pocket and then shrugged on my jacket, which wasn't heavy enough to offer any true protection from the cold, but was better than nothing. The last thing I grabbed was my gun which I kept in my hand as I exited the vehicle.

I hadn't made it more than a few steps when I heard someone shout, "Don't move!"

I instantly froze as I sought out the owner of the high-pitched voice. I finally spotted my quarry by the side of the cabin. I should have been unnerved by the sight of the revolver being pointed in my direction, but instead, I felt a sense of calm wash over me.

This was what I was good at.

Stick me in a room full of people I was expected to socialize with, and I was pretty much just a body turning oxygen into carbon dioxide. But point a gun at me or come at me with a knife and I fucking came alive. I didn't seek death out, but I sure as hell got a twisted thrill when it came at me with everything it had.

Normally, I would have just lifted my gun and pulled the trigger before my assailant even had the chance to verbalize another useless threat, but when I realized who it was beneath the gray hoodie that offered no protection from the brutal cold, I stayed my hand.

Because the person pointing the gun at me wasn't the man I was looking for. Hell, he wasn't even a *he*.

No, I was staring into the wide-eyes of a fucking kid. And a girl at that.

I estimated her to be around fifteen or sixteen. Her long black hair was slung over one shoulder in a long braid and she was wearing a pair of tattered jeans. I couldn't tell what kind of footwear she had on because her feet were buried in the ankle-deep snow. Several pieces of firewood were scattered around her and I realized she must have been getting the wood from the side of the cabin when she'd walked around to the front and spied me.

I scanned the rest of the area for other people, but no one appeared from the cabin and I didn't see any other sets of footprints besides hers.

I eased my finger off the trigger of my gun, but didn't put it away. The girl may not have been a typical threat, but she still posed a danger to me, especially considering how violently her hands were shaking as she held the gun on me. I estimated we were more than fifty feet apart; her chances of hitting me were slim, but not impossible. And I didn't have a lot of places I could use for cover.

"I'm looking for Allen," I called as I held my hands out. I took a couple of slow steps towards her.

"Don't move!" she screamed.

I ignored the order and ever so slowly began closing the distance between us. "I just came to talk to him," I said. "Do you know him?"

"Stay away from him! Do you hear me?!" she shouted.

Her skin was flushed, though I suspected it had more to do with her emotion than the cold weather.

"I hear you," I said easily. "I just want to make sure he's okay."

"You're a fucking liar!" she screamed. "I know he sent you!"

I had no idea who *he* was, but before I could even ask, she wiped angrily at her face with one hand, holding the gun on me with the other. "Just leave us alone!"

Her voice was thick with emotion and I didn't need to see her tears to know they were there. My insides clenched at the fear I was causing her, but I didn't have a lot of options. I had closed the distance between us by more than half.

"I'm afraid I can't do that," I said quietly, not sure if she even heard me over the blowing wind.

"Please," she choked out and I saw her close her eyes for the briefest of moments. I used those few seconds to take several more steps towards her. When she opened them and realized how much closer I was to her, her panic kicked up to a whole new level.

"I'll shoot you!" she screamed. She waved the gun wildly as she took a few steps back.

"Lucy?"

I stilled at the sound of another voice and glanced over my shoulder to see a man standing hunched over near the front door of the cabin. I automatically pointed my gun at him as I tried to assess the change in circumstances, but the move set the girl off.

"No!" she cried out and then the gun went off. Her shot went wild and sailed past me and slammed into the side of my truck. In the several seconds that passed, I did two things. I determined that the man was unarmed and not an immediate threat and that the girl was in a state of shock from what she'd done. I used the latter to my advantage and ran towards her. She screamed when she saw me coming and pointed the gun at me, but her slight hesitation as her finger searched out the trigger gave me the time I needed. As our bodies collided, I tried to brace her fall as I knocked the gun free from her hand, but I couldn't prevent some of my weight from crashing down on her as we both hit the ground. She let out a whoosh of air as the wind got knocked from her.

"Lucy!" I heard the man scream, and I barely had time to recover before his body slammed into mine. I automatically rolled, taking the man with me. Despite the fact that I still had ahold of my own gun, he came at me with punch after punch. But the guy clearly didn't know the first thing about fighting because every swing failed to make contact with anything that would have caused me enough injury to loosen my hold on him or my gun. His struggles irritated me more than anything else, so I did the only thing I knew would end the whole thing and put my gun to his head. As expected, he froze instantly, his eyes going wide with fear. I used his stillness to study him as best I could, considering the heavy snow that was falling around us. I guessed him to be my height and older than me by at least ten years, but he was leaner than me. Not skinny, just average build. His hair was dark brown and he was wearing jeans and a sweatshirt... like the girl, he was completely underdressed for the elements. The only feature on his face I could make out with any real clarity were his startlingly green eyes, even though one was swollen shut. Nearly his entire face was covered in bruises and his lip was swollen and split. Dried blood clung to a gash near his temple and I sucked in a breath when I saw the bruises on his throat.

Bruises I'd seen more times than I could count when I was a child.

Whoever had put the marks on his neck hadn't just been trying to hurt him...they'd been trying to choke him. Either into submission...or worse

I knew without a shadow of a doubt that at least some of the blood Ronan and I had found in the house had come from this man. And I knew Ronan had likely been right...he wasn't running from the law. He was running from something much, much worse.

"Do it," the man whispered harshly, his voice sounding scratchy... an aftereffect of being strangled probably.

I forced my eyes to his. His hands were fisted by his sides and he was sucking in deep breaths.

"Do it," he repeated. I stiffened when I saw his hand reach for my gun, but I knew by the way he was moving that he wasn't trying to disarm me. His cold fingers closed over my hand and I felt one finger press against the one I had resting on the trigger. I could say that after all the things I'd seen in my life, not much surprised me, but between the girl holding a gun on me and this moment, I was pretty much incapable of speech.

"Because that's the only way I'm going back to him this time," he declared. His voice dripped with a curious mix of determination, fear and resignation.

Before I could respond, I heard the girl yell, "Ethan!" and then she was coming at me, though her moves were sluggish as she continued to struggle to catch her breath. I easily caught her arm as she took a swing at me and I shifted off the man in one swift move and dragged the girl back against my chest, pinning her arms by wrapping one of mine around her.

"No!" the man shouted and he struggled to his feet, though he swayed wildly once he managed to stand. "Please," he whispered.

The girl struggled in my grasp. My patience was nearing its end and I snapped, "Be still."

I had no idea what the fuck was going on and I was freezing my ass off.

"Please," the man implored. "Don't hurt her…just…just leave her here and I'll go back with you. Tell…tell Eric I won't run again. I swear it."

"Ethan, no," the girl cried out.

"Sweetheart, stay still, okay? It'll be over soon."

The girl was shaking her head against me and I could hear her crying. Frustration coursed through me as I tried to ignore the girl's anguish and the terror in the man's eyes as he silently begged me.

I was about to explain to both of them that I wasn't whoever it was they believed me to be, but the man – Ethan – suddenly lost his balance and crumpled to his knees. His eyes rolled backwards just as the girl shouted "Ethan!" and I quickly released her and lunged forward to catch him before his head could make contact with the ground. The girl was by my side in an instant, tears streaming down her face.

"Ethan," she cried as she brought her hands up to his face, but seemed to struggle with where to put them.

"Lucy," I said as I tucked my gun in my waistband and lifted Ethan enough so his face lolled against my chest. "Lucy, look at me," I said when the girl didn't respond.

Her wet eyes lifted to mine and I felt my gut clench at the unspoken plea there. Whoever this man was to her, she obviously cared about him a great deal.

"I'm not here to hurt either of you," I said as I put my free arm beneath Ethan's legs. While I knew it would be easier to carry him over my shoulder in a fireman's carry, I didn't want to risk injuring him more. "I need you to open the door for me," I said as I motioned to the cabin. "We need to get him warm and dry."

I didn't wait for her to answer as I lurched to my feet. Ethan wasn't a small man and with my numb hands and the deepening snow, I knew it would be a struggle just to get him the short distance to the cabin.

Lucy hesitated and then ran towards the cabin, glancing over her shoulder at me every few seconds. I followed at a much slower pace and dropped my eyes to Ethan's battered face, hoping like hell he'd wake up.

But he didn't.

And I was fucking clueless what to do next.

CHAPTER 1

CAIN

It felt like hours had passed before I managed to carry Ethan over the threshold of the cabin. Lucy was standing just inside the door, her jeans and tennis shoes covered in snow. I scanned the living room that the front door opened into and saw only a couch and chair in front of the fireplace. A small fire was burning in the hearth, but it looked like it was going to go out any minute.

"Where's his room?" I asked as I used my hip to nudge the door closed since Lucy seemed frozen in time.

"The rooms are back there," she said after a moment and then pointed to a hallway just beyond the small kitchen. "But he's been lying on the couch because the heat isn't working."

I debated for a moment as I glanced at the too-small couch and then strode towards the hallway. I entered the first bedroom I found and ignored the chill in the air as I said, "Pull back the covers."

Lucy did what I told her. I was about to put Ethan down when I realized his clothes were covered in snow. I debated for a moment and then carefully laid him down by the foot of the bed so his body was on top of the decorative quilt covering the bed. "Ethan," I said as I gave him a gentle shake, but he didn't respond. My fingers shook as I searched out his pulse and I sighed inwardly at the strong beat I felt beneath my fingers.

"Is he..."

I'd forgotten Lucy's presence. Her shaky voice had me lifting my gaze to her. "He's alive."

She nodded, but didn't seem relieved. I couldn't really blame her since Ethan hadn't woken even once since he'd passed out. Ethan's chilled skin reminded me that I needed to focus and I quickly began undressing him. It took a little bit of effort to work the shirt off over his head and I heard Lucy gasp when the man's chest was exposed. Angry bruises covered both of his sides, proof that he'd taken multiple kicks to the ribs. His stomach was also bruised.

"Ethan," Lucy whispered brokenly just before a sob tore free of her throat.

I ignored her and began working Ethan's pants loose. I didn't miss the fact that as distressed as Lucy was, her cheeks colored when I pulled the pants down to reveal Ethan's briefs and she turned her back on us. I'd had the brief and disturbing thought outside that maybe the young girl was in an illicit relationship with the older man, but her behavior had me reconsidering. If they were lovers, she certainly wouldn't be embarrassed to see him in any state of undress.

"Lucy," I said, but she didn't acknowledge me and I could hear her softly crying. It took several more calls of her name before her teary eyes shifted to me. "Does this place have warm water?"

Lucy looked at me and nodded her head, but didn't react otherwise. She seemed completely lost. "Can you bring me some along with some clean washcloths or towels?"

"Um, yeah," she murmured and then she cast Ethan a quick glance before she hurried from the room. I used the time to pull Ethan's pants the rest of the way off. His briefs were dry so I left them on and maneuvered him to the head of the bed. But as I turned him to get him beneath the cover, my eyes caught on the bruises covering his back...and then several large spots of blood on his briefs. My chest tightened at the possibility of what that blood meant. I could hear the water running in the kitchen, so I worked quickly to pull Ethan's briefs down and off his body entirely. I nearly threw up at the sight of dried blood along the crack of his ass and across the backs of his upper thighs.

White hot rage went through me as I accepted what I was seeing, but the sound of the water turning off in the other room had me quickly rolling Ethan onto his back and covering him with the blanket as I tucked the bloodied underwear beneath the pillow. Lucy appeared at my side a moment later with a large Tupperware container full of water and a hand towel.

"I couldn't find a washcloth," she whispered, her voice hoarse.

"This is fine," I acknowledged.

The girl's hands were shaking violently as she handed the items over. "Is he..is he gonna die?"

"No," I automatically said, though I had no idea if that were true or not. The bruises on his back and torso meant he could have internal bleeding of some kind and the head wound was potentially a whole other issue. I searched out my phone so I could call Ronan, but I had no signal.

Fuck, we were on our own.

"Is there a phone here?" I asked.

Lucy shook her head.

"What about your cell phone?"

The girl hesitated before saying, "We got rid of them on the way up here."

Right, so they couldn't be tracked.

"Ethan...Ethan said he was okay...that nothing was broken and he just had a concussion. He told me to wake him up every couple of hours if he fell asleep and ask him questions like who I was and stuff."

"How long have you been here?" I asked as I began washing Ethan's face to get rid of the dried blood.

Lucy didn't respond and I glanced up to see her eyes filled with fear and confusion. "Who are you?" she whispered and I could hear a mix of terror and hope in her voice.

"My name is Cain. A friend of Ethan's sent me," I hedged.

"Ethan doesn't have any friends," she automatically responded.

"Someone he worked with at the hospital was worried about him when he didn't show up for work yesterday or today. He sent me to make sure he was okay."

"How...how do I know you're telling the truth?" she asked warily.

I sighed, though I couldn't really fault her for her suspicions. "Because if I'd wanted to hurt you guys, I would have done it already. If I wanted to take you back to whoever did this" – I motioned to Ethan's battered face – "We'd already be halfway down the mountain."

Lucy was silent for a long time and I was certain she wasn't going to answer me when she finally said, "We got here yesterday."

"Has Ethan been out the whole time?" I asked.

She shook her head. "He sleeps off and on and I wake him up like he told me to. He didn't want to eat anything, but he's been drinking water whenever he wakes up."

"What about you?" I asked.

"What about me?"

"Are you hurt anywhere? Did the man who hurt Ethan-"

"No," she interjected. "Just Ethan."

I waited for her to say more, but she remained silent.

"You said the heat isn't working, but there's power?"

Lucy nodded.

"Okay, stay here with him. I'll check it out."

I didn't wait for Lucy to respond as I left the room and did a quick tour of the small cabin. It was surprisingly modern for its remote location and the fact that it wasn't running on a generator was both good news and unexpected. Whoever owned the place had had the money to get hooked into the electrical grid. The problem with the heat was an easy fix because it turned out to be nothing more than a blown fuse. Within a minute of me resetting the fuse and turning the switch on the thermostat, the heat kicked in. I did a quick study of the kitchen and saw there were a few things in the fridge that looked like typical gas station convenience food fare. Blessedly, the freezer was full and the pantry next to the fridge was also stocked. If the storm trapped us up here a for a few days, we'd be okay at least.

I returned to the bedroom and saw Lucy kneeling next to the bed, her head resting on Ethan's chest. Her hands were wrapped around Ethan's lax fingers.

As I neared her, I realized she'd fallen asleep. I approached her, but stayed near the foot of the bed as I softly called her name. As expected, she jolted awake and her panicked eyes scanned the room before settling on me.

"Lucy, why don't you go change?" I said as I glanced at her wet pants and shoes. "Maybe lie down for a bit?"

"No…no, I can't leave him," Lucy whispered tiredly as she rubbed at her eyes.

I took a chance and stepped closer and was pleased when she didn't shrink away from me. I suspected she needed a comforting touch, but I just couldn't bring myself to do it so I said, "I promise to stay with him and I can come get you if he wakes up."

She began shaking her head as tears filled her eyes and I knew she had to be as mentally and emotionally exhausted as she was physically.

"Lucy," I said and I waited until she looked up at me. "He's safe. You're both safe," I murmured.

She let out an ugly, choked laugh/sob combination. "He'll never be safe."

I didn't miss the fact that she was referring to Ethan and not herself with the statement. Frustration coursed through me. I wasn't equipped to deal with this shit. Ronan would have known what to do. Hell, any one of my teammates would have been better at dealing with the emotions of a teenage girl.

"I can tell you two have been taking care of each other for a long time," I finally began. "When he wakes up, he's going to be worried about you…if he knows you got some rest…"

Lucy's warm brown eyes slid closed for a moment before she stumbled to her feet. I was half tempted to reach out to steady her, but my body recoiled at the prospect and I took a step back instead. Logically, I knew she was no threat to me, but my brain had stopped working on logic a long time ago when it came to other people.

"He'll want to know where I am when he wakes up," she said shakily.

I nodded. "I'll come get you right away."

"I'll be right next door," she said, her voice actually sounding a little fierce. My respect for her went up another notch at the unspoken message. I had no doubt she'd come after me again if I even looked at the man in the bed wrong.

Once Lucy had left the room, I returned to Ethan's side and snagged the stained underwear from beneath the pillow and placed it on the pile of clothes I'd removed from Ethan's battered body earlier. I grabbed the hand towel and gave it a good wringing out before I gently rolled Ethan onto his side so I could clean the blood from his backside and legs. I made quick work of the task and then I got him settled under the covers again before snagging his clothes off the floor along with the dirty towel and water and taking them to the kitchen. I'd found the laundry room off the kitchen when I'd gone in search of the fuse box so I quickly tossed Ethan's clothes into the washing machine and got it started. On my way back to his room, I grabbed a glass of water and shrugged off the light jacket I'd been wearing. I had a change of clothes in my bag in the truck, but I didn't want to risk leaving the cabin for the length of time it would take to grab it. In addition to the water, I grabbed one of the kitchen chairs.

Once I was back in the room, I put the water down on the nightstand and settled the chair next to the bed. I studied the man in the bed for several long minutes as I thought about what to do next.

I guessed him to be older than my own 25 years but maybe not by ten years or more as I'd initially suspected. He wasn't quite as tall as my own six feet and looked skinnier than he probably should be. With the bruises on his face, I couldn't make out much more than a firm, chiseled jawline and pale, full pink lips.

Full?

What the hell?

A twinge of discomfort went through me at the word my brain had decided to use to describe the man's mouth. I brushed it off and leaned forward to put my hand on his shoulder, ignoring how warm his skin now felt compared to the iciness of before. "Ethan," I said softly as I gave him a little shake. I didn't like how long he'd been out and while I knew nothing about head injuries, the fact that he'd told Lucy to wake him up every couple of hours gave me the encouragement I needed to keep at it. Relief went through me when his eyelids began to twitch.

Thank fuck.

Now maybe I could finally get some answers.

CHAPTER 2

ETHAN

The pain had me wanting to scream out loud, but I knew that would only make things worse, so I swallowed it down and fought back the tears that threatened to fall.

He liked the tears just like he liked the screams. They were like throwing gasoline on a fire. But the silence...

"Ethan, you need to wake up."

The voice was wrong and he was being way too gentle. The weight of his hand on my shoulder was too light.

Why wasn't he digging his fingers into my skin? Why didn't it feel like he was trying to snap the bone in two?

"Lucy's really worried about you."

That was enough to have me fighting the pain and exhaustion that were keeping my eyes sealed shut. It felt like there was sand scraping beneath my lids every time I tried to force them open and I couldn't stop a tear that escaped my eye.

God, I just wanted to fucking sleep.

But even as a tidal wave of darkness began to welcome me, I remembered Lucy's terrified scream as she'd been knocked to the ground.

Shock reverberated through me as everything became clear. That moment hadn't been a nightmare. I bolted upright. "Lucy!" I yelled as light flooded my eyes like little shards of glass. Pain shot through my head and a violent wave of nausea went through me. I tried to contain the bile that crept up the back of my throat, but it was impossible and I could do nothing but lean over and expel what little was in my stomach.

"Easy," came a deep voice that was much too smooth and filled with worry to be Eric's. Not to mention the fact that Eric would have been more likely to slap me for throwing up in his immediate proximity instead of resting his hand on my back.

On my very naked back.

What the hell?

"Ethan?"

Lucy's voice was like a balm and, despite my messed-up vision, I managed to focus on her as she came tearing into the room. I bit back a moan of pain when she threw her arms around me and she instantly tried to step back. "Oh my God, I'm sorry."

But I held onto her and managed to shake my head. Just knowing she was safe made the agonizing pain searing my ribs worth it. "It's okay," I rasped as I held onto her, hoping she'd get the message that she was fine where she was. Her hold on me eased considerably, but she didn't release me entirely. I finally realized I was sitting in a bed and that it wasn't just me and Lucy in the room. My grip on Lucy tightened when my eyes connected with icy blue ones that were studying me intently...well, my one eye because I was coming to realize my other eye was swollen shut. That or I'd gone blind in that one.

I felt the need to put Lucy behind me to keep her safe, but not only did my position not allow it, there was little I could do to protect her from the huge man.

Story of my fucking life.

The man who had to be several inches taller than me wasn't quite as heavyset as Eric, but his body looked rock hard and unforgiving. His blond hair was short and streaked with hints of gold, contrasting his pale blue eyes. The set of his jaw was tight and his eyes were inscrutable as he unfolded what looked like a hand towel in his hands.

Big hands that had held me down and put a gun to my head…that had held Lucy…

I ignored the fact that I was both too weak to put up any kind of defense as well as the knowledge that I was very much naked beneath the blanket and tried to maneuver myself so that I was between the man and Lucy. The man's eyes narrowed just a little bit and then he was moving towards us. Panic clawed at me and I began searching for anything I could use as a weapon, but all I saw was a glass of water on the nightstand. I grabbed it, not caring that the contents spilled onto me and the bedding. I used one arm to keep Lucy back as I raised the glass in what I hoped was a threatening manner, but more likely just showed I didn't have a clue what I was doing.

Maybe if I broke it, I could use it to cut something vital.

I didn't have strength for shit, but one well-placed swipe of the glass was all it would take. With that thought in mind, I slammed the glass down on the side of the nightstand. The top of it cracked and broke into several pieces, leaving me a huge chunk to work with.

"Stay back!" I ordered the guy.

Frustration went through me when he didn't even hesitate for a second and just kept coming at us.

"Ethan," Lucy interjected, but I shook my head which caused a blinding pain to shoot through it, so much so that I had to close my eyes. Another bout of nausea ripped through me and a double dose of humiliation swamped me as I felt the glass being calmly plucked from my fingers just before I leaned over and threw up again. This time all I did was dry heave which caused my ribs to scream out in agony.

"Ethan," Lucy whispered and I could hear the tears in her voice.

"Lucy," the man said. "Ask him the questions. I'll be right back."

I managed to look up long enough to see the man drop the hand towel over the small puddle of puke on the floor next to the bed and then he was grabbing the few large pieces of glass up and carrying them out of the room.

My last line of defense…

"Ethan," Lucy said again, her voice still tinged with panic. "What's my name?"

"Lucy, we need to get out of here," I mumbled as I began searching the room for my clothes. Confusion took over as I tried to remember where I was and then a moment later, the memory would return. It kept coming like that, flash after flash, until I was sure I was going to be sick again. "Not safe," I managed to get out right before my body gave up the fight and I slumped back against the pillow. "I'm sorry... should have kept you safe."

I felt small hands touching my face as the blanket was drawn up to my chin. I was dimly aware of Lucy's quiet cries, but I was riding the edge of consciousness so I couldn't find the strength to respond.

"Ethan, what's my name?"

I wanted to laugh, but I knew no sound came out. I knew her name. Why was she asking me that?

"Ethan, please, tell me my name."

I forced my eyes open and saw Lucy had moved so she was kneeling on the bed next to me.

"Lucy Palmer," I said tiredly.

"What day of the week is it?"

That required more thought. We'd arrived on a Wednesday...the same day Eric had once again found us.

God, was that just yesterday?

"Thursday?" I asked, hating how muddled my head felt and trying to remind myself that we didn't have time for this – we needed to run, damn it.

"Lucy," I heard the man's voice call and I managed to open my one good eye long enough to see that he was once again standing in the doorway, a glass of water in one hand and a plastic container in the other. "Go get some rest," the man said as he entered. Lucy was clutching my hand, which was one of the few parts of my body that didn't actually throb with pain and I couldn't help but tighten my fingers around hers. I wanted to tell her to run as soon as she got the chance, but I knew she wouldn't. She'd never leave me behind.

"Lucy," I tried vainly to say, but my tongue felt thick in my mouth.

Lucy stood and then leaned over me to kiss me on the forehead. "I don't think he wants to hurt us, Ethan," she whispered. "Do you want me to stay?"

I managed to focus long enough to notice how gaunt and pale she looked and guilt went through me as I realized she probably hadn't gotten any rest since we'd fled the house near Cougar Mountain the day before.

"No, go lie down," I managed to get out. "I'll be okay."

She nodded and then kissed me again. "Love you," she murmured against my forehead.

"Right back atcha, Kiddo."

She smiled at that because she hated when I called her that, even though she really didn't. She held my hand for several long seconds before releasing me and turning to leave the room. Her eyes shifted briefly to the man, but she didn't seem afraid of him, despite what had happened outside. I couldn't say the same since I could still feel the barrel of his gun pressed against my forehead. Yeah, I'd had a weak moment when I'd actually wanted him to pull the trigger, but I hadn't really meant it...not deep down where that untouchable need to survive still lived.

I watched as the man approached me. "Can you sit up a bit?" he asked, his voice raspy. I was surprised at the tingle that shot down my spine as he stood over me. It was an unwelcome feeling since this man scared the hell out of me. Not to mention that damn tingle had been what had led me eagerly down the path to hell four years ago.

I nodded even as pain shot through my head and body. I tried to use my hands to lever myself up enough so I could lean against the headboard, but it felt like cement was running through my veins. My gut clenched when the man suddenly sat down on the bed next to me, his ass brushing my side through the blanket. I nearly bit my tongue in two when his big arm suddenly wrapped around my chest and he lifted me to a sitting position. I was so stunned by the move, that the pain in my ribs was secondary to everything else.

The man had lifted me like I weighed nothing and he'd managed to do it in a way that had only caused a dull throb to skitter across my torso. The fact that he'd done his best not to hurt me further was lost on me because all I could focus on was his strength and the damage it could inflict on me if I did or said something to anger him.

And I knew it wouldn't take much.

It never did.

The man handed me the glass of water. "Rinse and spit into this," he said as he held up the plastic container. I did as I was told because I was good at that and also because I really wanted the vile taste of puke out of my mouth. I rinsed a couple times for good measure and tried to put the glass and the container on the nightstand, but the man took them from me and placed them there himself.

"How are you feeling?" he asked.

I found myself struggling to answer because all I could do was focus on his left hand which was fisted.

Fine...tell him you're fine.

But my voice failed me. What if "fine" wasn't what he wanted to hear? One blow and I'd be out for sure. And then Lucy would be alone with him.

Except if I didn't answer him, maybe that would piss him off too.

Fuck, at least with Eric I knew how to react. I wanted to laugh at the realization that my ex might actually be the lesser of two evils at the moment. But all it took was the memory of his weight on top of me yesterday as I'd begged for mercy and the sensation of my life leaving my body as his big hands had wrapped around my throat.

"Ethan, breathe," the man said gruffly and I jerked my head up, not realizing I'd still been staring at his hand. Or that I'd been holding my breath.

I sucked in a deep breath, ignoring the pain it caused and then tried to focus on the man's face. But I couldn't stop from dropping my gaze to his fisted hand again. Maybe if I could see the blow coming, I'd have a chance.

"I'm okay," I whispered, though that was the furthest thing from the truth I could have said.

I wasn't okay. I hadn't been okay for four fucking years.

"Ethan," the man said again and I looked up to watch him studying me intently. I couldn't read what he was thinking, but I highly suspected he had no trouble with knowing what was going through my head. "Take these," he said and he slowly lifted his fisted hand and opened it to reveal two white pills.

Humiliation scoured through me as I realized he'd had his hand fisted because he was holding them.

"They're ibuprofen," he added. "I found them in the bathroom cabinet…I can bring the bottle to show you."

I swallowed hard and shook my head. I could tell what they were just by looking at them. He dropped them into my hand and then reached for the water. I fought back tears of exhaustion as I swallowed the pills down.

"Who are you?" I finally managed to ask. If he'd been one of Eric's men, he wouldn't have given a shit about my comfort. And since Eric had found us yesterday, it made no sense that he'd send someone up the mountain after us when he could have just as easily come himself.

Unless he hadn't been able to walk out of that house yesterday…

The prospect was both terrifying and thrilling. And the fact that it was both bothered me more than I wanted to admit.

"My name is Cain. Ronan Grisham sent me to check on you."

"Dr. Grisham?" I said in surprise. That was the last thing I expected to hear.

Cain nodded. "He was worried when you didn't show up for work."

That made no sense to me at all. Unless…

"Look, I told him that nurse was mistaken. I didn't do what she said," I managed to get out even as terror threatened to clog my throat. If I was arrested for what I'd done to that patient, it would all be over. Panic for Lucy welled inside of me.

"So you didn't save that patient's life?" Cain asked.

I dropped my eyes and shook my head. "It was chaotic…the nurse just got confused. I…my job was just to transport patients…"

"So I suppose next you'll be telling me that you trashed that house and that this," – he waved his hand over my body – "happened during a mugging."

Since nothing I said would make sense, I did what I did best and kept quiet.

"You're a shitty liar Ethan...or do you prefer Allen?"

I forced myself to look at Cain as I spoke. "Tell Dr. Grisham I'm fine and I appreciate his concern. Now, I'm really tired. Have a safe trip down the mountain."

I was proud of how steady my voice sounded even though my gut was threatening to humiliate me with another upchucking episode.

Cain didn't respond, nor did he move.

Fuck, why wasn't he moving?

If he didn't leave, I couldn't go to plan B which was to grab Lucy and get the hell out of there.

Cain's expression didn't change at all as he stared at me and this time I made myself hold the eye contact despite my instinct to look down. Submission was something Eric had demanded, but I'd be damned if I was going to kowtow to this man too.

"Okay, Doc, have it your way," Cain murmured as he reached for the water and handed it to me. I wasn't able to hide the flinch that went through me at the nickname so I tried to cover it by taking the glass from him and swallowing a few sips. He was guessing I was a doctor – he had no way of knowing for sure.

"But we're going to have this conversation every time you wake up and there will be a point where you tell me who did this to you," he added as his eyes swept my body.

Despite the pain I was in, I still felt heat suffuse my entire system at the move.

I waited for Cain to get up, but he didn't. Instead, he reached for the water glass. Our fingers brushed for the briefest of moments and I felt a zap of electricity shoot up my arm. I suspected if my body wasn't as messed up as it was, my dick would have responded to the contact.

Thank God for small favors.

"For Lucy's sake, I need you to tell me how badly you're injured," Cain said softly. "It might be tough to make it down the mountain in this storm, but if you need a hospital..."

Storm?

Ignoring the pain in my head, I jerked my head to the side to look out the single window in the bedroom and felt my heart clench at the sight of wind whipping snow around outside. If the weather kept up, we could be trapped here for days, longer even. And it was clear Cain had no plans to go anywhere anytime soon.

"Doc," Cain said.

But I couldn't look at him. Because along with my terrible fear of him, I felt the need to unburden myself too. To admit how fucking scared I was that one wrong step meant disaster…for me, for Lucy.

Except I couldn't trust this man. I couldn't trust Ronan Grisham, no matter how friendly he'd always been to me, despite my lowly status as a transporter.

But I also knew the jig was up. Just like Ronan, this man wasn't going to believe I hadn't performed that procedure. Or that I hadn't been using an alias at the hospital.

"I have a concussion so I need to be woken up every couple of hours and asked questions. If my speech is slurred or I can't answer them correctly, it could mean there's bleeding in my brain. Also, if I start seizing or you can't wake me up…"

I let my words fall off because what else was I supposed to say? If any of those things happened, it was unlikely I'd survive long enough to make it down the mountain and to a hospital.

"My ribs are likely bruised and some might be fractured, but there shouldn't be any risk of them causing my lungs to collapse. At this point I don't think I have any internal bleeding, but that might change if I start coughing up or vomiting blood or if there is blood in my urine. I need to stay hydrated as best I can. The ibuprofen will help some."

I expected that to be the end of it and waited for the weight on the bed to change, but it didn't. I stubbornly kept my eyes on the window, trying to lose myself in the swirl of snow and wind. I couldn't help but wonder how something so beautiful could be so deadly at the same time.

Like Eric.

"Ethan."

My belly flip flopped at the way my name sounded on his lips. Soft, intimate. Like he was more than just a complete stranger seeing me at my weakest moment. I made myself look at him and was surprised when he was the one to drop his gaze. The hardness that seemed to be a constant feature softened quite a bit and I actually steeled myself for what was to come because I knew it wouldn't be good.

I knew what pity looked like and that was the last thing I wanted.

"When I was undressing you, I found bloodstains in your underwear."

And with that one statement, what little warmth I'd been feeling disintegrated and all I felt was obscenely cold.

Cain's eyes lifted and held mine, but I felt no comfort in it. All I felt was numb.

"I just need to know if the damage-" Cain began, but I cut him off.

"It's fine," I bit out. "It will heal on its own in a few days."

My throat felt like it was going to close off, it was so damn tight. "Is that it?" I asked, forcing my gaze to remain on him. I found myself wanting to make him more uncomfortable so he'd finally leave. The plan worked, because Cain stood up.

"Yeah, that's it. I'll be in the living room if you need me and I'll come check up on you in a couple of hours."

I wanted to tell him to stay away from me, but I didn't. He'd do whatever he wanted.

As he turned his back on me, another round of humiliation went through me and I felt a tear escape my eye. I wanted nothing more in that moment then to crawl under the blanket and stay there, but there was one thing I needed from this man so I quelled what little pride I had left and called his name.

CHAPTER 3

CAIN

"Cain."

I stopped at the sound of my name and turned around, though I didn't want to.

I was still reeling from the discovery of how badly I'd wanted to comfort the man in the bed as he'd had to indirectly admit to being raped and what that admission had cost him.

I didn't comfort people. I just didn't. I did my job and nowhere in my job description did it require me to make someone feel better. I was here to keep the man safe and report back to Ronan so he could figure out the next steps. I'd asked about the rape because I'd needed to know if his injuries were any kind of potential problem, not because I wanted to tell him how sorry I was that that had happened to him or that if I ever came face to face with the man who'd done that to him, I'd rip his fucking head clean off his fucking body.

Even if that was exactly what I wanted to do.

Even now, it took everything in me not to fist my hands as rage coiled deep inside me. And that was only because I'd seen how Ethan had reacted to the sight of my fisted hand earlier.

"Yeah?" I managed to say.

I saw Ethan wipe at his uninjured eye and didn't miss the dampness that was left behind.

"Don't tell Lucy."

I nodded. "I won't." Ethan's eyes shifted back to the window. "Get some rest, Ethan."

He nodded, but didn't make a move to lie back down. I left the room, closing the door enough to give him some privacy, but leaving it open a crack so I could hear him if he called out. My next stop was the other bedroom. The door was open so I could easily see Lucy lying on the bed, her back to me. She'd taken off her coat, but her shoes were still on. Since they'd been wet, I knew they had to be uncomfortable for her to keep on, but I suspected she'd done so deliberately.

Because being on the run meant you literally needed to be able to run at a moment's notice.

I closed the door just like I had Ethan's, leaving it open a crack, and then went to the kitchen to gather my thoughts. The storm outside was starting to pick up and I knew it wouldn't be long before it was considered a blizzard. If we got significant accumulation, it would make it nearly impossible to get down the mountain. On the drive up, it had looked like the narrow road had been plowed throughout the winter which once again led me to believe whoever owned the cabin was either well off enough to hire a private party to do the plowing or they had the means to do it themselves.

I debated what to do for a moment and then searched out my phone. There was still no reception so I began looking around the cabin until I found what I was looking for.

The keys to Ethan's SUV.

I snatched them up from where they were sitting on a side table near the door and then headed outside. Since my own truck couldn't handle the snow as well with an empty bed, I climbed into the rusted-out SUV. Pleased to see it had four-wheel drive, I started it up and then scanned the interior to see if there was anything inside of the vehicle that would help me figure out who the two traumatized people in the cabin were. A search of the glove box showed nothing except the owner's manual for the car and the window sticker from the dealership it had been purchased at. I glanced at the sticker long enough to see that the asking price for the rattrap of a car was way more than it was worth and to see that the dealership was located in Scottsdale, Arizona.

It took me nearly twenty minutes to get down the mountain far enough to where I could finally get a weak signal on my phone and another ten minutes to actually find a spot where I could safely turn the SUV around on the narrow road. Once I was back on the road and facing the direction of the cabin, I put the SUV in park and then dialed Ronan's number. It was late afternoon so I wasn't sure if he'd still be at the hospital.

I lucked out when he answered with a curt, "Yeah."

"Hey, I made it."

"And?"

I sighed. "I'm still trying to get a handle on what's going on, but the guy – his real name is Ethan – is hurt pretty bad. He's not alone either. He's got a teenage girl with him...Lucy."

"Tell me about his injuries."

I gave him a rundown of what Ethan had told me and then said, "If this blizzard keeps up, I won't be able to get him down the mountain at all. Should I risk bringing them down tonight?"

"No," Ronan said. "I've been monitoring the weather...the storm should ease in a few hours. Give him a few days to recover and then bring them down. What's his relationship to the girl?"

"No idea," I said. "Neither of them are talking much. Don't think it's sexual though. He mentioned a guy named Eric...not sure if he's an ex or what, but..."

"But what?" Ronan asked, picking up on my hesitation.

I debated how much to tell Ronan, surprised at my own need to protect Ethan's privacy. But Ronan wasn't just any guy off the street. He would determine what help, if any, we offered Ethan so he needed to know everything I did.

"I found proof Ethan was sexually assaulted."

Ronan was silent for an extended period of time, but I didn't continue because I knew he was likely trying to decide the best course of action. Not to mention the innate fury he'd be feeling.

Like what I'd felt.

The reminder that I was having trouble separating my emotions from the facts was like a cold slap in the face.

"What did he say about it?" Ronan asked.

"Not much. Just that his injuries would heal within a few days. He asked me not to tell the girl."

Another long pause and then, "Okay, bring them down as soon as he's up to traveling which, with his injuries, will be at least a few days if not more. Bring them to my house in Queen Anne."

I was surprised Ronan was willing to have the pair at his house with his family, but it was just further proof that he didn't believe Ethan to be any kind of threat. And after seeing things for myself, I no longer believed him to be any danger to anyone, but he certainly had danger following close enough on his trail that it could end up putting Ronan's family in jeopardy.

"Okay," I responded, since I wasn't going to question the logic behind Ronan's decision.

"I'll see what I can find out about them on my end."

"Understood," I said. "My phone doesn't have reception up here so I probably won't be able to check in until we're on our way back to the city."

"Okay," Ronan murmured. I had no doubt he wasn't thrilled about that since he liked knowing what was going on with his men, especially when they were on the job. And even though he'd handed control of the team over to Memphis Wheland, his second-in-command, Ronan still kept his thumb on the pulse of his organization and the men who were a part of it.

"I'll be careful," I offered, hoping to ease his mind. It had been a strange thing for me to understand that Ronan cared about me beyond being one of his operatives, but I'd gotten used to it in the three years since I'd joined the team.

"Yeah," Ronan said with a sigh. "If I don't hear from you by Monday, I'm sending the cavalry."

I chuckled. "Deal."

I said my goodbyes and then made my way back up to the cabin. The snow was still flying around, but it seemed to be a little less heavy than it had been and I hoped Ronan was right that the storm would pass soon. While I wanted to believe Ethan's injuries weren't life-threatening, I didn't want to be put into a position where I had to risk his and Lucy's lives by getting them down the mountain quickly enough to get Ethan the help he'd need.

And that was even assuming I could get him down fast enough.

The weight of the unknown was heavy on my shoulders as I made my way back towards the cabin. I parked next to my truck and got out, pocketing the SUV's keys. I searched out my bag from the backseat of the truck and then headed towards the door. I was glad the cabin was feeling warmer than it had before when I'd entered, but made a mental note to grab some of the firewood from outside just in case we ended up losing power. I dropped my bag on the kitchen table and then went to the back rooms to check on my charges. But I didn't make it past Ethan's room because instead of finding him asleep in bed like I would have expected, I saw his naked body lying sprawled on the floor just feet from the door.

"Fuck," I muttered as I pushed the door open and dropped down next to him. Relief tore through me when I felt for a pulse and found it. It seemed strong which gave me hope.

"Ethan," I said softly as I shook him. He didn't feel feverish which I hoped was another good sign, but he was once again out cold. I remembered his words about him being in trouble if I couldn't wake him up. I shook him harder than I probably should have. "Ethan, wake up," I ordered as the fear began to filter through my veins.

Ethan let out a little moan before opening his eyes. "What..." he said in confusion.

"What happened?" I said as I wrapped my arms around his shoulders and helped him sit up.

He seemed groggy, but his words were clear when he said, "Need to get Lucy out of here before he comes back."

I wondered if the *he* he was referring to was me or the fucker who'd hurt him.

"Who?" I asked.

"Promised I'd keep her safe," Ethan murmured tiredly. "He doesn't know she knows."

"Knows what?" I asked even as I put my arm beneath Ethan's legs.

Ethan just shook his head and then his eyes drifted shut. I lifted him and struggled to my feet. I managed to get him back in the bed and covered up and then sat down on the edge of the mattress and shook him until his eyes opened.

"Ethan, I need you to answer some questions," I explained. "I need to make sure you're doing okay."

He nodded slightly and I was relieved to see that he was able to focus on me. He appeared to be more awake than when I'd found him. I ran through some basic questions including asking him what my name was, where we were and who the president was and he answered them all without hesitation. But the second I asked him about what had caused him to get out of bed, he clammed up again and I knew it was because he *had* been hoping to get himself and Lucy away from me.

Once Ethan was asleep again, I went to check on Lucy, who was still in the exact same position, before heading to the kitchen to try and find something for dinner. The bag in the refrigerator from the convenience store had a couple of unappetizing looking sandwiches in it along with a bottle of soda as well as a bottle of water. I searched the contents of the freezer and then the pantry and finally settled on something simple and that had been a staple in my house when I'd been a kid, both because it was easy and cheap. It wasn't often that I cooked these days, so it felt awkward at first, but I soon found myself falling back into the routine.

As I worked, my mind drifted to the past, but I shoved the offending thoughts away. I'd stopped living in the past a long time ago.

The creaking of a floorboard automatically had me reaching for my gun. My eyes met startled brown ones and I immediately lowered the gun.

Fuck, I needed to get a grip.

So much for not letting my brief walk down memory lane get to me.

"Sorry," I murmured as I shot Lucy a glance. I tucked the gun in the back waistband of my pants and covered it with my shirt.

Lucy didn't say anything as she leaned against the wall near the entrance to the kitchen. She still looked wiped out, but she seemed steadier on her feet than she'd been. At some point she'd changed her shoes because instead of wet sneakers, she was wearing shoes that looked like some kind of cross between boots and slippers. Her jeans had been swapped out for a pair of leggings.

"He's still asleep," Lucy murmured.

I nodded. "I talked to him about twenty minutes ago, so he should be okay for a bit."

The awkwardness between us grew and I was once again reminded that I wasn't equipped to deal with a teenage girl.

I wasn't equipped to deal with a lot of things.

"Can I help?" she asked.

I didn't relish the idea of the girl joining me in the narrow kitchen, but the fact that she was even willing to interact with me was an opportunity I couldn't pass up. If I could get her to open up about what was going on, at least I'd know what I was dealing with.

"I think I saw some garlic bread in the freezer," I offered.

I forced myself to remain still as Lucy moved past me. I hated that even the sensation of her body passing in close proximity to mine had me wanting to reach for my gun.

Or the knife in the butcher block that was just in front of me.

I shook my head and tried to focus on getting the spaghetti noodles in the boiling water, but as my body began to lock up, I knew it was pointless. Luckily, it didn't take her long to grab the bread as well as the soda from the convenience store bag and she seemed clueless to my internal struggles as she brushed past me again and made her way to the counter on the other side of the stove. She was still too close for comfort, but I forced myself to remain where I was.

We worked in silence as she got out a cookie sheet and got the bread in the oven. I already had the sauce and noodles going so she went to sit down at the kitchen table.

"You're not going to leave us alone, are you?" she finally asked.

Her bluntness was a surprise.

"All we want to do is help you and Ethan," I said softly.

"Why?" she asked, the doubt in her voice clear.

"Because you need it," I answered simply.

The girl fell silent. I waited until the noodles were simmering before turning the stove down enough so the water wouldn't boil over and then I forced myself to go sit down at the table across from her. I liked that she didn't seem as frightened of me as before, but she was definitely wary as her eyes kept darting up to meet mine as if to prove to me and herself that she wasn't afraid of me.

Brave girl.

"Who is he, Lucy?" I asked. "Who's after you and Ethan?"

She shook her head. "Not me," she murmured. "He doesn't give a shit about me. He just wants Ethan."

"Who?"

She didn't respond right away, but I was caught off guard by the tears that started to slip from her eyes. She tried to dash them away, but they kept coming. "He was going to kill him," she whispered. "He was on top of him and Ethan couldn't breathe…he wasn't going to stop this time."

"This time?" I prodded, but Lucy shook her head again and stiffened her jaw.

"I should go check on him," she said softly as she used her sleeve to wipe at her face. I didn't say anything as she hurried past me.

I forced myself to get up and finish making dinner, but Lucy didn't return to the kitchen and I didn't blame her.

My appetite was gone too.

CHAPTER 4

ETHAN

What did I tell you, Ethan?

I knew that tone in his voice. It was the tone he used when he didn't really want or need an answer to his question. Not answering would earn me a fist to the face just the same as answering would.

It didn't really matter if I wanted to try answering him or not, because I couldn't. I couldn't do anything but lie there under his body, his legs on either side of my hips holding me down with his greater weight as his big hands tightened around my neck. I didn't wait for him to let up the incessant pressure on my windpipe because I knew this time he wasn't going to.

I could see it in his eyes.

I'd pushed him too far.

I wanted to welcome death as darkness began to prick the edges of my eyes. But that need to take another breath, to see another day kicked in as it always had – the same as it had the first time Eric had knocked me to the floor and begun pummeling me with his booted feet, the same as it had that last night I'd seen him…the night he'd asked me why I hadn't answered my phone when he'd called earlier that day.

I hadn't answered him that time either.

But unlike that night, this time I wouldn't be waking up on the cool tile of my kitchen floor.

Ethan, please, I don't know what to do...I'm so scared!

Lucy.

With everything I had left in me, I clawed at the hands around my throat and when they wouldn't budge, I went after his face.

"Ethan, stop!"

I wanted to say 'Fuck you' to him, but the words wouldn't come even as a sliver of air finally seeped into my tortured lungs.

"Ethan, wake up!"

Lucy?

"Lucy, run," I gasped, but even those few words cost me too much.

"Damn it, Ethan, open your eyes!"

The rough order broke through my muddled mind and even though I'd sworn I'd never take another order from the bastard again, my eyes automatically opened and I jerked upright. The weight from my hips was gone as were the hands around my throat. I used that to my advantage and began striking out with my fists. Even if I just left one bruise on the fucker, it would mean something.

He'd see it and for however long it graced his skin, he'd say to himself, 'Ethan did that to me.'

I wanted to shout out loud when my fist connected with flesh, but the thought was short-lived as my wrists were instantly wrapped up in a brutal hold that I had no chance of escaping from.

"Don't hurt him!" I heard Lucy scream. Why hadn't she run like I told her?

"Ethan, open your eyes now!"

I wanted to scream at him that they were, but it finally registered that they weren't, though I'd thought they were. I opened them for real this time and was immediately rewarded with a flash of light so strong that bile rose in my throat and I was helpless to stop it. I couldn't even lean over so I wouldn't puke on Eric because it all happened too fast.

So much for being strong for once in your life.

I wanted to cry at the self-inflicted jab, but I was still too dizzy to do anything but hang there, puke in my lap and God only knew where else, light seeping through my painfully dry eyes and the sensation of manacles on my wrists.

"Ethan," I heard Lucy whisper. I wanted to tell her to run again, but I didn't even have enough energy to open my mouth, let alone try to form words.

"Lucy, get him some water."

Awareness returned as the heavy timbre of a voice I didn't recognize seeped into my brain.

"Ethan, just take deep breaths."

I did as the voice told me and then I focused on the hands that were still holding my wrists. They were warm and calloused, but they weren't…hurting me.

Other things started to slowly come into focus for me even though I hadn't managed to open my eyes again. It wasn't the hardness of a floor beneath me, but the softness of a mattress…much softer than the mattress from the house Lucy and I had spent the last month in. The scent of mildew wasn't heavy in the air and there was no bitterly cold breeze washing over me from the gaps between the windows and their frames.

Confusion settled over me as I tried to process everything. I hurt like I usually did after one of Eric's "lessons", but why was I still even upright after throwing up on him?

Maybe I hadn't puked?

My eyes focused enough to see that I had, in fact, retched all over myself and the blanket that was half-on, half-off my lap.

My naked lap.

What the hell?

"Ethan, take another breath."

I forced my gaze up and instantly met icy blue eyes that didn't look as hard and unforgiving as I suspected they could have.

Cain.

Awareness returned in waves as I realized where I was.

"Lucy," I whispered, pleased that at least this time I could get the words out, though my voice sounded like I still had Eric's hands wrapped around my throat.

"I'm here," Lucy said in a rush as she returned to the room, a glass of water in hand. Cain released one of my wrists long enough to cover my lower half completely and, despite the fact that it caused some of the spit I'd puked up to drip over my skin, I was grateful. "Here," she said as she handed me the glass. Her face was flushed and I could see she'd been crying recently because her eyelashes were wet.

"Are you okay?" I managed to ask her after taking a sip of the cold water. I was sure nothing had ever tasted so good before.

"Am I…" Lucy said, her voice choked. "I'm okay," she managed to get out with a vigorous nod. She dashed at her eyes again.

"Lucy, can you go make Ethan some soup? There was some chicken noodle in the pantry…strain out everything so there's just the broth."

I was dimly aware that Cain still had ahold of one of my wrists. I should have pulled free of him, but I didn't.

I didn't ask myself why I didn't.

Lucy nodded and then she leaned down to wrap her arms around me. She didn't say anything and her hold was incredibly gentle which was odd for her because she'd always been big on hugs.

Bone-crushing, all-in hugs.

"I'll be back in a minute," she said.

The fog was finally starting to recede and I watched as she left the room, looking back at me every couple feet as if to make sure I was still there.

"Ethan," Cain said quietly and I forced myself to look at him.

"What happened?" I murmured as I took in the tangled bedding at my waist. There were a couple of pillows tossed recklessly on the other side of the bed and even one on the floor.

"You were having a nightmare," he said. He finally let go of my other wrist and I cursed the fact that I missed his touch.

He started to pull the blanket from my lap, but I latched on to his arm to stop him. The second I did, his whole body went tight and all the warmth I'd seen in his eyes fled. As badly as I wanted him to not move that blanket, my self-preservation instincts kicked in at the hard look in his eyes as they met mine and I jerked my hand from his arm.

I'd just made a terrible mistake and it was going to cost me. I knew it just by looking at him.

But he didn't lash out at me. There was no punch to the face, no grabbing of my chin and squeezing it until my eyes bled with uncontrollable tears. He didn't do anything at all. He just sat there, coiled tight like a snake about to strike.

"We need to get you cleaned up," he finally said, his voice sounding tense, but not angry. His hand was still on the blanket, but he didn't move it.

It finally registered that he was talking about the vomit I'd spewed all over my lap earlier. Humiliation coursed through me as I nodded my head. "Right," I whispered. "I...I can do it," I said, though, in truth, my body hurt too much to imagine doing even the simplest of tasks. Taking that sip of water had cost me dearly. I didn't even remember putting the glass on the nightstand, but it was there so either I had done it or Lucy had.

God, why couldn't I think more clearly?

"Do you think you can make it to the shower?" Cain asked as he peeled the blanket away from my lap. Even though all I'd spit up was a mix of saliva and water, it was still a mess. I probably should have been more bothered by the fact that I was now completely exposed to Cain, but somehow the sight of my naked body bothered me less than the sight of my sick clinging to my skin and the blanket.

I felt tears prick my eyes. A shower sounded like a combination of heaven and hell. From the moment Eric had pulled free of my body the day before, I'd wanted nothing more than to scrub away every remnant of his touch from my skin.

I shook my head.

"What if I help you?" Cain asked.

I managed a nod because despite the shame of what that meant, I really wanted that shower.

I didn't look up from my lap as Cain's weight shifted off the bed. I felt one of my arms being lifted and draped over a pair of wide shoulders.

"Swing your feet over," Cain said quietly. I managed to stifle my cry of pain as my body rejected the move. I felt an arm go around my waist and then I was being carefully pulled upright. I immediately felt the urge to vomit again, but luckily, I managed to quell it. Cain did most of the work after that. With every step we took as he practically carried me to the bathroom, I was dimly aware of his clothes scraping over my bare skin.

Blessedly, it wasn't a long distance to the attached bathroom. Cain had me sit on the closed toilet. It occurred to me that I should probably make use of the facilities while I was in there, but the idea of telling Cain that had me keeping my mouth shut. Luckily, the lack of food and water had made it so it wasn't a pressing need. Not to mention that my ass hurt so bad that the idea of using the bathroom left me cold all over.

Another round of tears threatened as I settled my hands on my lap to try and cover my flaccid cock. I kept my eyes on the ground as Cain got the shower going. A sliver of relief went through me when I saw that the owner of the cabin had installed a handrail in the shower. Which meant even if I needed help getting into the shower, at least I'd be able to stand on my own once I was in there.

And that meant only another minute or two of humiliation and then I'd finally have a few moments to myself to try and pull it together.

That was my thought.

Reality, as usual, turned out to be a cruel bitch.

Because as soon as I latched my hands on the rail and Cain removed his arm from my waist, my knees buckled. I would have hit the tile had Cain's reflexes been even a little slower.

I lost it at that point. I was just done.

Utterly done.

The sobs crawled up from my belly so painfully that no amount of wishing them away would have mattered.

I had nothing left.

I stood there, naked and broken with water raining down on me and finally wished Eric had finished what he'd started yesterday.

He'd won.

Even if I was still pulling oxygen into my lungs, he'd won.

I let my knees buckle hoping Cain would just let me slide to the ground and leave me there in peace, but I wasn't that lucky. I waited for him to pull me back out of the shower, but he didn't. Nor did he say anything. I was barely aware of him shifting his body a few times, but I didn't have the energy to look at him or even beg him to leave me alone.

All I had was grief.

Grief for everything I'd lost. Grief for the man I'd once been…that foolish, stupid man who'd walked blindly to the gates of hell and begged to be admitted.

Cain finally moved me, but it wasn't to help me out of the shower. No, it was to move me forward, and to my disbelief, I felt his big body pushing up against me as he climbed in with me, fully clothed.

A new round of wracking, painful cries erupted from my throat at the gesture and I wanted to both tear myself away from him and lean back against him at the same time.

"Just let it out, Ethan," Cain whispered and I swore I felt his lips against the spot where my neck met my shoulder. "I've got you."

I shook my head because I couldn't let myself believe that.

That he had me.

His hold on me was strong, but gentle. Every part of my body hurt, but the pain was secondary to how warm I felt. From the water, from him. Both of his arms were wrapped around me, one at my waist, the other across my chest. I was still clinging to the handrail, but as the terror that had plagued me since the moment my eyes had met Eric's again the day before – no, since the moment I'd realized what a terrible mistake I'd made when I'd let the man into my life four years earlier – began to fade away, I lifted one of my hands to cover the one Cain had pressed right over my heart. I held it there for a moment, knowing I needed to move it, but not wanting to. The pulses of warmth that began to fire through my body, all centered from that one spot where our hands were touching gave me renewed energy, enough to let my breathing even out and for the sobs to fade away unnoticed.

Several long seconds passed before I heard Cain say, "Open your hand."

I did as he said. The hand he had around my waist disappeared and I immediately felt the loss, but I understood the purpose a moment later when he squeezed some body wash into my hand. I used my hand to reach all the places I could, focusing on my lower body where I'd vomited on myself. I was careful not to touch my dick since I didn't want to risk getting even a hint of a hard-on, even though I doubted my body was capable of sexually responding to the close proximity of Cain's.

Once I was finished, Cain handed me the small bottle of body wash. "Put some in my hand," he murmured. My insides tightened at that, but not only because I was nervous about what I knew was coming. The bottle was pretty full so fortunately it didn't take much energy to squeeze some of the gel into his palm. I didn't miss the fact that his hand was so much bigger than mine.

Like Eric's.

An unwanted shiver washed over me. But it dimmed when I felt Cain put some space between us without releasing his hold on me completely. I held on to the rail to keep myself upright as his hand washed parts of my back. His touch was gentle, but impersonal, which I was both glad for and a little disappointed by.

I tensed when Cain's hand skimmed my lower back, but when he brushed the top of my ass, my body locked up tight and I couldn't stop the whimper that slipped from my throat.

"I won't hurt you, Ethan," he said as he stopped his movement. "You had some blood on you that I couldn't reach yesterday with the hand towel."

I wanted to die as I realized what he meant.

I managed a nod, but nothing more.

He made quick work of cleaning my crack and the backs of my thighs. I suspected under normal circumstances, his touch would have turned me on. But all it did was bring back the tears I'd manage to stifle earlier. At least I had the water from the shower to mask them.

He was done within a minute and then he was turning us so the water could wash away the soap on my back. He turned off the water a moment later and then he was easing me out of the shower. I noticed his shoes on the floor and realized that taking them off must have been what he'd been doing earlier right before he'd gotten into the shower with me.

A towel was wrapped around my body as Cain sat me back down on the closed toilet. I was glad to have something to cover up with. He used a second towel to dry off the exposed parts of me. He never looked at me while he worked, which I was supremely grateful for.

"Do you need to use the bathroom?" he asked as he tossed the towel aside.

I shook my head. "But…my teeth. Can I brush them?"

Cain nodded and then began searching the cabinets. He found a new toothbrush and worked it free of its packaging. He put some toothpaste on it and then handed it to me. As I brushed away the lingering taste of puke, he cleaned out a plastic cup that had been holding the cabin-owner's toothbrushes and then filled it with water. He handed it to me so I could rinse and luckily the sink was close enough that I didn't need to stand to spit out the water.

"Anything else?" he asked.

I shook my head. As he helped me to stand and began to lead me from the bathroom, I caught a glimpse of my reflection in the mirror and stumbled to a halt.

I didn't recognize the man looking back at me.

There was nothing of myself, even beyond the bruises, swollen flesh and blackened eyes. It wasn't the first time I'd seen the damage Eric had wielded, but it was the first time I was seeing it through someone else's eyes.

Cain's eyes.

His gaze met mine in the mirror, but I couldn't bear to see the pity I knew would be there, so I dropped my eyes and got us moving again, using one hand to hold my towel in place. Lucy was waiting by the bed, her hands twisted as she watched us approach. She'd swapped the blanket out, though I wasn't sure where she'd gotten the new paisley comforter that was on top of the mattress. The sheet hadn't been changed, but since I hadn't actually puked on it, it hadn't needed to be. There was a bowl of broth on the nightstand.

Just the idea of eating had me wanting to throw up all over again, but I quelled it. Cain helped get me in the bed and didn't loosen the towel from around my body until he had me covered up again. At some point, I'd really need to ask for my clothes back.

Cain didn't speak as he disappeared into the bathroom, towel in hand. His clothes were sopping wet. I hadn't seen a bag in the bathroom so I had no idea if he even had a change of clothes.

"Here," Lucy said as she held up the bowl and handed me the spoon. Her hopeful eyes were on me as I forced myself to eat a few spoonfuls. In between bites, Cain left the bathroom and disappeared from the room all together. Exhaustion was starting to filter through my body and I barely managed to keep my eyes open long enough to answer the questions Lucy asked me about who she was and what year it was. I wanted to tell her I was sorry I hadn't done a better job of looking out for her, but I couldn't find the strength to speak the words. Everything hurt as I lowered my upper half down on the bed and the last thing two things I registered as my eyes drifted shut were Cain returning to the room wearing fresh clothes and the realization that I hadn't thanked him.

CHAPTER 5

CAIN

What the fuck had I been thinking?

I hated the agitation that had become like a living thing beneath my skin. I was known for my coolness under pressure, but now…now I felt like I was going to crawl out of my own skin.

I shoved the offending blanket off my lap and got off the couch. Even with it being pitch dark outside, not to mention cold as fuck, I tore open the front door and went to stand on the porch. The snow had stopped and like Ronan had said, the accumulation hadn't been bad. We'd be able to get down the mountain just as soon as Ethan was up to making the trip.

Even the man's name had me itching to put my hands on something.

Or someone. No, not some*one*…

Fuck!

I began pacing the small porch in the hopes the cold would ease the tension running through my frame. The icy air pricked at my arms and feet but, despite the fact that I was wearing just a T-shirt and jeans, I still felt hot all over.

Why the hell had I touched him?

And why the hell couldn't I stop thinking about it?

Lucy and I had been finishing up dinner when we'd heard moaning coming from the back of the cabin. By the time we'd reached Ethan's room, he'd been screaming the word "No" over and over again. Several pillows had been shoved across the bed and to the floor as Ethan had thrashed around and the blanket had been draped precariously over his lap. As I'd rushed into the room, his screams had stopped and he'd started wheezing like he couldn't breathe. Panic had rushed through me as I'd wondered if one of his injuries had worsened, but I hadn't had time to give it much thought because as soon as I'd put my hands on him, he'd lashed out at me. He hadn't hit me at first – no, he'd clawed at my neck as I'd tried to get ahold of his arms. Even now, I could feel the scratches just beneath my shirt collar where the fabric had shifted during the struggle and his nails had raked over my skin. Just before I'd caught his swinging fists which had come way too close to hitting Lucy who'd gone around to the other side of the bed and climbed onto it in the hopes of waking Ethan up, his fist had connected with my jaw. The blow hadn't been enough to deter me, but unlike when he'd taken swings at me when I'd first arrived and encountered him and Lucy in the front yard, this time he'd managed to leave a mark on me.

Lucy and I had both yelled at him to wake up, but it wasn't until he'd heard Lucy's voice that he'd spoken again.

But just to tell her to run.

To save herself.

To leave him behind.

I shook my head as thoughts about everything the man had endured at the hands of another continued to torment me. Watching him try to hold himself up in that shower, the bruises standing out like swathes of night against his pale skin, the remnants of blood staining the backs of his thighs…I'd been moving before I could even consider what I was doing.

It would have been easy to pull him back out of that shower and just let him use a washcloth to clean off where he'd vomited on himself after being jolted from his nightmare. But I'd seen that blood and I'd wanted it gone. I couldn't explain why…not because what had happened to him disgusted me or anything. No, it was seeing the proof of how badly he'd suffered that had kept me in that shower with him, even as my mind had rebelled at the feel of his back pressed up against my front...his hand clutching my arm where I'd held on to him.

I'd wanted to wash away that proof so that I wouldn't ache inside for what had happened to him. So that I'd be able to think about things other than hunting down the man who'd dared to even lay a finger on him. But there was no washing away the bruises that littered his body like an artist's canvas.

And his sobs...

His soul-crushing, defeated sobs.

The ones I'd felt everywhere.

I'd never heard that level of agony. I'd felt it myself, but I hadn't ever given in to its need to escape my body. No, I'd used it as fuel instead. But with Ethan, I'd wanted the tormented cries gone, just like the blood and any other possible remnants his rapist had left behind as well as the fucking bruises. I'd wanted him to be free of all of it.

Though I had no idea why...

It wasn't like I'd never been around victims before. Hell, my entire childhood had revolved around watching my mother use creative means to hide the bruises that had mottled her skin just like Ethan's did his.

But from the second I'd wrapped my arm around Ethan's too-thin body and told him I had him, something had happened.

And it wasn't something good.

No, it was never good if it stayed with you...if it kept you awake at night.

If it made you start questioning things.

Weird things.

Like why jabs of electricity had fired up from my palm through my entire arm as I'd washed Ethan's back. Like why I'd been tempted to let my hand linger on Ethan's ass after I'd swiped my fingers through his crack, brushing his hole for just the tiniest of moments. Like why it had been so fucking hard to breathe when he'd finally given in to whatever had been holding him back from sinking into my hold, his fingers digging into my arm where he'd clutched me like I was the only thing in the world.

And like why I'd had to escape that room as soon as I'd gotten Ethan settled back in the bed.

Not because my clothes had been sopping wet, though I was more than grateful that I'd had that fact to use for cover.

No, the same thing that was currently keeping me from falling asleep had also had me rushing out of that bedroom.

I was hard.

Rock hard.

Harder than I'd ever been.

It had to be because Ethan's body had been smoother than I'd expected it to be…that the slope of his back had been soft and gentle and that his ass had been perfectly rounded…

"Fuck," I muttered as I stopped at the edge of the porch and stared out into the inky blackness that surrounded me. I tried to focus on the bite in the air and the cadence of the forest as it settled around the cabin, but all I could hear was the sound of Ethan's breathing as I held him. All I could feel was the warmth of his skin…

"Jesus," I snapped and then I was doing something I couldn't even believe I was really doing. I stormed off the porch, not caring that I had no shoes or socks on. The snow was several inches above my ankles, but I barely registered the bitter cold hitting my skin as I hurried around the side of the cabin. I had my pants unzipped and my cock out by the time I was out of sight of the front door and I leaned heavily against the wall as I began stroking myself. The second my hand came into contact with my dick, I felt my balls draw up tight. I tried to call up any one of the women I'd been with in the past, but all I saw behind my closed eyelids were vibrant green eyes. All I felt was impossibly smooth, wet skin beneath my hand. And beneath my lips was the sweetness of Ethan's flavor as I pressed my mouth against the softness of his shoulder.

A ragged groan tore free of my throat as I came hard and fast. My knees buckled as the orgasm wrenched through me and I had to lean against the cabin wall to support myself. Hot cum spewed all over the wall and my hand and it felt like it was never going to stop shooting out of my dick. I buried my mouth against my arm to stifle my moans of pleasure as wave after wave of violent bliss tore through me. When it was finally over, my hand and dick were soaked in ropes of cum and I was struggling to catch my breath. I had no idea how much time passed before the cold finally began to register. My feet felt like blocks of ice as I stripped off my T-shirt and wiped off my still half-hard cock and hand and tucked myself back into my jeans. I returned to the cabin reluctantly and went to the small half-bath to clean up as best I could. I told myself to return to the couch and try to get some sleep, but my body had other ideas because, before I knew it, I was in Ethan's bedroom standing over him. At some point, he'd turned on his stomach in his sleep and the blanket had gotten kicked down enough so it was only covering his lower body from the ass down.

I shook my head as I stared at his back.

There was nothing feminine about him.

Not one goddamn thing.

I reached down to grab the edge of the blanket and pulled it up the length of his back. I didn't have to let my fingers connect with his skin as I covered him, but I did. And sure enough, energy sparked to life every time my body made even the barest contact with his.

Disbelief washed through me as I settled the blanket over his shoulders.

This can't be happening.

But I knew it was. And I knew it wasn't some trick of my imagination because even as I stood there and stared at the look of peace in Ethan's face as he slept, I felt my dick stirring to life again.

I wanted him.

A man.

I turned away from him even as my body urged me to crawl into bed next to him and wrap myself around him so I could absorb some of that same peace he'd finally managed to find in sleep. I knew I wouldn't be as lucky because by the time I reached the couch, I was once again hard and I knew it wouldn't matter if I jacked off again or not.

Because in my gut I knew that as long as I was around Ethan, it would likely become my new normal.

And that just wasn't going to fucking work for me.

∼

Two days later and I was as close to losing it as I could possibly get. I'd managed to avoid Ethan for the most part once I'd accepted that no amount of questions or reassurances that I was just trying to help were going to get him to open up to me. So I'd turned him over to Lucy's care and had only interacted with him when he'd needed help getting to the bathroom. Blessedly, he hadn't needed me in the shower again since enough of his strength had returned that he could take care of the task himself, not to mention that I'd found a small stool in the laundry room that I'd put in the shower for him so he could sit if he felt weak at all. He did, however, need my help getting back and forth to the bathroom. Luckily, I'd had the sense to give him a pair of my sweat pants which had a drawstring in them so he could keep them on his smaller frame. I'd also loaned him a T-shirt which was too big for him, but to my relief and probably his too, he'd worn it anyway. Only now, along with thoughts of what his chest and back would look like when the bruises disappeared, I was wondering if my shirt would smell like him when he gave it back to me.

I was as close to obsessed as I'd ever been about something in my life. So much so that I was hypersensitive to everything around me and instead of actually waiting for danger to seek us out, I kept looking for it instead. Just this very afternoon, I'd nearly taken out the driver of the truck that had ambled down the narrow path leading to the cabin. I'd barely managed to stash my gun at my back after I'd realized the guy was just there to plow the road. The man had waved at me, seemingly unsurprised that the cabin was occupied. Up until that point, I'd been okay with giving Ethan a few more days to recover before we headed to Ronan's house, but the sight of that driver had me on edge and since neither Ethan nor Lucy would tell me who the cabin belonged to and if they had permission to be there, I'd decided we needed to leave sooner rather than later or risk running into the angry homeowner or worse, the cops.

I'd been fortunate to find an outlet for my pent-up energy earlier in the afternoon when the sun had come out and the temps had risen above the freezing level. There'd been a pile of uncut firewood by the cut wood next to the cabin and after searching out the axe in a small shed behind the building, I'd taken out all my frustrations on that pile of wood. My muscles had burned afterwards, but the discomfort had helped since I hadn't been able to work out as much as I'd wanted in the past four days. I'd managed to do some strength training in the small living room, but it hadn't been enough to take the edge off. And since I couldn't risk leaving Lucy and Ethan alone in the cabin, I was pretty much stuck inside of it with them 24/7.

While Lucy had seemed receptive to my presence the first couple of days, her demeanor had changed in the last two. She'd gone quiet again, barely speaking to me beyond one-word answers. She spent most of her time in her room or Ethan's. She took the food I made each night for dinner, but she ate in Ethan's room and I suspected it was at some point over one of the meals that Ethan had reminded her that they couldn't trust me. Ethan had finally started eating more substantial things, but I left all that to Lucy to deal with since I had no desire to spend more time in the man's company than I had to. In fact, I had officially started counting the hours until I could get him and his young charge turned over to Ronan.

As I tried to get comfortable on the too small couch for what thankfully would be the last time, I heard Ethan's door open. It was just the barest of squeaks, but I'd become so in tune to the sound that it never failed to register. Under normal circumstances, I would have waited for the footsteps that signaled Lucy was returning to her room from Ethan's. But it was well after two o'clock in the morning and I'd heard Lucy head to bed hours earlier.

I quickly climbed to my feet, instantly concerned that Ethan needed something. But my worry turned to something else when I saw a figure round the corner from the back hallway into the kitchen. The cabin was almost completely dark except for a small night light plugged in near the stove. It was enough light to confirm it was Ethan I was seeing, but that he clearly hadn't seen me. His moves were slow as he entered the kitchen, but he seemed steady on his feet. I kept my presence to myself since I assumed he was just getting himself something to eat or drink, but the second he began rifling through the drawer nearest the stove, I tensed. From the way he worked to make sure there was next to no sound as he opened the drawer and searched through it, I realized he was looking for something. A mix of fury and fear went through me as it registered what he was looking for and I instantly moved forward, my bare feet silent on the tile floor. Ethan had just pulled the second drawer open when I snagged his wrist and yanked his arm behind his back.

He let out a sharp cry of pain as I snarled, "They're not there, asshole! You want to take me out, you're going to have to find a different weapon!"

"Please," Ethan whispered as I shoved him hard against the counter and grabbed his other hand so I could make sure he hadn't found something in the drawer to use against me. His hand was empty so I yanked him upright and turned him around. He tried to lash out at me, but it was easy to subdue him by putting my hand around his throat. As infuriated as I was, there was enough light cast across his features to remind me of the bruises that still covered much of his face and I automatically eased my grip on him. Ethan's hands came up to close over my wrist at his neck, but he didn't struggle beyond that.

"Did you really think it would be that easy?" I snapped.

"I don't know what you're talking about!" Ethan managed to say, though his voice sounded scratchy.

"Right, and next you're going to tell me you were just looking for a spoon or some shit like that!"

"My keys," he bit out as his breath began to come in ragged gasps. Since my hold on his neck wasn't putting any real pressure on his throat, I knew his reaction wasn't because he couldn't actually breathe.

Which meant he was panicking.

Because I was doing to him what that fucker had done to him just a handful of days ago.

I commanded my mind to release him, but a part of my brain hesitated and I knew why. Just as I began to reach my hand down to quickly check Ethan's clothes for any hidden weapons, the overhead light came on.

"What are you doing?" Lucy shouted and then she was coming at me.

"Don't fucking move!" I yelled at her because I was too close to the edge. If she put her hands on me, I wasn't sure what would happen. Luckily, my tone registered with her and she stopped several feet short of us.

And I knew Ethan had finally seen what he likely couldn't have in the dark. It was the same thing I knew he'd seen several days earlier when I'd been moving the blanket off his lap after he'd vomited on himself and he'd grabbed my wrist. "Do what he says, Lucy," he managed to say between panicked breaths.

Lucy held back, the stark fear in her eyes clear as day. I ignored the guilt of knowing how badly I was scaring her and focused my attention on Ethan, though I kept Lucy in my periphery in case she tried anything.

"I'm not going to hurt you," I said as calmly as I could, my eyes on Ethan's. I needed him to calm down or I'd never be able to search him. And if I couldn't search him, I couldn't release him.

Ethan managed a nod, but I could tell he didn't believe me.

"I just need to make sure you aren't armed. I'll let you go as soon as I'm done."

"I'm not, I swear it."

I didn't bother telling him he could swear it until the cows came home. Instead, I held him there, my grip on his neck as loose as it could be while still keeping him under my control. I hated the sight of the dark bruises beneath my fingers, but I had no choice.

He'd started this by betraying me.

Several long seconds passed before Ethan finally seemed to realize I wasn't letting him go, but that I also wasn't restricting his airflow. His breathing evened out and his grip on my wrist relaxed, though he didn't remove it.

"I'm going to search you now," I warned him. Lucy hadn't moved even an inch.

"Okay," Ethan said, his voice sounding a little more even.

He was still wearing my sweats and T-shirt. I made quick work of skimming my hands down his sides. Luckily, I was still too on edge for my body to react in any kind of way as I ran my hand over his ass and along his legs and groin before reaching up beneath the shirt. When I was satisfied that he wasn't armed, I released him and stepped back. Ethan immediately moved away from me and put himself between me and Lucy. He reached his hand behind him to grab Lucy's, but when she made a move to hug him, I shook my head. "Don't."

Lucy froze and a muffled sob left her throat. As badly as I wanted her to find the comfort in his arms that she so clearly needed, I couldn't risk it. It would be too easy for her to transfer a weapon to him.

I shifted my eyes back to Ethan and said, "Don't force me to search her too."

Ethan's gaze widened. His previously swollen eye had returned to its normal size, so it was startling to see how sharp and bright his green eyes really were.

"Go back to bed, Lucy," Ethan said softly.

"No," the girl immediately said, but Ethan quickly turned to face her. Unlike the other times I'd heard him talk to her, he seemed clear-headed and firm as he repeated the order. His words weren't harsh, but he clearly was letting her know there was no room for argument.

Lucy nodded, but didn't move right away.

"I'll come check on you in a few minutes," he said softly.

Another nod and then she was moving. Once she was gone, Ethan warily returned his eyes to me. "I wasn't looking for a weapon," he said. "I was looking for my car keys."

I didn't believe him, of course, but I didn't say that. The part about his keys might be true, but I had no doubt if he'd been able to find a knife, he would have used it to his advantage.

"And what were you planning to do with your keys?" I asked coldly.

He didn't answer, not that I needed him to. It didn't take a genius to figure out he'd been planning to take Lucy and try and make a run for it. The fact that the girl had been dressed in street clothes instead of the leggings and sweatshirt I'd seen her wearing the last few nights had been telling enough. And while Ethan was still wearing my clothes since I hadn't returned his to him, he'd managed to put on his shoes which had been in his room.

"Sit," I said as I pointed to the kitchen table. He immediately stiffened at the order, but he did what I told him. Part of me hated that he did because I knew what it meant.

He was scared of me.

Not that I could blame him considering what had just happened, but I'd tried not to hurt him despite what he'd done.

I sat down across the kitchen table from him. He refused to make eye contact with me so I took a moment just to study him. He was still a mess since most of the bruises were an angry purple-blue color, but where his skin wasn't bruised, he looked less pale than he had that first day. And while his movements were slow, he didn't seem to be struggling with any nausea or dizziness like he had the first couple of days.

"So your big plan is to run again?" I asked. "Because that's been working so well for you up until now," I added.

No response. No stiffening of his body, no uptick in his breathing, no flash of anger in his eyes. It was like all his effort was centered on not reacting in any kind of way. I couldn't help but wonder if that was how he'd learned to cope. Maybe staying silent and being invisible had saved him in the past.

But I doubted it. It hadn't ever worked for my mother.

Even the brief thought had a renewed level of rage going through me. But this time it wasn't directed at the man across from me.

When he remained stubbornly silent I sighed and said, "Go back to bed, Ethan. Starting tomorrow, you're Ronan Grisham's problem. See if you can convince *him* you don't need help."

I started to get up so I could go back to the couch.

"You don't know a thing about me," Ethan suddenly spit out. I glanced over my shoulder at him and was pleased to finally see some fire in his eyes. I slowly lowered myself back into the chair.

"What I know is that you're scared shitless and I suspect you have every reason to be. I think you're too afraid to ask for help because getting it means you're also getting something I think scares you almost as badly as the motherfucker who stole it from you in the first place." I didn't expect him to respond so I answered his unspoken question. "Hope," I said softly.

Ethan let out a harsh little laugh. "Hope," he murmured. "Hope is the last thing I want," he said as his gaze reconnected with mine. "Eric is going to kill me. Not maybe. Not probably. Not if. He *is* going to kill me. Having hope means making mistakes…it means trusting people who will either end up hastening your death or who will pay the price themselves. Do you and Dr. Grisham really want to be either one of those people?" he asked angrily.

Eric.

Finally, a name to go with the faceless fucker.

"And what about Lucy?" I asked. "Which of those people is she?"

Just like that day in the front yard when he'd put his finger over the trigger of the gun I'd held to his head, Lucy proved to be the chink in his armor because he dropped his eyes. "You said he didn't know Lucy knows. Is *he* Eric?"

There was nothing at first. No comment, no shift in expression. But just before I was about to move on to my next question, Ethan gave me the briefest of nods.

"Who is he?" I asked.

Ethan shook his head. "No, it's my turn," he said. "I get to ask a question."

I wasn't really interested in playing a tit for tat game, but if it got him to give me a little more information, I could work with that. I expected his first question to relate to what Ronan's and my plans for him were, so I wasn't at all prepared for him to say, "What made you think Lucy and I are any kind of threat to you?"

CHAPTER 6

ETHAN

I couldn't help but think that if Cain held his jaw any tighter, it would end up snapping clear in two, but I kept that thought to myself as I watched the traffic fly by us on the Interstate. He'd had the same expression after I'd asked him my question the night before. He'd reminded me that Lucy had held a gun on him that first day, but when I'd pointed out that even armed, she'd been no match for him and I hadn't been able to even land one decent blow on his body as he'd subdued me, he'd fallen silent. Several long minutes had passed before he'd softly ordered me to go back to bed. As eager as I'd been to escape him only moments before, I'd actually hesitated and I'd forced myself to go to Lucy's room to check on her before going back to my own to try and sleep.

The second he'd grabbed me in the darkness of the kitchen as I'd been rummaging through the drawers, I'd immediately thought he was Eric and the panic had nearly crippled me. It had hurt when he'd yanked my arm back behind me like he had, but the second I'd cried out in pain, he'd loosened his hold, easing the pressure on my shoulder joint. But while the pain had dissipated, my fear hadn't, even after I'd realized he wasn't Eric. Because I'd seen the fury in his eyes. Along with something else…

It was the same darkness I'd seen when I'd grabbed his hand as he'd tried to move the blanket off my lap just before he'd helped me into the shower. Just like that day, I'd sensed the danger I was in. He'd had control of himself, but I'd instinctively known there was something just beneath the surface. Like someone had lit a match and was holding it just millimeters above a geyser of gas...all it would take was for one of those droplets to push just a little higher than the rest and it would be over.

I'd seen similar reactions in some of the trauma victims I'd treated, especially when they came into the ER unconscious only to wake up surrounded by strange hands and voices. They often lashed out in defense before I or another staff member could convince them they were no longer in danger.

It was that revelation and the fact that Cain hadn't hurt me despite his obvious anger that had made it possible for me to relax in his grip and get myself under control. Lucy's presence had almost set him off again, but I'd grudgingly respected his ability to maintain that iron grip he had on himself. But he'd also been short on patience and I'd had no doubt that for whatever reason, he really had believed there was a possibility Lucy had some kind of weapon and that she'd give it to me if we'd been given the chance to come into contact with one another beyond holding hands. Sending her back to her room had been one of the hardest things I'd had to do, but her safety had been my main concern so I'd done it. And luckily, she hadn't argued with me, though she rarely did.

Because she trusted me implicitly.

It was one of the many reasons she also hadn't put up much of an argument when I'd told her we couldn't trust Cain, which meant we couldn't share anything about ourselves with him. I'd seen the disappointment in her eyes and I'd understood it completely because, despite what I'd told Cain about hope, I'd felt it resurface for the briefest of moments when he'd held me in that shower.

Lucy had also agreed to my plan for the night before. When I'd told her we needed to leave while Cain was asleep, she'd informed me that Cain had taken the keys to the SUV at some point and she wasn't sure what he'd done with them. I'd had to hope he hadn't had them on his person when I'd started my search for them while Lucy had waited in her room for me to come and get her, but I hadn't had a chance to find out since he'd grabbed me right after I'd started checking the kitchen drawers for them. It had been a fool's errand to think I could be stealthy enough to get past a man like him, but desperate times…

Despite Cain's rough handling after he'd accused me of trying to find a weapon to use against him, I hadn't truly been afraid of him when he'd told me to sit at the table. That was one of the main reasons I'd been able to keep from telling him what he wanted to know.

Early on in my relationship with Eric, I'd been a terrible liar and on the few occasions I'd tried to lie about something to protect myself from his punishments, he'd seen through me easily. Even when I'd started telling him the truth, it hadn't mattered because he'd already made up his mind at that point if he was going to believe me or not and he usually didn't. While I'd gotten more skilled at lying about things, near the end, it hadn't mattered what I'd said to Eric…he'd made up his mind about hurting me long before the first blow fell.

If Cain had threatened me with violence, I would have caved. I simply didn't have the strength to stand up to him…not the physical strength and most definitely not the mental strength. Hell, all he would have had to do was make one subtle comment about Lucy and I would have sung like a bird.

But the fact that he hadn't offered up any kind of threat had emboldened me and I'd clung to my secrets. It had been a liberating feeling and I supposed that was what had bolstered me enough to dare to ask him why he thought Lucy and I posed him any kind of threat.

He'd let Lucy and me sleep in this morning, but by mid-morning we were locking up the cabin. I hadn't been foolish enough to hope he'd let me and Lucy follow him down the mountain in our car, but I had been expecting that I'd drive our SUV while he kept Lucy with him while he drove his truck. It was an idea I'd been wholeheartedly ready to argue with him about since whatever meager trust Lucy had initially had in the man had been wiped out by his actions the night before, but he'd surprised me again by saying we were all going in his truck and he'd arrange to have the SUV picked up. He'd seemed surprised at my lack of argument until he'd seen the way Lucy had flinched away from him as he'd motioned for us to head out of the cabin. He hadn't said anything, but I hadn't missed the mix of hurt and guilt in his eyes.

I'd ended up sitting up front because I'd wanted Lucy to have the room to stretch out in the backseat so she could get some sleep. Her constant weariness was always at the forefront of my mind, but I knew there wasn't much I could do for her besides try to make sure she got as much rest as possible. Between the events of the day Eric had reappeared in our lives and the hell we'd been living the past six months as we'd tried to stay a step ahead of the man, she was enduring something no fifteen-year-old kid ever should. I'd taken her to keep her safe, but I couldn't help but wonder if I'd done the right thing.

I cast a glance over my shoulder at Lucy and saw that she'd taken my suggestion to lie down once we'd gotten down the mountain and onto the Interstate. She still had her seatbelt on, but she'd managed to find a position where she could stretch her legs out on the seat while using her duffle bag as a pillow of sorts. Her eyes were shut and while that in itself wasn't a guarantee of sleep, the relaxed expression on her face was.

I finally let my mind drift to what was about to happen. I knew nothing about Ronan Grisham other than him seeming like a decent guy…and a reasonable one. My hope was that I could convince him that Lucy and I were better off on our own and I wasn't above begging the man not to tell anyone about us. I had no intention of telling him who Lucy and I were, but I'd started spinning a tale in my head that I hoped he'd buy. I'd already discussed it with Lucy and I knew she'd do what I told her and not say anything at all. I refused to let my mind go to a place where he called the cops. Technically he could do that anyway, even just for the procedure I'd performed on the patient the week before. And while I couldn't regret my actions since the man had lived, I knew if he did make that call, I'd have to tell the cops the truth and hope like hell they believed me over the version of events Eric had come up with.

If it meant going to jail or being sent back to where Eric could get to me, I no longer cared…as long as Lucy was safe. And if telling my story to anyone who would listen, including the media, would help, I'd do it in a heartbeat. Hopefully someone would question things enough to see the truth and to make sure Eric couldn't get to Lucy.

"Relax, Ethan," Cain murmured. Despite his low voice, I still jumped. He shot me a glance that showed he wasn't exactly surprised by my reaction. "I'm not taking you to the executioner," he drawled.

"You seem like a smart man, Cain," I returned as I turned my attention out the window. "But you'll forgive me if I say you don't know what the hell you're talking about."

I heard the man sigh, but I didn't care. Did he really think I was going to thank him for intruding in our lives like this? Frustration welled inside of me as I thought about everything I'd lost in the past few years. As hard as these last six months of being on the run had been, at least they'd been my choice.

"You and Ronan," I whispered as I willed the tears away. "You have no right to do this."

I hated how my voice caught. I kept my eyes on the window even as I felt the car slow and we took the next exit off the Interstate. I didn't know Seattle all that well, but I knew enough that we weren't anywhere near the city. I tensed up when Cain turned onto a quiet looking road and then turned again on a side road with nothing but farm land around. He pulled off to the side and threw the truck into park and turned it off. He snatched the keys out of the ignition and quietly said, "Get out of the truck, Ethan."

Fear ratcheted down my spine as I realized I'd finally managed it. I'd said something that had made him cross that line. I wanted to cry as I got out of the truck and closed the door as quietly as I could. No way I wanted Lucy to witness this. I went to the back of the truck where Cain was waiting for me and I could see that he was pissed. He looked a lot like he had that first day when Lucy and I had gone after him in the snow.

I knew that if I apologized, I might have a chance of making this all go away. It hadn't always worked with Eric, but Cain seemed more in control of his emotions. If I was sincere enough...

But I shook my head. No, I wasn't going back to that part of my life. Let the asshole hit me...it would be proof that everything he'd said was a lie. That the way he'd held me in that shower had been a lie.

Just let it out, Ethan...I've got you.

"Lie," I whispered under my breath so he wouldn't hear.

I forced myself to look at him and settled my eyes on the small bruise on his jaw. I hadn't realized it at the time, but Lucy had told me later that I'd struck Cain when he'd been trying to wake me up from my nightmare. I'd been stunned to learn that not only had I managed to leave a mark on him, but that he hadn't hit me back. The guilt I'd felt at actually even inflicting the smallest amount of pain on him had consumed me, but when I'd tried to apologize to him the next day when he'd helped me to the bathroom, he'd brushed off my words like they were nothing...like the bruise was nothing.

Though I supposed to a man like him, it was nothing.

Even now, he seemed to tower over me and I couldn't stop from staring at his hands. Maybe if I saw them close into fists, I'd somehow be able to prepare myself for the blow...

"Stop that," Cain said harshly. I forced my eyes up to his and saw the glittering anger there. I dropped my eyes again and hunched in on myself. I knew it was a self-defense mechanism that I'd learned early on – making myself as small a target as I possibly could – and I hated that I relied on it even now after promising myself I didn't care what he did to me, but old habits died hard.

I sensed rather than saw Cain moving towards me and I reflexively backed up until my back hit the back of the truck. I turned my head to the side but didn't cover it with my hands like I wanted since that would only make things worse. Submissive was one thing, cowardly was another.

Eric hated cowards.

"Don't make me him," Cain said roughly as his body crowded mine. The heat coming off him was intense and even as I waited for him to grab me, I felt part of my body wanting to seek out more of that warmth.

It was sick.

I was sick.

"Ethan," Cain said softly and then his fingers were at my chin...not to grab it, but to tip it up. "I'm not him," he whispered.

I nodded, though it was more of an instinctive thing than anything else. When Eric got all quiet and reflective, I found that agreeing with him typically worked better than silence. "I know you're not."

It wasn't until I felt Cain's thumb stroke over my jawline that I forced myself to look at him. As soon as I met his gaze he said, "Ethan, I'm not him."

He held me there like that, refusing to let me look away. I wanted to repeat my own statement to assure him that I knew that, but the lie wouldn't fall from my lips, so I only nodded.

I felt his warm breath skitter over me as a sigh escaped his lips.

He didn't believe me.

I really *was* a bad liar.

I expected him to release me and step away, but I was surprised when his fingers drifted down to my throat. His thumb flicked back and forth over a spot near my pulse and then his entire palm flattened against the spot just above my T-shirt collar.

The T-shirt that had only stopped smelling like him the day before.

"Did I hurt you last night?" he asked me softly. His eyes weren't on mine anymore. They were on my neck.

"No," I murmured as I sensed the change in him.

It wasn't a real lie...he'd hurt me for a handful of seconds, but compared to what I was used to, it had been the equivalent of having my hand gripped just a little too hard during an overeager handshake with someone.

His eyes lifted to mine again and then his finger was on the move, rubbing back and forth over my skin in an almost soothing manner. I briefly wondered if the man might be gay, but he threw off so many mixed signals that I really had no idea. I certainly wasn't going to risk having my ass handed to me by testing to see if he was or wasn't, no matter what kind of havoc his touch was wreaking on my senses.

"Ethan, I need you to give me your word that Lucy is with you by choice and that you haven't touched her."

I stiffened at that. I knew, in theory, that some people who looked at our situation might think my relationship with the young girl was inappropriate and there were even some out there who'd been convinced it was, but actually hearing the words made bile creep up the back of my throat.

"I swear on my life that I would never hurt her. I've never laid a hand on her in anger or in any other way that you're thinking," I managed to get out.

Cain's eyes lifted to meet mine and he studied me for the longest time.

Making sure I was telling the truth, no doubt. I held my ground because of all the things I wanted…no, *needed* him to believe about me, it was this.

Cain finally nodded and then his hand was cupping my neck as he fiercely whispered, "I know you won't believe this, but I'm going to say it anyway. I don't lie, Ethan, and I detest people who do. If you can't tell me the truth, then don't say anything at all."

I managed a shaky nod, though I had no idea why I was even responding to the crazy statement. People lied every second of every day.

But in my gut, I knew he wasn't talking about the little white lies people told each other every day to keep the peace or to make their lives easier or to not hurt the feelings of someone they cared about. No, what he was talking about went deeper.

I wanted to believe him…badly. But, how could I?

"Why are you telling me this?" I asked.

"Because I'm about to make you a promise that I want you to hang onto for as long as it takes for you to tell Ronan everything."

I shook my head because there was no way in hell I was telling the man anything beyond the lies I'd come up with about who Lucy and I really were. So what if Cain would hate me for it? I didn't owe him anything.

Cain stopped my shaking head by cupping the back of it in a way that I was forced to keep my attention solely on him.

"If you think for even one second after you and Ronan are done talking that you're not better off accepting his help, I will help you leave. No matter what. Even if Ronan says you're not going anywhere...if he calls the cops...doesn't matter. If you want to go, I will get you and Lucy out of there and I will take you wherever you want to go, no questions asked. And you will never have to see any of us ever again."

The promise was a startling one and I couldn't believe it. But the way he was holding onto me, his eyes boring into mine, I so badly wanted to.

I tried to pull away, but he wouldn't let me. His body pressed against mine as he continued to hold on to me. I started to put my hands at his waist simply because I didn't know what else to do with them, but he stiffened as soon as I brought them up so I immediately dropped them again.

"That's why," Cain whispered as his gaze fell to my hands and stayed there for several long seconds. I had no clue what he was talking about, but then he was looking in my eyes again. "Your question last night about seeing you as a threat. I can see that your hands are empty and I know you're no threat to me, but my brain still thinks you are. It's telling me to search you for a weapon again, even though I know you don't have one."

His voice was so low, I barely heard it.

But I had and I was reeling from his admission.

"I let someone get too close once and it cost me everything," Cain murmured. "I'm not going to make that mistake again."

I nodded, even though I didn't truly understand what he meant. But whatever had happened to him, it had left its mark in a big way and I understood his message loud and clear.

Hands off. Full stop.

"Swear on the most important person in your life that you're telling me the truth about letting me and Lucy go," I said. It was a stupid demand, but I needed it just the same.

"I can't," he said quietly.

I immediately tried to escape his hold, but he refused to release me. "I can't because I don't have anyone important in my life." He paused for a moment before he finally said, "This truck…this fucking truck is the only thing I have that I give a shit about. So if you want me to swear on a piece of metal that I meant what I said, I'll do it."

I didn't miss the shimmer of amusement in his eyes as he said the words and for some reason, that helped more than anything else. It was one of the few times I'd sensed any emotion behind his icy veneer.

"No," I said as I relaxed a little in his grip. "I don't need that."

Cain nodded and released me. I missed his touch almost immediately which made no sense to me, but since nothing had made sense to me since this man had stormed into my life, it didn't really matter. I'd do something I hadn't thought I'd ever do again and I suspected would likely come back to bite me in the ass.

I'd trust him.

~

"Please, have a seat."

I glanced over my shoulder at Lucy as she followed the young man and three kids towards the kitchen. Her eyes connected briefly with mine and I gave her a reassuring smile before I entered the room and went to the couch Ronan Grisham was pointing to and sat down. We were in some kind of sitting room or den. There were several nice pieces of oversized leather furniture surrounding a huge flat screen TV. Late afternoon light was filtering in through the window so I could easily make out the half dozen pictures on the bookshelf along the far wall. Most were of the three kids I'd been introduced to a few minutes earlier as well as Ronan's young husband, Seth, but there were also pictures of several other people, kids and pets. I hadn't known Ronan was a family man, though I'd heard through the rumor mill at the hospital that he was married to a man. I'd also heard and seen the infinite amount of respect the man had garnered.

I'd been a nervous wreck when we'd arrived at the stately home fifteen minutes ago. It was located in a nice neighborhood just north of the city and while it wasn't the biggest house on the block, it was still more than I'd ever dreamed of one day owning.

Lucy hadn't been doing much better than me, so I'd held myself together for her and I hadn't been surprised when she'd clung to my hand as I'd followed Cain into the house. We'd first been greeted by a huge German Shepherd that Ronan had later introduced to us as Bullet. The dog had been friendly and I'd enjoyed watching the fleeting smile that had graced Lucy's lips as the dog had eagerly lifted a paw in greeting. She'd shaken it before letting her fingers stroke over the well-behaved animal's big head. Ronan had appeared a moment later and while his eyes had narrowed slightly when they'd fallen on me, he'd smiled kindly before holding out his hand to me. I'd realized as soon as he'd called me by my real name that at some point Cain must have called him and told him what it was. A large African American man who Ronan had introduced as Phoenix had been with him and I'd immediately found myself shrinking back against Cain who'd remained behind us, probably to keep us from darting out the door. Phoenix had extended his greetings, but he hadn't tried to force a handshake on me which I'd been extremely grateful for. The tension had been thick in the air until we'd encountered Ronan's husband and three children.

I was caught off guard by both the age gap between Ronan and his husband, Seth, as well as the age of their oldest child, a girl named Willow. Since Seth was in his early twenties at the most, I suspected at least Willow was adopted since she was close to Lucy's age. I suspected the same of the middle child, Niccle, who was around eight, but I knew it was possible that the youngest child, a boy, could have been either man's biological child. In theory, the older ones could have been Ronan's children from a previous relationship, but I doubted it.

Seth had been welcoming, though he'd been careful to limit the physical contact with me and Lucy. I hadn't missed the way nearly everyone had stared at my face when they'd seen it and, for the first time, that'd had my insides flooding with shame. It wasn't like I could pass off my injuries from something as benign as a fall.

The youngest, Jamie, had asked his Daddy Seth what had happened to me, but Seth had merely said I had some "owies" that needed some extra special care. The little boy had gone on to suggest his Daddy Ronan fix them before he'd asked me if I wanted to see his Spiderman doll. Seth had asked both me and Lucy if we needed anything to eat or drink. I'd been the one to suggest to Lucy that she go have some hot chocolate when the oldest girl offered it because I didn't want Lucy hearing my conversation with Ronan. There were a lot of things the girl knew, but plenty she didn't and I wanted to keep it that way. Lucy had been reluctant, but she'd nodded. I'd reassured her that I'd see her soon and then I'd watched her follow the small group along with the dog down the hall towards the kitchen while Ronan had motioned to a door to my left.

Ronan sat on the couch across from me while Phoenix took up an armchair nearby. Cain remained near the door. I liked that I could still have my eyes on him as we talked, though I wasn't sure why. Maybe I needed to see if there was any point where I'd see something in his gaze that told me the words he'd said to me earlier were a lie.

Not that it mattered since between the three men in the room, I wasn't going anywhere unless they decided to let me go.

"Thank you for coming, Ethan," Ronan began. "I know it couldn't have been easy for you."

I bit back the retort I was about to spew out that I didn't really have a choice in the matter and just remained quiet.

"Before we talk, I would like to know if I can take a look at your injuries."

"I'm fine," I assured him.

"I don't doubt that," he said calmly. "But the doctor in me won't be able to relax until I know for sure." He paused before saying, "I think you know what I mean."

REVELATION

I wanted to believe he was only guessing with the implication, but I doubted it. I supposed it could have been the procedure I'd performed on that patient that had tipped Ronan off, but I doubted that too. In my gut, I knew that Ronan knew I was a doctor. I had a sneaking suspicion he knew more than that.

"Okay," I finally said, though in truth, I didn't want him touching me. Not that I had anything against him personally. I just didn't want anyone touching me.

I saw Ronan nod at Phoenix who immediately left the room. I saw Ronan's eyes connect with Cain, the silent message clear. I was about to tell him I wanted Cain to stay when Cain said, "I'll stay."

To give Ronan credit, he barely reacted, but I didn't miss the subtle shift in his eyes as he looked from Cain to me and back to Cain. For my part, I was beyond relieved that I hadn't needed to ask the man to stay myself.

Since I didn't even know why it was so important that he did.

"Is that okay with you, Ethan?"

I quickly nodded, keeping my eyes off Cain so Ronan wouldn't think my behavior odd. I endured Ronan's touch as he quickly examined the bruises on my jaw and neck. He ran through the standard questions I would have asked one of my own patients. When he asked me to remove the T-shirt, I did so reluctantly. He took a stethoscope from a small bag next to the couch and listened to my heart and breathing and then went through taking the rest of my vitals. He rattled off the different diagnoses as he worked, looking to me with each one to see if I concurred or not.

I did…on every single one.

I was glad when he didn't ask me to remove my pants, instead having me roll them up to take a look at a gash on one of my legs. The exam took a good fifteen minutes before he seemed satisfied.

"Do you need anything?" Ronan asked. "Something for the pain?"

I shook my head. While I was still really sore and likely would be for a while yet, I needed my wits about me. But there was one thing I needed if I could just find the courage to admit to it. I cast a brief glance at Cain and was surprised to find him watching me, his expression unreadable. He hadn't moved even once from his position near the door, but I'd still felt oddly comfortable having him there.

"Do you need Cain to step out for a moment, Ethan?" Ronan asked as he waited patiently. The man was way too perceptive. Few people likely would have known I was working up to something.

"No," I shook my head. I forced myself to make eye contact with Ronan as I softly said, "Can you draw blood?"

Ronan nodded, but waited for me to continue on my own.

"I need to be tested for STDs," I finally managed to get out just before I shot another look in Cain's direction.

I couldn't tell if his expression was unreadable anymore because he was no longer looking at me.

I couldn't say I really blamed him. After everything I'd let happen to me, I couldn't look at me either.

CHAPTER 7

CAIN

The reminder of Ethan's rape had me so enraged that I had to look away from him so he wouldn't see the fury in my eyes and somehow think it was for him. I'd already seen him look at me once today like I was no better than the piece of shit who'd hurt him and I couldn't go through that again. Watching Ethan stand before me quietly as he'd waited for my fists to fall, resigned to his fate, had been a brutal wake-up call for me. I'd never claimed to be an easy man to deal with, nor a particularly gentle one. But I'd also never hurt someone who didn't deserve it. So to be placed in that same category had hurt like a motherfucker. And in that moment, nothing had mattered but making Ethan understand I would never do that to him. Yes, I'd hurt him briefly when I'd sought to disarm him the night before, but I'd still been careful not to do anything that would have left him with any kind of lasting pain.

But between him and Lucy looking at me all morning like I was leading them to the slaughter *and* that I'd be the one to deliver the fatal blow had been a unique form of torture.

So I'd done the one thing I could think of that might buy me the sliver of trust I needed to make all this easier for the both of them.

I'd told Ethan the truth.

About the fact that I didn't lie and when I'd finally answered his question from the night before.

It had been a strange thing to speak the words aloud...to admit for the first time what drove my aversion to being touched. I suspected Ronan and Memphis knew because they knew about my past, but I hadn't actually ever told them what I'd told Ethan.

"I'll run this under my own name," I heard Ronan say to Ethan once he'd collected the blood. "I'll need a urine sample too at some point," the man said softly and I watched Ethan nod his head. The little bit of unbruised skin on his face went bright with color and I wished there was some way I could spare him the humiliation.

I saw Ronan nod at me and I knew what he wanted. I opened the door and motioned to Phoenix who went and sat back down in one of the armchairs near Ethan. I felt my gut twist uncomfortably at how close the two men were, but I didn't want to admit what the cause of the uncomfortable sensation was.

But just because I didn't want to think about it, didn't mean I was safe from the thought.

I knew Phoenix was gay. He was also a very good looking man and his presence here meant Ronan had plans for him with this case. It should have been a relief because it would make things that much easier when I asked Ronan to reassign me.

It wasn't a relief.

Not even close.

"Ethan, I would like to start by saying nothing you tell us leaves this room," Ronan said. "My men and I are here to help you."

"You're a doctor," Ethan said softly. "Why do you even have men?" he asked, his voice laced with distrust.

"Because I've been where you've been. Alone. Scared. Broken," Ronan said softly. "Someone helped me fight back and I decided to pay that forward. In a perfect world, there'd be no need for the men who work for me, but you and I both know that very little about this world is perfect and sometimes things like justice need a helping hand."

Ethan didn't respond at first, but I felt a shimmer of electricity flicker through me when his eyes met mine.

And then I saw it.

That moment where he was giving me exactly what I wanted, along with proof that he was fucking terrified. I didn't need to hear the words to know what he was saying.

I'm trusting you. Please don't let me down.

I gave him a nod, ignoring the fact that Ronan and Phoenix were both watching us.

I've got you, Ethan.

Ethan dropped his eyes and took a deep breath. "My name is Ethan Rhodes. Up until about six months ago, I was working as an ER doctor at George Washington University Hospital in Washington D.C."

"And Lucy?" Ronan asked when Ethan didn't continue.

"She's my ex-boyfriend's stepdaughter."

"Eric Palmer?" Ronan asked softly.

Caught off guard, Ethan managed a nod and then said, "How did you know?"

"After Cain told me yours and Lucy's first names, I had one of my people do a little digging. She found a BOLO alert on you."

"What…what is that?" Ethan asked.

"It means 'Be on the Lookout.' It's used to inform law enforcement to be on the alert for suspects, missing persons and people of interest. It allows police officers to detain someone until the interested party can be notified," Ronan explained.

Ethan paled, but nodded. "Is it…is it for kidnapping?" he asked.

"No, it's not a warrant. You're named as a person of interest in transporting a minor across state lines."

"Person of interest?" Ethan asked, his voice shaky.

"You haven't formally been charged with the crime," Ronan said.

"Why wouldn't Eric just have me charged with kidnapping?"

"My guess is your ex wanted some wiggle room…he needed help finding you, but didn't want you to be formally charged."

Ethan shook his head. "He wants to control the outcome," he murmured.

"It's a calculated risk. If you're arrested and charged, you're more likely to tell your side, but as a POI, he can work something out with you and drop the charges if things go his way."

Ethan nodded. "He doesn't want me in jail. He wants things to go back to the way they were. And when things quiet down…"

I remembered Ethan's words from the night before. He'd been so certain Eric would kill him. He'd actually accepted it as a foregone conclusion.

"Start at the beginning, Ethan," I said softly as I watched Ethan try to hold himself together. I was tempted to go sit next to him on the couch, but I knew it would look strange, so I stayed where I was.

"Um, I met Eric a little over four years ago. I was a second-year resident at that time."

"Second year?" Ronan interjected. "Most people your age would have still been in medical school at that time."

"Yeah, um, I skipped a couple of grades when I was a kid. I graduated high school when I was sixteen."

Ronan nodded.

"Eric came into the ER with a broken wrist. He'd been chasing a suspect. When he tackled the guy, he fell wrong…"

"Your ex is a cop?" I asked.

Ethan nodded. "For Metro PD…Metropolitan Police Department in D.C." Ethan dropped his eyes again and said, "He started flirting with me, though I didn't really realize it at the time. I was…I was kind of clueless when it came to that kind of stuff," he said softly. "When he asked me out, I was so surprised. I told him no because I didn't think I was allowed to date a patient. He came back the next day and asked me out again…said I wasn't his doctor anymore." Ethan paused before softly whispering, "He was so charming."

Silence fell across the room and I had no doubt Ethan was remembering that day because a wistful expression fell over his face. It took him several long moments to continue.

"Things were good at first. He was patient and sweet. I wasn't very experienced so I wanted to move slow. He did too. He said I was worth waiting for. It was three months before we even…you know," Ethan murmured as more color flooded his face.

"Things started to go bad about a month after that. He hit me for the first time after he accused me of cheating on him. Another doctor had given me a ride home from work when I was having car trouble. I didn't even know how Eric knew and when I asked, he hit me and told me not to try and change the subject. I was so stunned that I didn't know what to do. He apologized the next day…told me it was just because he loved me so much and the idea of me with someone else drove him crazy. He swore he would never do it again and I believed him. *I needed to believe him,*" he added, his voice low.

"About six months into our relationship, Eric was involved in something pretty big. He and some other officers were providing support to the Secret Service for this rally for one of the presidential candidates running for office that year."

I knew instantly what Ethan was talking about and what would come next because it had been big news at the time.

"Eric intercepted a guy who'd managed to get past security and was running towards the stage. He…he had a bomb strapped to his chest. Eric tackled him and kept him from detonating the bomb. It was…it was a big deal."

"I remember that," Ronan said softly. "It was all over the news."

Ethan nodded. "Everybody called him a hero. And he was," Ethan murmured. "He saved a lot of lives that day. No one…no one knew what he was really like." I saw Ethan dash at his eyes. Even though he'd only mentioned the one violent episode, I knew he'd left countless more out.

"The press was how I found out he was married…to a woman," Ethan said softly. "I'd had no idea. But things started to make sense after that. Why he never wanted to go out in public with me, why he rarely spent the night. I confronted him about it and told him I didn't want to see him anymore. It…it didn't go well for me." Ethan fell silent for a moment before continuing.

"I found out his wife was actually his second wife. His first had died about a year after Eric married her – some kind of drowning, I guess. His second wife was named Patricia Fields and I guess she was a pretty big deal. A lawyer for the White House or something. They'd been married for three years. Patricia had a daughter from a previous marriage."

"Lucy," Ronan murmured.

Ethan nodded. "She told me later that Eric adopted her about a year after the marriage. Lucy's dad died of a heart attack when she was nine. I guess Patricia was well-off – family money or something. After I found out about Patricia, Eric would talk a lot about how she never let him forget it was her money and not his. The things he said about her..." Ethan shook his head.

"Do you think he was abusing her too?" I asked.

Ethan glanced at me and shook his head. "I don't think so. Lucy said he never laid a hand on her. They fought a lot, but for some reason, Eric never went after her like he did me."

Yeah, because Eric had had Ethan to use as a punching bag. I had no doubt the fucker had taken every violent thought he'd had about his powerful wife and vented it on Ethan instead. A glance at Ronan told me he was thinking the same thing.

"The episode with the bomber got Eric a pretty big promotion at work. He became some kind of liaison with the Secret Service. It meant meeting a lot of important people. He...he was on cloud nine," Ethan murmured. "Which meant things got better for me for a little while and I thought maybe the worst was behind us. He'd told me he was planning to divorce Patricia all along but that now he needed to wait until the press died down. He said he'd come out too...that he'd proudly tell the world about us. He became that guy who'd swept me off my feet again and we were really happy for a few months. But when the attention started to wear off..."

"The abuse started again," Ronan said softly when Ethan seemed reluctant to continue.

Ethan nodded. "It was worse than ever," he whispered. "He began controlling everything in my life. He tracked my phone, my car. He took over my finances and monitored my email. If I went somewhere

I wasn't supposed to, he accused me of going to meet a lover. If I spent money on something he didn't authorize, he wanted to know what it was. If someone from work called me, he wanted to know why. My work schedule was always unpredictable, but he accused me of lying about the extra hours I'd work. He was sure I was cheating on him," Ethan whispered.

"But I wasn't…even if I'd had the chance, I wouldn't have. I…I wouldn't do that," he said as he looked at me and then Ronan.

"I tried to leave him a few times, but he wouldn't let me go. I think people at work started to figure things out. I couldn't always hide the bruises. I started calling in sick when the beatings became too much, but when my boss said he'd have to let me go if I kept doing it, I knew I needed to do something. Work was all I had left…I couldn't…I couldn't lose that too."

Ethan paused for a moment and I saw Ronan get up and go to a small refrigerator that was part of a built-in bar along the far wall. He returned with a bottle of water and set it in front of Ethan along with a box of tissues.

"Thank you," Ethan whispered. His fingers were shaking as he tried to open the bottle of water. It took him a few tries before he managed it. He wiped carefully at his face with a tissue before he continued.

"I started planning my escape about eighteen months ago. Eric would only give me a certain amount of money each week to live on. He'd forced me to add him to my accounts so he'd be able to see if I took any money out of them, so I never did. Instead, I began shopping at places where I'd be less likely to get receipts…like farmer's markets. I bought as much of my food there as I could and then kept the leftover money. Eric believed me when I told him that I wasn't able to get receipts for the things I'd bought and he wasn't around often enough to see that I wasn't buying as much as I said I had. I took the change and opened a safe deposit box at a bank a few miles from my work. I only ever took the bus to that bank and I left my phone at work when I would make my weekly runs so Eric never found out about it. I…I started hiding proof there too."

"Proof?" Ronan asked.

A quick nod from Ethan. "Um, yeah, I started recording Eric when I knew I was in trouble for something. They had these small digital recorders at work that we used to use for transcription before the electronic charting system was implemented. I...I took one and I set it up in my room...I taped it to the back of my bookshelf. I'd turn it on when I knew Eric was coming over. Most of our fights ended up in my room," Ethan said softly before dropping his eyes.

I stiffened at that because I knew what he meant. The idea that he'd been repeatedly sexually assaulted broke open something so deep inside me that I barely managed to stifle a moan. I noticed Phoenix watching me with curiosity so I forced myself to focus on Ethan while trying to school my reaction.

"I'd use the computers at work to transfer the recordings to CDs... I didn't store them electronically because I was afraid Eric would somehow be able to find any kind of cloud account. I put the CDs in my safe deposit box. I put medical proof in there too."

"What kind of proof?" I asked, though I already knew.

I could see the shame creep into Ethan's eyes and I hated that he couldn't look at me as he spoke.

"Mostly just pictures I took of my bruises in the mirror, but one night after a particularly bad fight, I had to go to the hospital because I knew he'd done damage that I couldn't treat myself. I went to a hospital in Maryland because I knew they might call the cops even if I told them not to. I convinced them not to, but asked them to take pictures and document my injuries-"

"What kind of injuries?" I asked.

Ethan's eyes flashed to mine and he shook his head.

"What kind of injuries, Ethan?" I asked, softening my voice. He held my gaze for a long moment before speaking. But he refused to keep looking at me.

"He broke my arm and two ribs. I needed stitches here," Ethan murmured as he touched a spot behind his ear. "I was bleeding... rectally...but it didn't stop on its own so I was worried he'd done more damage than usual..."

As Ethan's voice fell off, I felt my body lock up so tight that I knew I needed to get out of there.

"Ronan, I think Ethan needs a break," I cut in before Ethan could continue his story.

Ronan's eyes met mine and I knew that he knew what was going on with me, but he merely nodded. "I think that's a good idea. Ethan, do you want to go check on Lucy?"

Ethan nodded. "Yes, thank you."

"How about we meet back here in fifteen minutes or so?" Ronan suggested.

I managed to keep control of myself as I nodded. I was out of the room like a shot as soon as the other men stood up. I had one destination in mind and as I made my way there, I was supremely grateful that I'd been in the house enough to know where things were.

Ronan and Seth's home gym wasn't huge, but it didn't matter because it had two things I needed in the moment. One, it was in the basement which afforded me the privacy I needed. Two, it had a weight bag that could take the brunt of my anger. I didn't bother with gloves as I approached the bag. I didn't even need an image of Eric's face, which I had yet to actually see but that I vaguely remembered from the news reports years earlier, to spur me on as I slammed my fist against the heavy bag. No, all I needed was the image of Ethan's battered body and the sound of his broken sobs as I'd held him in that fucking shower.

Within minutes, my body ached from the relentless punches, but it wasn't enough. I wasn't at all surprised when Phoenix appeared and silently went around to the other side of the bag and held it so it wouldn't swing as much when I slammed my fist into it. Five minutes later, sweat was dripping down my face and my entire body burned.

Unfortunately, so did the rage.

"Better?" Phoenix asked as he stepped around the bag to watch me as I snagged a towel off a rack against the wall.

"What do you think?" I asked.

"I think you need to go change," he said softly. "I've got an extra shirt in my bag over there," he added. I followed his gaze to a black bag sitting on a shelf near the door. It didn't surprise me that the man had already made use of the gym. He was built like a fucking tank.

"Thanks," I muttered.

I went to the bathroom attached to the gym and stripped off my sweat-stained shirt. I turned on the tap and got my towel wet so I could wipe away the worst of the sweat. A quick dunking of my hair under the cool water helped counter some of the heat and tension still running through my body. By the time I returned to the gym, Phoenix was waiting for me, bottle of water in hand. I took it and drained it with just a few swallows. I wasn't surprised when he handed me another bottle.

"You want to talk about it?" he asked.

"What's there to talk about?" I asked in irritation. "Don't pretend that shit doesn't piss you off too," I added.

Phoenix looked at me patiently before saying, "We've heard "that shit" before. First time you've needed to take the fucker out *before* the vic is even done telling their story."

"He's not a victim," I interjected before I could even consider what I was saying. I didn't know why the term bothered me so much since I knew it hadn't been meant as a criticism. But just knowing how much Ethan had likely left out of his story and remembering how he'd fought back that day I'd woken him from his nightmare had started making me think of him as a survivor.

I felt a wave of discomfort go through me as Phoenix studied me. I'd worked with the man several times and knew how good he was at reading people.

"We should get back," I said. But sure enough, as soon as I tried to move past him, he stepped in my path, though he was careful not to touch me. He'd made the mistake of touching me on our second assignment together and it hadn't been pretty.

"You know you can talk to me, right?" he said softly.

Too softly.

Fuck, had he picked up on something? My behavior upstairs had been over the top, especially for me, but surely he couldn't see *why* I'd reacted the way I had.

"I'm fine," I said, forcing myself to remain calm.

"I don't buy that and you know Ronan won't either."

I did know that and while Phoenix was likely to let me off the hook, Ronan wouldn't. Especially if he thought my behavior would be any kind of detriment to the job.

Which meant I needed to get a handle on myself.

"Nothing to tell," I finally said as firmly as I could. As confused as I was about my physical reaction to Ethan, I wasn't about to give voice to those feelings. It had been a temporary thing brought on by the close quarters. And the fact that it had been a while since I'd been with a woman.

Phoenix said nothing as he moved out of my way. I hurried back to the family room and found that Ethan and Ronan were already sitting down again in the same positions. Before I could give it too much thought, I went to sit on the same couch Ronan was sitting on. I ignored my inner voice telling me I should have sat down next to Ethan. I also ignored Ronan who I knew was looking at me just like Phoenix had downstairs.

Once Phoenix entered the room and closed the door, Ronan nodded at Ethan to continue. I steeled myself for what was to come next and locked eyes with Ethan just before he opened his mouth.

CHAPTER 8

ETHAN

My body felt hot all over as Cain's gaze swept over me. It didn't take a genius to know what he was thinking, especially considering at what point of my story he'd interjected the suggestion of a break.

How could you let him do that to you?

It was a question I'd asked myself over and over that night and in the months that had followed as I'd continued to work my plan to get free of Eric. As a doctor, I'd encouraged victims of domestic abuse and sexual assault to come forward and press charges. I'd taken pictures of broken, battered bodies and performed exams on people at the most vulnerable times in their lives. But it wasn't until that night as I'd limped into the ER, blood and tears coursing down my face and the proof of Eric's depravity pooling in my underwear, that I'd truly understood what my patients had been feeling and why so many had remained silent. Since I'd known that calling the cops was one of the first things the hospital staff would do when they got a look at me, I'd told the nurse who'd been sitting at the triage desk that I'd leave if the police were called. I'd spent the rest of the evening enduring being put back together and listening to the same argument I myself had often given to my patients. I'd been strong up until they'd asked me that one question that had hurt more than any injury Eric could have inflicted upon me.

Is there someone we can call for you, Ethan?

There'd been no one.

Because I'd pushed them away.

For Eric.

"Ethan," I heard Cain say softly and I looked up to see him and Ronan watching me with concern. I finally noticed that Cain had some bruising on his knuckles that hadn't been there before and his hair looked damp. His shirt was different too.

"Sorry," I murmured as I realized I'd gotten lost in the past. "After that night, I had to take some time off work for my injuries to heal. I was hoping the medical records and recordings would be enough proof to convince Eric to stay away from me, but I still needed money to disappear…to start over somewhere. I…I got better at not pissing Eric off as much, but it was taking a toll on me and people started noticing. But I was able to put them off with excuses about stress and being tired. About three months before Lucy and I took off, Eric's former partner on the force came into the ER to be treated for a burn to his hand. He was one of the only people who knew about me and Eric…I'd seen him a couple of times when Eric would do one of his random check-ins to make sure I was at home or work like I'd said I'd be. His name was Tom Douglas."

I paused as a wave of pain went through me. "He was really nice," I whispered. "Eric had hit me the night before so he saw the black eye and asked me about it. I told him what I'd told everyone else…that I'd taken up a self-defense course and had gotten hit while sparring with a partner, but I knew he didn't believe me. I could see it in his eyes. He told me he could help me if I just told him the truth. I denied it at first, but he kept telling me it wasn't my fault…that Eric was sick in the head and he'd help me get out of the situation and he'd make it so Eric could never hurt me again." I felt tears sting my eyes as I softly said, "So I told him. Everything."

"Did he tell Eric?" Ronan asked.

I shook my head. "No, not like you're thinking," I said when I heard the anger in the man's voice. "He tried to keep his promise."

"What happened, Ethan?" I heard Cain ask, his voice gentle, like it'd been in the shower when he'd held me.

"He was killed in a home invasion two nights later. His wife too. I saw it on the news." I wiped away the tears that started to fall. "I didn't know the truth until Eric came to see me the next day."

"Eric killed them," Ronan offered.

I nodded even as fresh tears fell. "Eric told me they were dead because of me. That if I'd just kept my mouth shut, their daughter wouldn't be an orphan…she was sleeping at a friend's house that night." My voice broke as I said, "She was only twelve years old."

"It's not your fault," I heard Ronan say. A fresh tissue was thrust into my hand, but I had no clue who put it there. I didn't bother correcting Ronan.

It was absolutely my fault.

"He beat me so bad I could barely walk."

"What about his admission?" Cain asked. "Did your digital recorder capture it?"

I shook my head. "No, I'd taken it to work that day to get the recordings transferred and left it in my locker."

"I went back to work about a week later after telling my boss a family member had died and I needed some time off. I was working my regular shift when this girl showed up in the ER complaining of stomach pains. I knew she was faking right away because her symptoms made no sense. I thought maybe she'd been assaulted or something and was making up the stomach pains as a way to work up to admitting to what had really happened to her."

"Lucy," Cain murmured.

I nodded. "I didn't know that's who she was though. She'd given a fake name at the check-in desk. When she wouldn't tell me what she was really there for, I told her I'd have to call children's services since the number she'd given us for her parents was fake too. That's when she told me who she was and that she knew who I was."

"How'd she find out about you?" Ronan asked.

"She'd heard her mother and Eric fighting. Her mother had accused Eric of cheating, though she'd had no clue he was cheating with a man apparently. I guess Lucy's mom was threatening to divorce Eric, but he'd threatened to expose her drinking problem which would have ruined her career. And since he'd adopted Lucy, he could have fought for custody if they separated. Lucy hated Eric...had from the moment her mother met him. So she started following Eric – one of her friends was old enough to drive – in the hopes that she could catch him in the act and give the information to her mom for the divorce."

"And Eric led her to you," Ronan offered.

"Yeah. The day she saw me was the day after Eric had beaten me for telling his partner about what he was doing to me. Lucy saw him grab me through the window. Later, after Eric had left, I'd gone outside to get my mail and she saw the bruises. I think that's why she didn't go to her mom right away."

"So she came to see you in the ER so she could talk to you?" Cain asked.

"I think she just wanted to feel me out at first. You know, decide if I was a bad guy or not. I told her she needed to stay out of it. I was terrified what would happen if she confronted Eric. I made her promise me she wouldn't. But she kept coming back to the hospital to see me. I think...I think she needed someone to talk to."

"Did Eric ever hurt Lucy or her mother?" Ronan asked.

"I don't think so," I said. "She said Eric mostly ignored her and the fights with her mother were loud, but he never laid a hand on her."

"What happened that forced you to take her?" Cain asked.

The fact that he'd phrased it that way warmed something inside of me. Maybe because I hadn't been sure these men would believe me, but Cain...I could see by the way he was looking at me that he did.

"It was late one night when I heard someone knocking at my door. It was Lucy. She was crying and shaking. I asked her what was wrong and she just...she just blurted it out," I said softly as the memory of Lucy's tear-stained face washed over me.

"*He killed her, Ethan. He killed her,*" I murmured. I forced my eyes up and saw all three men watching me intently. "Lucy's mother," I clarified. "Lucy told me she was supposed to be spending the night at a friend's house but that she'd gone home to get her phone. She was in her bedroom when she heard her mom and Eric fighting in the hallway outside her room. She decided to try to get the fight on video so she could finally get her mom to see how messed up their relationship was. The house they lived in was really big and the bedrooms were on the second floor. She saw Eric and her mom right in front of the bannister that overlooked the first floor. Neither of them saw her – I guess she only had her bedroom door open an inch or two. Anyway, I guess Lucy's mom had somehow found out Eric was into men because she threatened to expose his secret and the fight got physical. He...he pushed her over the bannister."

Ronan and Cain both stiffened as they realized the implications of what I was saying.

"I saw that story," Ronan murmured. "He said her death was an accident...that she had a drinking problem."

I nodded. "She was legally drunk, but I believe Lucy's story that he pushed her."

All three men nodded.

"Lucy stayed hidden in her room until Eric went to call 911. Then she took off. The friend she'd been spending the night with was waiting in the car. Lucy had her drive her to my house...I'd told Lucy never to call me because Eric monitored my phone calls and I'd figured he might monitor hers too."

"What did you do?" Cain asked.

"I asked her to let me see the video, but on the way out of her house, she'd dropped the phone on the sidewalk. It wouldn't power on anymore."

"Did she upload the file to her cloud?"

I shook my head. "She'd turned that feature off when she found out Eric was snooping through her stuff on the cloud." When neither man asked me additional questions, I continued on my own. "I was afraid for Lucy...what Eric would do to her if he found out she'd witnessed the murder. I knew we had to run. She didn't have any other family and without the phone, I knew the cops wouldn't believe her. All the cash I'd been hiding from Eric was in the safe deposit box, but I was too afraid to wait for the bank to open. On the way out of town, I stopped at an ATM and got as much cash from my debit card as I could. Some of my credit cards were designed to let me get cash from the ATM so I used those too. Since Eric knew how to track my car, I ditched it in a parking garage and we walked to the bus station and grabbed a bus headed for New York. We switched buses a few times before settling on one bound for Minneapolis. Eric found us within three days," I said softly. I shook my head. "I still don't know how he did it. I'd gotten rid of my phone, hadn't used my credit cards, hadn't called anyone or checked my email…"

"He could have used the security cameras at the bus stations to figure out your destination," Cain said quietly. "And if you got a hotel room near the bus station, it would have just been a matter of showing your pictures around…"

Humiliation spread through my limbs. "I never thought of that," I whispered.

"Why would you?" Ronan asked gently.

I managed a nod. "Lucy and I had been out getting her some clothes when we saw Eric outside our hotel room talking to the manager. We left everything behind and ran. Luckily, I'd kept most of the important stuff like my cash and safe deposit box key on me so I didn't lose much. We took the bus to Kansas City, then Dallas. Even though I hadn't known how Eric had found us, I'd decided taking the bus wasn't safe so I bought this really cheap car for cash. We drove to New Mexico and hid out there and waited. When Eric didn't show up, I started looking for a job, but it was tough without any kind of ID. I worked odd jobs for a little while and after a month we ditched the car and moved again…being in one place too long made us both nervous. Lucy changed her hair color and we avoided being seen together in public. Whenever I was working, she spent most of her days at the public library. A few months ago, we went to Arizona and I managed to find a job as a caretaker for a man named Arthur Stillwell. He'd had a stroke a few months earlier and needed help getting around. The position was a live-in one so Lucy and I had a place to stay."

I shook my head as I said, "I was so stupid...I thought we were old news at that point since it had been four months since we'd run, but I was wrong. Arthur saw us on a news report and confronted me. I...I was so sure he was going to call the cops, but he didn't. He believed me," I murmured. I could feel tears threatening as I whispered, "He wanted to help us."

"What happened?" Cain asked. "Why did you leave?"

"Eric found us. No idea how. He was waiting outside the library I used to take Lucy to. She liked to read a lot and I was also trying to keep up with her schooling, so she'd use the books to do assignments I'd give her. But she never checked anything out even though Arthur offered to let us use his library card."

"Did Lucy use the computers at the library?"

I shook my head. "No. I think she would have needed a library card to use them. And she knew not to check her email."

Ronan glanced at Phoenix. "Can you ask Lucy to come join us?" The big man nodded and then left the room.

"Did Eric find out about Arthur?"

I shook my head. "No, I've kept in touch with Arthur using those disposable phones that you buy and load minutes onto. I bought a few using cash in Arizona as Lucy and I were leaving. I use one to call him once a month and then I throw it away."

"Why take the risk to keep in touch with him?" Cain asked.

"Um, Lucy's phone. We kept it with us the whole time even though we couldn't get it to work. I thought...I thought that there were people out there who could fix it. But I was worried about carrying it with us since it was the only leverage we had against Eric to keep Lucy safe. Just like my safe deposit box, I wanted something I could hold over his head to get him to leave us alone. So I left the phone with Arthur and gave him instructions to mail it to my brother if he didn't hear from me by the last day of every month. I included a letter telling my brother everything just in case something happened to me..."

I saw Cain's jaw tighten, but he didn't say anything.

"So Arthur still has the phone?"

I nodded. "He gave me his son's social security card before we left along with his ID...his son died a while back when he was about my age. He thought it would help me find decent work long enough for me to earn some money before the HR department figured out the social security number wasn't mine." I glanced at Ronan. "His son's name was Allen."

Ronan nodded since he knew Allen was the name I'd used to get the job at Ronan's hospital as a transporter.

I paused in my story when Lucy entered the room, followed by Phoenix. She looked terrified and I immediately opened my arms when she hurried to me. I could feel her shaking against me so I kissed the top of her head and murmured, "Everything's okay, Lucy. Ronan just has a couple of questions for you."

She nodded against me. I felt her silent tears burning through my shirt so I grabbed a couple of tissues from the dispenser and pushed her back enough so I could see her face. I clasped the sides of her face with my hands and said, "We're safe, Lucy. I promise."

Another nod and then she was wiping at her eyes. She leaned against me as she faced Ronan and Cain. Her body was rife with tension and fear, but she held her ground.

"Lucy, when you were using the library in Arizona, did you ever use the computer?"

She began shaking her head, but stopped suddenly. "Um yeah, once," she murmured. She shifted to look at me. "But I didn't use the card Arthur gave me and I didn't check my email. The person who'd been using the computer before forgot to log out so I was using their card," she said quickly.

I nodded reassuringly.

"What did you do on the computer?" Ronan asked.

"I...I read some news stories about what happened to my mom. I looked at some of my friends' profiles on Facebook."

"Did you interact with them?" Cain asked.

She shook her head. "No, I didn't log into my account. I just checked their timelines…a lot of them were worried about me. They were saying Ethan kidnapped me," she said softly. "It…it wasn't true so I created a new email account with a fake name and emailed my friend, Jackie, and told her to tell people I'd told her I was running away…I thought it might confuse the police," she said as she looked at me hopefully. "Eric didn't know Jackie – she was an online friend. I swear, Ethan, she wouldn't have told him I talked to her."

"I know, Lucy. It's okay," I said as I stroked her hair.

"If he'd contacted her, she would have told me," Lucy said.

I nodded.

"Lucy, have you been in touch with Jackie again?" Ronan asked.

"Just once after we left Arizona and got to Seattle. I never told her where I was, though."

I watched as Ronan pulled out his phone and dialed a number. "Daisy, I need you to check an email for me." Ronan paused long enough for Lucy to tell him the email address for the account she'd created. Several long moments passed in tense silence as we waited while Ronan listened to whatever the person on the other end of the phone had to say. His expression was grim when he got off the phone and I felt a wave of unease go through me.

"Okay, Lucy, thank you. That was very helpful. Would you mind hanging out with Seth and the kids for a while longer while we finish up here?"

She looked at me and I nodded. "Go on, we're almost finished."

Her slim arms went around me and my heart clenched when she whispered, "I love you, Ethan."

Even though we hadn't been together long, our reliance on each other as we'd fled the same evil had made us something more than two people on the run together. She'd filled a hole inside of me and I'd hoped I'd done the same for her. "I love you too, Kiddo," I said softly as I pressed a kiss against her temple.

I waited until Lucy was gone before I faced Ronan. "What?" I asked.

"When she set up her new email, she had to enter her regular email address as a recovery email. That linked her new account to her old one which made it traceable."

I closed my eyes as what he was saying began to make sense. "So that's how Eric found out about the library in Arizona and that we'd come here."

"Was Lucy using the library here too?" Cain asked.

I nodded. 'Since I had Allen's ID, I figured it was okay to use it to get a library card. We'd been so cut off from everything for so long, that I wanted her to have something normal." I let my eyes settle on Ronan. "Thank you for not telling her about the email. She'd…she'd never forgive herself if she knew…"

I shook my head, unable to complete the thought.

"I'll have my tech girl delete the email account. We'll tell Lucy that for now, it's safer that she doesn't create any new accounts, no matter what."

I managed a nod. "Thank you."

"Ethan, tell us about the day Eric found you again," I heard Cain say.

It was the last thing I wanted to do. I was so damn tired and raw that the idea of having to revisit those moments even for a few minutes was taxing. But I also needed to be done with this.

Unfortunately, I had no idea what would happen once I *was* done.

Would Cain keep his word to let me and Lucy go?

Or would it be just another broken promise in a line of many?

CHAPTER 9

CAIN

My heart hurt for Ethan because he just looked so damned tired. A part of me wanted to tell Ronan that we'd heard enough, but another part of me needed to hear every detail of what Eric had done to the man before me. I'd use it as fuel when I confronted the fucker. And I *would* confront him. Of that, I had no doubt.

"After I performed that procedure on that patient, I knew the jig was up. I told Lucy when I got home that we'd need to leave the next day. I ended up sleeping in later than I'd meant to the next morning. When I woke up, I found a note from Lucy saying she'd finished packing her stuff and had walked over to a friend's house to say goodbye. I packed up my own stuff and then drove to the gas station to fill up the car and get us some snacks for the road. When I got back to the house, Eric was waiting inside," Ethan said softly.

"He was on me before I even realized what was happening. He hit me a few times and then kicked me. Then he started breaking things. He accused me of taking Lucy to humiliate him. Said I was trying to brainwash her against him. I managed to get to my feet while he was trashing the place. I flipped the light switch near the front door so the outside porch light would turn on – it was a signal Lucy and I had worked out. If the light was on, it meant she should run...go to the police."

My insides clenched as my admiration for this man rose several more notches. Even with his own life in jeopardy, he'd put Lucy's safety first.

"I tried talking Eric down...telling him I was sorry, but he was in a rage. He dragged me to each room as he..."

Ethan's voice dropped off and I didn't need him to finish his statement. I remembered the blood all over that house. I had no doubt it had only come from Ethan.

"My room was already trashed when he dragged me into it. He... he threw me face down on the bed and told me I was his...always his. Then he pulled my pants down...I was too out of it to fight back," Ethan murmured. "When he was finished, I managed to pull my pants up before he knocked me to the ground. Then he was on top of me, his hands around my throat. I knew he wasn't going to let me go this time. I could see it in his eyes. I was...I was relieved," Ethan admitted as tears slipped unchecked down his face. "All I ever wanted was to be free...I just never thought he'd be the one to give that to me."

Rage surged through me, white-hot, and I barely managed to stay where I was. My fists were clenched, but there was nothing I could do to relax them. I wanted blood. Period.

"How did you get away?" Ronan asked.

Ethan let out a strangled laugh. "Lucy," he managed to get out as he wiped at his face. "She saw the light on, but ignored it and came inside. She hit him over the head with a cast iron skillet. Knocked him out cold, then helped me to my feet. I told her to grab the safe deposit key I'd taped underneath one of the dresser drawers and then we ran. She drove because I couldn't. I was too out of it to do anything. She told me when we got to the cabin that it belonged to her friend's family and that the girl had said we could use it. The girl's parents were out of the country for another couple of months so we'd be safe there. Her friend told the guy who plowed the road that we were there with her parents' permission so he wouldn't call the cops. She also told Lucy about the gun her parents kept at the cabin for protection."

Ethan took a few deep breaths and then lifted his eyes to Ronan. "She can't know I was raped," he said, his voice firm.

While Ethan had made the same request of me, I knew his demand held even more weight now since Lucy's email account had likely been what had led Eric to finding them.

"She won't," Ronan said just as firmly.

Ethan nodded.

"Ethan, I'd like for you to let us help you," Ronan said.

Ethan began shaking his head before Ronan even finished. "No. Two people are dead because I accepted help." Ethan's eyes shifted to me. "I want to go."

I knew what he was asking of me. I felt Ronan's eyes on me and while I knew I was about to do something that would cost me my job, I did it anyway. I stood up and said, "Okay," and motioned to the door.

Ethan glanced uncertainly around the room before he climbed to his feet.

As he neared me I said, "Be sure about this, Ethan. It's not just your life that you're putting at risk." I knew it was a low blow, but after having seen the connection between Ethan and his young charge, I was only speaking the truth. "She's put herself in danger twice for you. You really think she's going to stop doing that just because you tell her to?" I asked.

Ethan stiffened at that and then glanced at Ronan. He was quiet for a moment before saying, "Can you keep her safe? Even if Eric comes at you with everything he has?"

Ronan stood. "We can keep you both safe, Ethan. Whether that means proving to the world who Eric really is or just making it so he's no longer a part of it, he'll never get near either of you again. You have my word on that."

Ethan was clearly overwhelmed and torn. I couldn't stop myself from reaching out to clasp his face with my hand so I could force him to look at me. I leaned forward enough so only he could hear my next words. "I've got you, Ethan," I whispered.

A choked sob tore from his throat as he let out a jerky nod. He stepped away from me and went to sit back down.

I was too on edge to sit so I moved to stand behind the couch.

"Um, what happens next?" Ethan asked as he wiped at his face with his hands.

"I'd like to arrange to get Lucy's phone from your friend and we'll also need the contents of your safe deposit box. My suggestion would be for Lucy to stay here with my family while one of my men escorts you to get the phone and the contents of your safe deposit box in D.C." Ronan glanced between me and Phoenix. "Cain and Phoenix will act as primaries on your case and I'll call in more men if we need it."

"Primaries?" Ethan asked.

"One of them will stay here to shadow Lucy whenever she leaves this house and one of them will escort you to Arizona and then D.C."

"I'll go with Ethan," I interjected before Ronan could continue. I ignored the heat that crawled up my neck as all eyes turned to me. Not only was I stepping on Ronan's toes by making a decision that was solely his, I'd just revealed a pretty big fact about myself.

That I was way more emotionally invested in this case than I should be.

I remained silent as Ronan's eyes returned to Ethan. "Both Phoenix and Cain are more than qualified for this job, Ethan. Do you have a preference for who your primary is and whose Lucy's is?"

I held my breath as Ethan's eyes shifted between me and Phoenix.

"Phoenix should be Lucy's," he finally said as his eyes briefly met Phoenix's before meeting mine for a fraction of a second.

I tried not to react at all, but the fact that Ronan cast a glance at me showed it wouldn't have mattered if I had or not. He knew something was up.

"I'd like to recommend you rest up for a few more days," Ronan said. "That will give Lucy time to adjust to being with my family."

Ethan nodded. "Thank you. I'd like to be the one to tell Lucy about all of this."

To Phoenix, Ronan said, "Would you take him to Lucy, please?" To Ethan he said, 'Seth can show you to your rooms so you and Lucy can talk."

I kept my eyes off Ethan as he left the room, but didn't bother leaving myself since I had no doubt Ronan wanted to talk to me. The way he'd held my gaze as Ethan had gotten up to leave was proof enough of that.

"Do you want to tell me what's going on or do I need to guess?" Ronan asked.

I took a deep breath and went to sit down on the couch across from him. "Does it matter?" I asked. "I can keep him safe."

"I have no doubt about that," Ronan responded. "Does he know about your…preferences?"

I wanted to laugh at the polite word he'd chosen to describe my aversion to physical contact.

"He knows. I told him this afternoon." I paused and said, "I wouldn't hurt him, even if he…"

"Touched you?" Ronan finished for me.

I nodded.

"And what if he touches you in other ways?" Ronan asked.

"What do you mean?"

Ronan sighed. "I had the same problem," he said softly. "Though my reasons for it were different from yours, I suspect."

I found that hard to believe since I'd seen plenty of people touching Ronan in all sorts of ways. Even the thought of all those people doing the same to me had a shiver running up my spine.

"How did you get over it?" I whispered before I could even think better of it.

"By almost losing the one thing that meant more to me than anything else."

I had no doubt he was talking about his husband. Since that wasn't in the cards for me, I simply said, "I'm no threat to Ethan."

Ronan climbed to his feet. "It's not Ethan I'm worried about," he murmured. I didn't respond to his cryptic statement, nor did I move as he headed for the door. "Get some rest, Cain. We can discuss strategy tomorrow."

Once Ronan was gone, I went to my truck to grab my bag and then headed down to the gym. While I could've used the gym at the hotel

I'd been staying at the past few months, I was still too on edge from the encounter with Ethan to wait that long. I worked out for more than an hour before I finally felt some of the rage leave my system. After using the shower to get cleaned up, I was about to leave the gym and head for my truck when I noticed a figure out in the backyard. I recognized the long black hair instantly.

I was tempted to just continue on my way, but I knew I needed to mend some fences. I left my bag in the gym and walked out the double doors leading to the back yard.

Ronan and Seth's house was quite sizeable and sat on a good chunk of property on a bluff overlooking Elliot Bay. I walked to where Lucy was sitting on one of the swings of an elaborate play set. Her back was to me so she didn't see me coming, nor did she notice when Bullet left her feet to come greet me.

As I rounded the swing set, she startled and then hastily wiped at the tears that had been trailing down her cheeks. She went on instant alert as she eyed me suspiciously.

"He told you, huh?" I said softly.

Lucy hesitated before nodding.

I eased around the post I'd been leaning on and went to sit on the swing next to hers, hoping it would hold my weight.

"It's for the best, Lucy. We can end all this and things will go back to normal."

"Normal," she whispered. "My mom's dead and my stepdad killed her. I don't have a normal anymore." She dropped her eyes and leaned heavily against the chain holding the swing up. "I don't have anything anymore."

"You have Ethan," I offered.

She sniffed and said, "He only took me in because he had no choice. He has a whole life he gets to go back to," Lucy murmured. "He's not going to want a reminder of everything Eric did to him around."

"You're not a reminder," I pointed out. "Ethan loves you very much and I'm sure he'll do everything he can to make sure you two can stay together."

It was a point I really had no right to make, but I'd seen the way Ethan looked at the girl. Circumstances might have forced them together, but he'd given up everything for her and I knew he hadn't done that out of a sense of obligation.

There was no response from Lucy. It was a reminder of how badly I sucked at this communication shit. "I thought I was alone when I was your age too," I said softly. "My life changed in the space of a few minutes and everything I ever knew was gone just like that," I said as I snapped my fingers.

"What happened?" Lucy asked.

I glanced at her and said, "A miracle." As her brow furrowed in disbelief, I felt a smile tugging at my mouth. "My grandmother," I clarified. "I didn't even know I had a grandmother. There I was with nothing…scared and alone…broken," I murmured. "And she swept in and said she was my family now and that everything would be okay."

"And was it?"

Since I couldn't lie to her, I said, "It was as good as it could be."

The answer seemed to satisfy her.

"Lucy, I'm sorry if I scared you last night. I can't tell you why I reacted like I did because it's just not something I talk about…with anyone. But I hope you'll believe me when I say I never would have hurt you or Ethan."

She cast me a sidelong glance. "We weren't going to hurt you," she said softly.

I sighed and said, "Before all this shit happened with Eric, you probably never looked at other people and saw only monsters, right?" At Lucy's nod, I said, "All I see are monsters…until they prove to me they're not. I'm not saying it makes any sense-"

"It does-" she interjected. "I see Eric everywhere," she admitted. "In every face I see. It wasn't like that before…"

"Before he killed your mom."

She nodded.

"It'll get better," I offered.

Her eyes settled on me. "Will it?" she whispered, her voice heavy with doubt.

Since I couldn't make her that promise, I didn't.

"You'll keep him safe, right?"

"I will," I said. "I swear it."

She nodded again, but didn't say anything else. I got up to leave, but stopped when she said my name. I turned to look at her as a shy smile spread across her lips. "I'm sorry I shot your truck."

I chuckled. "I'm not," I said. "Reminds me how glad I am that you have shitty aim."

Her light laughter followed me back to the house.

CHAPTER 10

ETHAN

"Jesus, I don't think I can do this," I murmured as I leaned forward in the luxurious seat and wrapped an arm around myself in the hopes I could stave off the nausea that was threatening to crawl up my throat.

Cain didn't say anything for which I was glad for. Platitudes about how things would be fine wouldn't make me feel any better.

"How long has it been since you've seen them?" Cain asked when I finally straightened.

We were sitting on Ronan's private jet which had just started its descent and was scheduled to land at a private airport just outside of San Francisco.

Home.

"Almost four years," I said softly. I held my tongue as Cain got up from his seat and came to sit down next to me. I assumed he'd done it so he could hear me better over the din of the engines. But I couldn't help but fixate on the way his powerful thighs bunched beneath his snug jeans as he got himself buckled in. Or how close his arm was to mine despite the wide seats.

Things hadn't exactly worked out according to plan after I'd called Arthur from what Ronan had assured me was a secure, untraceable phone about a week after I'd told Ronan and his men my tale. Arthur had been horrified to have to tell me that my package with Lucy's phone had inadvertently been mailed to my family two days earlier when Arthur's daughter had come across it on his desk. Arthur had been in the hospital for a routine procedure so he hadn't been around to explain that despite the package being addressed and the postage already affixed, it wasn't supposed to have been sent. I'd assured Arthur that it was okay and that I'd retrieve the package from my family, but as soon as I'd hung up the phone, I'd nearly lost it. Not only had I not seen my family in years, they were about to get a letter explaining why I'd been absent out of their lives for so long including information about what Eric had been doing to me. Worst of all, the way I'd written the letter along with the instructions about what they should do with the phone had made it sound like I was gone.

The only saving grace had been that it had only been two days since the package got mailed to the PO Box my oldest brother, Devon, used for his business. I'd hoped by using the PO Box that I could control how the rest of the family found out the truth. As much as I'd hated dumping all of that responsibility on Devon, I'd known he'd be the best one to see that the phone made it to the right people and to console the rest of my family. I'd been forced to call him right after hanging up with Arthur so I could explain the presence of the package and make him promise he wouldn't actually open it. To say he'd been surprised to hear from me had been an understatement. Of all my family members, Devon was the strongest, the most sensible and the least likely to let his emotions rule his decisions. But that also meant he took shit from no one, including me. And while he hadn't made me explain myself over the phone, I had no doubt I wouldn't be so lucky in person.

"So Devon is your oldest brother?" Cain asked.

I nodded. "I have another brother, Garrett and a sister, Eden. They're both older."

"You're the baby of the family."

"Yeah. I was kind of unexpected." At Cain's questioning look, I explained, "I'm adopted. My mom's sister was a social worker. She got assigned to my case when I was a kid and that's how my mom found out about me."

"Your case?"

"Um, yeah, I was found at a bookstore one day when I was three. Someone left me in the children's reading area but they don't know who. I only knew my age and my first name so I couldn't tell them much. No one came forward when they ran my story in the local news." At Cain's frown I said, "I don't remember any of it. And I was really lucky to get the family I did. I had a lot of developmental delays so my parents had to work with me a lot to get me caught up to other kids my age."

"And then you went on to graduate high school two years early," Cain pointed out.

I smiled. "My parents were really proud of me for that," I said. "They were proud of me for a lot of things."

"But you weren't," Cain said softly.

"What?" I asked, startled. "No," I said quickly. "I was really lucky..."

"But it wasn't easy for you, was it?"

I was about to deny the comment, but then I remembered Cain's insistence that he hated liars. I didn't know why it was so important to me that he didn't put me in that category.

"No, it wasn't," I admitted. "I was a pretty awkward kid. My social skills weren't great and I had every childhood insecurity you could think of...acne, braces, glasses, a weight problem...I was pretty much a walking, talking cliché. By the time I walked across that stage to accept my diploma, I'd heard every nickname and then some. *Freak Show* was the worst," I murmured.

"Was college any better?"

I smiled ruefully and shook my head. "You ever hear girls talk about the Freshmen 15?" I asked.

Cain nodded.

"Well, for me it was like fifty pounds instead of fifteen and that's saying a lot for a kid who was already overweight to begin with. And since I was still sixteen, I hadn't managed to get rid of all that other stuff like the zits and the braces. Add in the fact that I was gay and my social life was pretty much doomed from the start."

When I saw his frown, I quickly backtracked and said, "But it wasn't all bad. I got really good grades and the demands of medical school helped me shed some of the weight."

"You're too thin," Cain suddenly said. His words caught me off guard.

"What?"

"You're too thin," he repeated as his eyes swept my body. I felt my insides light up at the move and I had to remind myself that he wasn't looking at me the way I really wished he would.

"Well, being on the run will do that for you," I joked, but he didn't smile. I dropped my eyes and felt my cheeks warm with color. "What about you?" I asked. "I doubt you were ever even a pound overweight in your life," I said jokingly.

Cain was quiet for a moment and I realized I'd crossed some invisible line. I opened my mouth to apologize, but he spoke before I could say anything.

"I was really big into athletics," he said. "Soccer, football, basketball, didn't matter – as long as I was moving and it kept me out of the house, I was good." He shot me a glance as he said, "I could have used someone like you."

What?

By now I was sure my cheeks were positively flaming and I was actually glad I still had some lingering bruising that might hide the proof of my embarrassment.

"For what?" I choked out.

"Tutoring. My grades were for shit. Almost got held back my freshman year."

"Did you find one? A tutor I mean?"

Cain shook his head. "It wasn't a priority after that."

The cryptic statement made no sense to me, but I didn't ask him what he meant because I could tell from the dark look in his eyes that he wasn't about to expound on it.

"How about college? Maybe you ended up with the Freshmen 1?" I said jokingly, hoping to draw back some of that lightness I'd seen in his eyes for the briefest of moments.

"Didn't go to college." I saw his fingers start to flex and un-flex and I found myself needing to remind myself that he wasn't Eric. His agitation wouldn't result in me with a split lip or bruised cheek.

"How come you stayed away from home for so long?" Cain asked.

The switch back to me wasn't ideal, but something about talking to him helped relax me.

"A few months after I met Eric, I brought him home to meet my parents...before I knew what he was really like. I thought myself so completely in love with him that I was blind to everything else. But my family didn't suffer from that affliction and instead of hearing what they had to say, I cut them out of my life."

"They didn't like him," Cain said.

I shook my head. "They saw things I refused to. Like how he'd put me down, how he talked only about himself, how he ordered me around. I was angry with them for not seeing how good he was for me. When he said things about my weight, I saw it as him caring about my health. When he put down one of my accomplishments, I saw it as him saying I could do even better. When he talked about himself, I just saw it as him being more interesting than me. I was just so blind," I murmured.

"Why?"

The bluntness of his question caught me off guard, but when I looked at him, I didn't see any judgment in his gaze. He looked...curious.

"I guess because he was the first person who ever truly wanted me. I mean, I knew my family loved me and stuff, but I felt like he saw me without the unconditional love that your family sees you with and he liked what he saw. He chose *me* despite all my flaws."

"Flaws?" Cain asked, his voice low.

"My weight, my awkwardness, my oversensitivity to things...he was always encouraging me to overcome those things to help me be better," I explained.

"Better?" Cain said softly.

"Yeah," I said, confused by his reaction.

Cain shook his head and made a move to unbuckle his seatbelt. I grabbed his arm without thinking. He stiffened and I instantly yanked my hand back. "Sorry," I quickly said.

"It's okay," he said after a moment.

When he started to unbuckle again, I said, "What did you mean by that?"

He didn't respond and I knew it was because he didn't want to lie to me.

"Please," I said softly.

Cain hesitated before finally settling his flinty blue eyes on me. "Seems like the fucker told you all that shit so you wouldn't realize how much "better" *you* were than *him*. I'm glad he failed…on all counts, Ethan. Except the weight," he added gently. "I wish he'd gotten that wrong too because I think you'd look just fine with a few extra pounds."

With that, he got up and went to the back of the plane. I sat there in stunned silence as I absorbed his words. He returned a moment later and wordlessly handed me a can of soda along with a bag of potato chips. My stomach growled at the sight of the salty goodness, but Eric's voice in my head was louder.

You like being a fat pig, is that it, Ethan?

Logically I knew I hadn't been fat when he and I had met and I certainly could use the calories now, but I couldn't make myself open the bag. Tears of frustration stung my eyes. I glanced at Cain who was watching me intently, but he didn't tell me to eat the chips.

Why had I been able to find the strength to leave, but I couldn't find the strength to open the damn bag?

"Talk to me, Ethan," Cain said softly.

"You'll think I'm crazy," I whispered.

"Are you afraid you're disappointing him somehow?" Cain asked. I flicked my gaze to his as the shame crashed over me.

I managed a nod, but my throat was too tight to actually speak.

"My father used to beat my mother."

The admission got my attention and I tore my eyes from the bag of chips.

"Just my mother," he said. "Not me, not my brothers and sisters. She'd bend over backwards to please him, but nothing she ever did was good enough. She could do something like cook him his favorite meal perfectly every single time, but there'd always be that one meal that wasn't quite up to par."

I knew from the inflection of his voice what he meant. How well the meal was or wasn't cooked had absolutely nothing to do with the outcome.

"He just needed an excuse," I murmured.

Cain nodded. "She did too. Because after he was done with her, she'd look at me and even while I was still cleaning the blood off her face, she'd say, 'It'll be better now.' The next day she'd have this look of peace on her face…like everything in her world was right again."

"You think I'm like her," I said, my insides falling at the comparison.

I flinched when Cain grabbed my chin gently in his hand to force me to look at him. "No, I don't. She wouldn't have even looked at the chips twice to wonder why she didn't want them. And she sure as shit wouldn't have the guts to do what you did for Lucy…for yourself. Eat the chips or don't eat them, Ethan. Just make sure your decision is for you and not *him*."

He released me and then opened his own bag of chips.

His admission both bothered me and explained a lot. I suspected there was quite a bit he hadn't told me, but I was shocked he'd said as much as he had. But his words were hard to hear because I didn't like knowing he had so much insight into things. It would be that much harder to hide the truth.

From him.

From myself.

I reached for the bag of chips and gingerly opened them. The first one tasted so good I wanted to cry. I waited for my stomach to reject the food in some kind of silent tribute to the past, but when nothing happened, I ate another.

And another.

I ate the whole bag within a couple of minutes and when Cain silently handed me another, I took that one and tore into it, eating the entire thing before settling back in the seat and watching the clouds give way to land.

And only one thing came to mind when the landing gear hit the runway a few minutes later.

Fuck you, Eric. I'm going home.

~

One look at my brother and I knew he hadn't kept his promise. But it was hard to care when he wrapped his big arms around me and held onto me like nothing else in the world mattered.

"Don't ever scare the fucking shit out of me like that ever again, do you hear me?" he growled in my ear as he held onto me.

I nodded. "Sorry," I croaked as tears filled my eyes.

Devon didn't seem to care that we were standing in the middle of the walkway leading to his house for all his neighbors to see. He just held on to me as I wept against his chest and then he was pushing me back so he could get a good look at me. I could tell he didn't like what he saw. While my bruises had healed quite a bit, they were far from gone.

"I'm going to kill him," he whispered.

I shook my head, but before I could even say anything, I felt him stiffen. I separated from him long enough to see his eyes were on Cain. I hadn't explained anything to Devon about Ronan and Cain and how they were helping me, but I knew I'd have to now.

"Devon, this is Cain. He's my...my..."

I was at a complete loss as to what to call him. Friend was probably a stretch. Bodyguard just sounded scary and would set my brother off even further, though since he'd read my note, I doubted he could get much more upset than he already was.

"I'm here to make sure Ethan stays safe," was all Cain said. He looked tense and I didn't miss the way he kept looking around the neighborhood.

Watching for Eric, probably.

We'd ended up circling the neighborhood several times before Cain had pulled the rental car into the driveway of my brother's sedate Craftsman style house. At 45, Devon was the perpetual bachelor, but it was a lifestyle he seemed content with. Although, since I hadn't seen him in almost four years, he could be married with kids for all I knew.

The realization of how much I'd missed had pain shooting through my veins.

"Can we go inside?" I asked since I wasn't sure I could keep it together and I didn't want to embarrass myself in front of the few neighbors who were out and about.

Devon nodded and put his arm around my shoulders as he led me up the walkway. His house looked the same inside as it had four years earlier so I suspected I hadn't missed a big event with him like a wedding or a new baby, but it didn't ease the knowledge that I'd been so blinded by my need to be with Eric that I hadn't been the brother I should have been.

"Sit," Devon murmured as he motioned to the couch. "Do you want something to eat or drink?"

"No," I said softly. Cain also declined and I felt him settle down on the couch next to me which left the armchair for Devon. I wasn't surprised when he turned it so he was facing me.

"Ethan," he said softly, though he was saying it more like he couldn't believe I was there.

I reached out to grab his hand. "I'm okay," I whispered.

He nodded. My big, tough brother looked so distressed that another round of guilt went through me. "You read it, didn't you?" I asked.

Another nod. "Four years, Ethan. And then six months ago, the cops show up here looking for you. Saying you'd taken the daughter of a man you'd been stalking."

I flinched because I hadn't realized that was the angle Eric had come up with. The irony was almost too much.

"I messed up, Devon...not with taking Lucy," I clarified. "The things I said to you guys…"

Memories of the cruel words I'd flung at my family as they'd tried to convince me Eric was no good for me filtered through me like little shards of glass.

"None of that matters," Devon said firmly. "We knew you didn't mean what you said."

I nodded and glanced at Cain. I hated that he would be seeing yet another side of me. I wondered if there'd ever be a chance for me to show him I was something besides a weak, stupid, foolish man.

"Tell me everything." Devon insisted. "From the beginning."

I sighed because I really didn't want to have to tell my story again, but I knew I owed it to him. "Can…can we wait until the whole family is together so I only have to tell it once?" I asked.

"Sure," Devon said softly. "I'll call them now and ask them to come over."

"Do they know I'm here?" I asked.

He shook his head. "I wanted to make sure you wanted to see them first."

Part of me didn't, but most of me did. I could only hope they'd be as forgiving as Devon. 'I do," I said.

"Okay," Devon responded and then he was getting up, presumably to make the calls.

"Devon, can I use your bathroom to clean up?"

He nodded. "You can use the one in the guest room next to my room." He looked at Cain. "I have a second guest room you can use tonight."

Cain rose to his feet. "We can't stay here tonight. It's not safe…Eric might be having the house watched."

I stiffened at that.

Devon rose to his full height and said, "I can protect my brother."

Before Cain could respond, I got up and stepped in front of Devon. "Devon, I trust Cain and if he says it isn't safe, it isn't safe. I can't," my voice broke. "I can't put you and our family at risk." When he didn't respond right away I whispered, "Please, Devon."

He didn't like it, but he nodded and then his arms were around me again. "Okay little brother, we'll do it your way. But when this is over, you come right back to us, do you hear me?"

I nodded and barely managed to hold back my tears.

"Go get cleaned up," Devon urged.

"Are you coming?" I asked Cain, more because I was afraid to leave him and Devon alone together than anything else.

"You go on. I'm sure your brother has some questions for me."

That was what I was afraid of.

I nodded and stepped past Cain. I accidentally brushed his hand with mine, but before I could apologize, he actually grabbed my fingers and gave them a gentle squeeze. Air rushed out of my lungs as heat and electricity shot up my arm and spread throughout my entire body. I looked up at Cain in surprise and was startled to see his eyes light up with…something.

But just as quickly as it was there, it was gone and he moved out of my way to let me pass.

By the time I got upstairs, my body started to give out on me and I was forced to sit down on the bed. Sitting down led to lying down and before I knew it, I was out. By the time I woke up, an hour had passed. I jolted upright, ready to jump off the bed and run downstairs to make sure Devon and Cain hadn't killed each other. But just as I swung my legs off the bed, I saw Cain sitting in a chair in the corner of the room, his eyes on me and his hand holding my letter.

My final farewell letter.

And he did not look happy.

CHAPTER 11

CAIN

Dear Devon,

I don't even know how to start this letter except maybe to tell you I'm sorry. And to tell you I'm at peace now.

You guys were right about Eric. I knew that even before I walked out of your lives that day and returned to D.C. with him. But I needed what I thought he was offering. Love, acceptance, validation, commitment...all those things Mom and Dad had. I wanted that for myself. I wanted to someday have a family like ours...where love is freely given, not earned. I wanted to someday give to someone else what our family gave to me.

I've done part of that, Devon. I found someone who needed me, but it wasn't Eric. Her name is Lucy. She's Eric's stepdaughter. I need you to keep her safe for me. She has no one left...Eric took her mother from her. Worse yet, Lucy witnessed it and she's suffering.

He'll kill her if he finds out she knows the truth about how her mother really died. I took her to protect her, but if you're reading this letter, I've failed. I can only hope Lucy got away. You need to find her, Devon. Please. Take care of her. The enclosed phone belongs to Lucy – she was able to record her mother's death with it. Use it to prove to the world Eric isn't the hero they believe him to be. Set Lucy free from the fear of being hunted.

If you can't get the phone fixed, there's evidence of Eric's crimes in my *safe deposit box at Meridian Bank – it's a few miles from my hospital. I put you down as an authorized user of the box so they will give you the key when you show them proof of who you are.*

Devon, the stuff you'll see and hear in that box...just remember that he can't hurt me ever again. And know that I was working to get free...to come home to all of you. To tell you how sorry I was for choosing him over you. I know now that it never should have been a choice. I deserved to be with someone who would have loved my family as much as me.

Tell Mom and Dad that I'll never forget what they did for me and that I will always be with them. Tell Garrett and Eden I'll be watching over them as they start their own families. And to you my brother, thank you for taking on this final burden for me...I was the luckiest little boy to have had you for a big brother. I know you'll be strong for our family as they try to get through this. And know that I'll be watching over you too...I'm strong enough to do that now.

Take care of Lucy.

I love you all very much.

Ethan.

I watched as Ethan's eyes shifted from the letter to me and back again. I'd read the damn thing three times already after I'd managed to coerce Devon into letting me look at it while he called his family. I'd been so disturbed after reading it for the first time that I'd had to find Ethan just to reassure myself he was okay. That had been thirty minutes ago.

It shouldn't have surprised me that he'd fallen asleep because as far as he'd come in the last two weeks, he was still struggling with his injuries. He moved easier and faster, but he tired easy and I often saw him flinching in pain if he turned or stepped wrong. His bruises had finally started to lighten and fade, but I still didn't really know what he actually looked like in person. I'd been so desperate to know what his face would look like without all the swelling and bruising that I'd actually gone online after he'd told me, Ronan and Phoenix his story just so I could look at his picture.

I'd already thought him beautiful, but the picture had confirmed it. The fact that I'd even thought of him that way was eating at something inside of me. I'd passed off my attraction to him as some strange fluke, but I knew it was bullshit. I *was* attracted to him.

Desperately so.

But it wasn't just his physical appearance that was drawing me in like a moth to a flame. His strength, his kindness, his ability to trust after everything he'd been through…his ability to trust *me* did something to me on a level I couldn't explain.

It had been brutal to watch him with that little bag of potato chips on the plane. I felt like I'd been given a glimpse of what Ethan was truly running from. The psychological damage Eric had inflicted upon him was so much worse than the bruises that would eventually heal.

I wasn't sure what had possessed me to tell him the truth about my own parents. Maybe it was because early on when I'd first encountered him in that cabin, I *had* subconsciously been comparing him to my mother. Like Ethan, my mother had been well-educated with a good paying job when she'd married my father. I had no doubt that my father's abuse had begun early with my mother, but for whatever reason, she'd never left him. Not even after bringing five children into the world who'd had to helplessly watch their mother endure the most brutal of beatings along with the declarations of love that always followed. But unlike Ethan, my mother hadn't stood up for her children when the time had come.

"Your family will be here in about twenty minutes," I said to Ethan as he continued to stare at the letter in my hand.

"Why did you read that?" he whispered.

I debated telling him the truth versus not answering him at all. I knew I was getting in way too deep with this man, but there was something inside of me that just couldn't disconnect from him.

He was changing me.

I could still feel the proof of that on my skin even hours later. Where he'd grabbed my arm on the plane to stop me from getting up…where his fingers had pressed against mine downstairs just before he'd gone to get cleaned up.

I wanted to touch him again.

I wanted *him* to touch *me* again.

And that made no fucking sense to me whatsoever.

"Because I need to know you, Ethan," I said softly.

He stood up and walked over to me. It should have bothered me that he was standing above me, putting me in the more vulnerable position. Yes, my gaze went to his hands automatically, reflexively, but it didn't stay there long before returning to his face, to his pretty green eyes that were even now filled with confusion.

"Why, Cain?" he whispered.

"I don't know," I admitted. I stood up, causing our bodies to nearly touch since Ethan didn't step back. I liked that he had to look up at me a little, though I didn't know why I liked it. He was drawing in deep breaths and I watched as his eyes dropped to my mouth.

I knew what he wanted.

Did I want it too?

Did I want to cross that line?

I'd only ever been with women, though in truth, after the age of fifteen when everything had changed for me, those women had been nothing more than warm bodies to slake a biological need. Something inside of me had ended up broken, because I'd never looked at women the same way again. I'd never looked at *people* the same way again.

And I'd never looked at anyone the way I was looking at the man in front of me. I'd never felt this ache to touch, to taste, to feel.

I didn't know how long we stood there for, but the silence around us was broken by the sound of the front door being opened and someone calling Devon's name.

Ethan's family was early.

"Oh God," Ethan whispered.

I had no doubt the turmoil Ethan was going through right now. I'd seen it in every line of his face as he'd encountered his brother again after so long. But I also knew that nothing he told his family would change the way they felt about him. I'd seen proof of that when Devon had started interrogating me the second Ethan had been out of sight. There hadn't been much I could tell him without divulging the true nature of Ronan's group, but I'd finally managed to convince him that I would bring his brother home to him. Only then had he gotten the phone for me along with the letter. I was certain I'd have to make the same reassurances to the rest of his family and while it made me nervous to be around so many people at once, I'd do it for Ethan. He'd need that strength in the coming days and weeks as we brought Eric to his knees.

"You've got me, right, Cain?" Ethan suddenly asked.

I ended up squeezing his hand again like I had downstairs.

"I've got you, Ethan."

Only when I said the words did he relax and nod. And then he was heading downstairs to face the family he so badly needed.

∼

"Jace, you have us?" I asked as Ethan and I got out of the car.

"I have you," came the response. "Parking garage," Jace said, his voice loud in my ear. I'd explained to Ethan that I would be wearing a communication device in my ear that would allow me to communicate with my teammate, Jace Christenson. Although I wasn't expecting trouble while we emptied out the safe deposit box, I'd decided that having a second set of eyes on us wouldn't hurt and since Jace was based out of D.C., it had made sense to call him, though I'd never worked with him directly.

Ethan was tense next to me as we crossed the parking lot next to the bank. I glanced up and saw a glimpse of Jace as he got set up on the top floor of the parking garage across the street from the bank. I could see he had a pair of binoculars, but his position didn't allow me to see much else. But I knew he'd come prepared to provide the support we might need if anything went wrong.

We'd landed at a small airstrip early that morning after leaving Ethan's family late the night before. The visit with his family had gone as expected. Shock, grief, excitement...the range of emotions as the Rhodes family had been reunited with their son had been endless... and powerful. I'd found myself envious at times of how close they were. As expected, there'd been no anger with Ethan and his sudden return, just pure happiness. So much so, that Ethan's mother had grabbed me in a giant hug because she'd decided I'd played some big role in bringing her son home to her.

Ethan had panicked when she'd hugged me, but I'd managed to maintain control of myself and I'd given him the smallest shake of my head when he'd tried to stop his mother. Luckily, she hadn't held on to me for long since she'd wanted Ethan back in her arms right away.

It had been brutal to watch his family learn the truth about what had happened to him over the years he'd been gone, and that hadn't even taken into account how much he'd left out. It hadn't really mattered because his family had suffered anyway. There'd been lots of tears and outrage, but there'd been a lot of joyous moments for Ethan too. He'd discovered his sister was married and pregnant and his brother, Garrett, was engaged. They'd shared dozens and dozens of stories in the few hours we'd spent with them and when it had come time to say goodbye, there'd been another round of tears and hugs and promises. His mother had hugged me again, but it had been easier the second time around because she'd been crying and begging me to promise to bring her son home. It was hard to consider a weeping, shaking woman a threat, so I'd held her and promised I would do exactly as she'd asked.

I'd decided that we should fly out right away rather than stay at a hotel on the off chance that Eric was watching the family. Ronan's tech girl was monitoring Eric's movements through his phone and credit cards, but he'd been quiet in the past two weeks.

Too quiet for my liking.

After landing this morning, Ethan and I had gone to a hotel near the airport after grabbing the rental car Ronan had had waiting for us. We'd checked in, but Ethan had been too on edge to sleep so I'd made arrangements with Jace to shadow us so we could get the task of retrieving the contents of the safe deposit box over with.

"You see anything?" I asked Jace.

Silence for a moment, then "No, you're good."

The location of the bank was in a quiet neighborhood of mostly Mom and Pop type shops and small businesses. There were a few people out and about which helped us blend in. I'd had Ethan wear a baseball cap and a windbreaker over his T-shirt. I'd debated having him wear sunglasses to try and hide some of the bruising on his face but had decided they'd look suspicious if he wore them inside the bank.

Ethan was tense as we reached the sidewalk and passed by a narrow alley before reaching the entrance to the bank. He already had the safe deposit key out, along with his ID. Since he'd ditched his ID after taking off with Lucy, Ronan had had to get creative and had a new one made for him using the picture from the Internet that the news agencies had used for their reports – it was the picture that had once been on the hospital website where he'd worked.

The bank was a small, outdated establishment, so it hadn't surprised me when Jace had let me know that his reconnaissance before our arrival had revealed the absence of metal detectors. Which meant I had the comfort of being able to carry a gun with me, though I had no reason to think I'd need it. The place wasn't busy at all when we entered so within a matter of minutes, an older woman in a crisp navy skirt and matching blazer was greeting us.

"How can I help you today?" she asked.

"I'd like to access my safe deposit box," Ethan said, his voice calmer than I'd expected it to be. Pride shot through me at how well he was handling himself because I knew he was scared shitless.

"Of course. I'll just need to see some ID," the woman said as she motioned to a desk. Neither Ethan nor I sat as she looked up Ethan's information and checked his ID. She glanced at him several times, her face pulling into a frown for the briefest of moments, presumably as she took in his battered face and tried to confirm it really was him.

"Right this way, Mr. Rhodes," she said as she got up and motioned for us to follow her to a side door. She led us to the room with the safe deposit boxes and used her key along with Ethan's to open his box.

She removed the long, silver drawer and placed it on a table in the middle of the room.

"I'll be outside if you need me," she said politely before leaving.

Ethan's hand was shaking as he tried to insert his key to open the box. I covered his hand with mine and said, "Deep breaths, Ethan."

He nodded and did as I said. Several long moments passed before he relaxed enough to work the box open. I saw him hesitate at the last minute before he lifted the lid. I had no doubt he was preparing himself for all the memories that would flood his brain the moment he opened the thing. I didn't rush him in any way and when he finally opened it, I waited for the inevitable fall. But when his mouth fell open and his eyes went wide, I stiffened and went around to his side of the table.

"Oh God," he whispered.

Shock tore through me as I saw what he was seeing.

An empty box.

Ethan shook his head. "It must be some kind of mistake," he murmured as he looked over his shoulder at the slot where the box had been removed from. He compared the number on the little door to the number on his key. "It's…it's my box but this makes no sense."

"We need to go," I said quickly as I grabbed his arm.

"We should talk to the lady-"

"We need to go right now, Ethan!" I ordered. "Jace, we're coming out."

I didn't hear a response and suspected the link was fucked up by the heavy metal of the vault surrounding us.

"Cain, what's going on?" Ethan asked, his voice heavy with fear.

"You said Eric was already inside the house that day you got home from the gas station, right?"

"Right."

"He found the key, Ethan."

"No," Ethan argued. "If he'd found it, why didn't he just take it?"

"Because he wanted a way to find you again if you got away that day."

Ethan came to a complete stop, his face a mask of shock, but I yanked him forward. "Stay calm," I told him softly once we reached the main lobby. The woman who'd helped us was on the phone, but as soon as she saw us, she put it down and rushed towards us.

"Can I help you gentlemen with anything else?" she asked eagerly. Too eagerly.

"No, thank you," I said easily. "Have a good day."

I practically dragged Ethan towards the door. I waited until we were in the vestibule to say, "Jace, it was a trap."

"Copy that," he responded quickly. "All clear out here."

"Ethan, lose the jacket and hat," I snapped as I tore my own jacket free and stuffed it into the garbage can next to the ATM machine. I did the same with Ethan's jacket and hat and then pushed out the door.

I turned us right towards the parking lot, but we hadn't gotten more than a couple steps before a police car rounded the corner in front of us, lights on but siren off.

"Keep walking," I said to Ethan as I grabbed his hand in mine and held onto it. I could feel the tremor in his fingers as he clasped my hand in an icy grip.

"Jace, we need a distraction," I said softly as I continued to move Ethan towards the parking lot. In my periphery, I saw the cops getting out of the car. One ran into the bank, but the other didn't follow him.

"Hey," the cop called out.

"Jace," I said desperately as I pretended to not hear the cop.

"Twenty seconds," I heard Jace say calmly. I could hear the sound of metal on metal and I knew he was likely putting together the long-range sniper rifle he was known to carry.

"You there, just a minute," the cop called again.

"Cain," Ethan whispered.

I knew we wouldn't make it to the parking lot. My eyes fell on the alley as I mentally counted down the seconds. If the cop saw Ethan's face and recognized it, this whole thing was over. Not to mention the ID he was carrying with his real name on it. I was armed, but killing a cop wasn't going to happen. I debated taking him out with just a few punches, but knew I'd waited too long to make my move when a second patrol car rolled up behind the first.

Desperation crawled through my mind. I needed to buy Jace fifteen seconds.

"Hey!" the cop shouted, louder this time. I still had a hold of Ethan's hand so I quickly tugged him into the alley. I pushed him against the wall, but before he could ask me what was happening, I sealed my mouth over his.

Ethan let out a startled gasp and went completely still in my hold. I could hear footsteps hurrying towards us.

"Kiss me back, Ethan. It needs to look real," I said as I reached down to pull his arms up so they were around my neck. I covered Ethan's mouth again, but this time, his lips didn't freeze beneath mine. I stifled a moan as his mouth moved against mine and then opened in invitation. I didn't need to taste him to make this whole thing look like it was the real deal, but I did anyway. Ethan let out a startled cry when my tongue licked over his and I felt his arms tighten around my neck.

"Hey, you!" I was dimly aware of someone saying as I pressed Ethan back against the wall, wrapping my arms around his waist.

"Five seconds," I heard Jace say in my ear.

I ripped my mouth free of Ethan's and used my hand to tuck his face against my shoulder so the cop wouldn't see it. "Uh, sorry Officer, just looking for a little privacy with my guy," I said with what I hoped sounded like an embarrassed chuckle. "Is there, ah, a problem?" I asked.

"Three."

"I need to see some ID," the man said, unamused. Another cop appeared at his side.

"Two."

"Um, yeah, sure," I murmured. I turned my body and tucked Ethan behind me as I pretended to go for my wallet. "Baby, he needs to see ID," I said to Ethan over my shoulder in the hopes of placating the cop.

The leather of my wallet hadn't even cleared my pocket when I heard the distinct pop in my ear followed by another one. A second later, an explosion rocked the air around us. I grabbed Ethan and pushed him against the wall, covering his body with mine. The cops started yelling and then they were running. I grabbed Ethan's hand and stuck my head out of the alley. I could smell and hear the fire before I even saw it. It was at least two blocks over in what looked like some kind of junkyard. Both of the cops who'd been talking to me were running in that direction, yelling into the communication devices on their shoulders. I tugged Ethan towards the car. Two more cops ran past us towards the fireball.

"What was that?" I asked Jace as I began trotting towards our rental.

The man snickered in my ear. "Propane tank," he said. "No casualties," he added. I merely smiled at that because I knew Jace would have taken every precaution not to injure an innocent bystander.

"I'll call you if we need anything else," I said as Ethan and I got into the car.

"You bet," Jace said and then the comm went silent. I removed it from my ear and focused on getting us out of there.

I managed to keep to the speed limit as I maneuvered the car through traffic and headed towards the road that would get us out of D.C. and back into Virginia and on our way to the hotel. But inside I was totally fucked up. Between the adrenaline rush of our close call and the lingering sensation of Ethan's mouth on mine, I was barely holding it together.

Ethan wasn't doing any better.

"Ethan," I said softly as I tried to calm myself.

"He won," he whispered. And then he went silent as tears tracked down his face.

I let him be and focused on getting us back to the hotel. About ten miles before we reached our destination, I pulled the car over long enough to swap the plates out. I always kept a spare set of license plates in my bag for times like this. With all the security cameras on the streets, I didn't want to worry about the cops knowing what car we were driving. And if they happened to figure it out, the fake plates would throw them off. I knew it was likely overkill, but I wasn't taking any chances. It would be easy to put the regular plates back on the car just before we returned it to the rental agency and since Ronan had rented the car under an alias, I knew we wouldn't be tracked that way.

I called Ronan as we neared our hotel to give him an update and told him I'd call him back later to discuss next steps.

Ethan still hadn't spoken by the time we reached the hotel. When I opened the door and moved out of the way to let him enter, he walked towards the bathroom. The mirror and sinks were outside the actual bathroom so I could see him as he leaned against the vanity and stared at his reflection. I closed and locked the door. Both sets of curtains were drawn so I opened the heavier, outer ones so light could filter into the room through the sheer inner curtains. I watched Ethan in silence as he studied himself in the mirror, his expression blank.

I was shocked when he suddenly lashed out at the mirror with his fist, like he was striking at himself. He let out a guttural scream and then he was tearing at the few items sitting on top of the counter like the complimentary toiletries and box of tissues. I strode up to him and wrapped my arms around him from behind, pinning his arms so he couldn't hurt himself.

"I tried so fucking hard, Cain," he shouted as his body shook and tears coasted down his face. "I can't...I can't do it anymore," he whispered harshly.

"Do what?" I asked softly.

"Be strong," he murmured. "Fight." He was silent for several beats before saying, "Hope."

"Look at me," I ordered softly. His eyes lifted to meet mine in the mirror. "You're not done, do you hear me?" I said firmly. "You're not done fighting and you sure as shit aren't done hoping. I've never met anyone as strong as you, Ethan."

Ethan held my gaze for a long time and then carefully pulled free of my hold. But he didn't walk away from me. Instead, he turned around to face me. "Please don't do this to me, Cain," Ethan whispered.

"Do what?" I asked.

"Make me want something I can't have."

My insides lit up, but before I could even move, he was pushing past me. "You're not gay, are you?" he asked when he stopped near the door.

"No," I admitted.

"Are you bi?" he asked.

I began walking towards him, not missing the way he tensed and his breathing ticked up.

"I don't know what I am," I said softly.

Ethan backed up until his back hit the wall next to the door. "That...that kiss wasn't real," he said half-heartedly just before I reached him.

"Yes, it was," I murmured right before I bent my head and sealed my mouth over his.

CHAPTER 12

ETHAN

I kept trying to tell myself it wasn't real, but the argument held no water because the sensation of Cain's mouth moving over mine as he kissed me was undeniable.

I'd never felt anything like it.

Not even with Eric.

Unlike in the alley, I didn't wait for Cain to tell me to kiss him back. I greeted his seeking tongue with fervor and followed it back into his own mouth as he drew back just a little bit. I didn't know what to do with my hands because I didn't want to ruin what was happening by touching him if that wasn't what he wanted. But Cain took the decision away from me a moment later when he grabbed my hands and pressed them against the wall next to my head. He laced our fingers together as he pressed his body against mine. I was at his mercy and I didn't care.

I welcomed it.

I barely felt the hardness of the wall against my back. I didn't hear the low din of the fan circulating air around the small room. I didn't register anything but Cain's mouth, his body, his smell.

I craved to touch him. To once again feel his hot skin beneath my fingers. There'd been a point when he'd kissed me in that alley where I'd forgotten all about the danger we were in and I'd clung to him out of need rather than fear.

A moan fell from my lips when I felt his groin brush mine.

He was hard.

It made no sense, which was why I knew I needed to stop. I'd been ruled by passion before and that was *nothing* like this. What would happen if I let this man take what was left of me...the few parts of me Eric hadn't managed to reach with his fists or his words?

But I couldn't force myself to tear my mouth from his. I couldn't make myself tug my hands free of his and I couldn't stop myself from canting my hips so my stiff cock could brush his through the too many layers of clothing separating us.

The simmering desire exploded into something a thousand times more intense when Cain suddenly released my hands and clasped my face with his hands and took complete control of the kiss, me, everything. I couldn't stop myself from wrapping my fingers around his wrists where he was holding onto me. I needed something to ground me, to keep me with him because it just felt that fucking good.

When we were both forced to come up for air, Cain hung there, his forehead pressed to mine, his mouth just centimeters from mine. He was breathing hard and his skin felt like it was on fire. I held there, unmoving, as I tried to get control of my lust.

"Ethan," Cain whispered. "I need you to do something for me."

"Anything," I said without hesitation.

"I need you to touch me, but I need you to promise you'll stop if I ask you to."

"I will," I said softly. "I swear it."

He nodded against me. I was surprised when he kept his forehead pressed to mine as he moved my hands down to his waist. His T-shirt was untucked so he used one hand to pull it up just a little before placing one of my hands on his waist. After he maneuvered my other hand to where he wanted it, he released his hold on me and placed his hands next to my head. His eyes were on my hands.

His skin was hot and tight to the touch. And soft. Much softer than I would have expected. I slowly slid my hands up his waist just a little, but stilled when I felt him tense up.

"Keep going," he murmured.

I left one hand where it was and moved the other. Within a fraction of a second, my fingers skimmed over a raised patch of skin just below his armpit. I didn't focus on the scar as I let my hand travel back down to his stomach. But as soon as I reached his abs, I felt another scar. When I moved my other hand, it quickly encountered a third scar, then a fourth. I finally let my finger follow the complete path of one of the scars. It was several inches long. Tears stung my eyes as I realized what they were.

"Knife?" I asked softly.

Cain nodded against me. "Butcher knife," he whispered, his voice harsh.

"Do you want me to stop?" I asked.

"No," he said and I stilled when he brushed a kiss over my mouth and let his eyes connect with mine. "Don't stop."

I took my time exploring his muscled chest and abdomen. Scar after scar met my seeking hands.

"Will you take this off?" I asked gently as I tugged on the hem of his shirt.

He sucked in a breath and I knew, just knew that what I was asking was something monumental. "I've got you, Cain," I whispered.

Cain closed his eyes and nodded just before he reached behind him with one arm and tugged the shirt off. I kept my eyes on him for the longest time before I finally looked down. Twelve scars mottled his entire torso.

"My back," he murmured.

I reached behind him to explore his back and felt three more scars. "Fifteen," I said quietly.

"That's how old I was," Cain responded. "He used our ages to decide how many times to stab us."

Nausea crawled through my belly.

"Us?" I whispered.

"Me, my brothers, my sisters." He fell silent for a moment before saying, "Hailey, nine, Daniel, six, Justin, three and Amanda…one."

I slid my hands up to his shoulders and then to his face until I was cupping his cheeks. "Who?" I asked. "Who did this?"

He didn't answer right away. His eyes were still closed and I could feel a fine tremor filtering throughout his body. "My father," he finally admitted.

Horror went through me, but I managed to keep from crying out my distress. I lifted enough so I could brush my mouth over his. I kissed him over and over again, telling him I was sorry between kisses. When his mouth finally opened beneath mine, I let my tongue slip between his lips and gently explored every part of his mouth. When my arms went around his shoulders, he let out his breath and pulled his mouth from mine. He crushed me in a bruising hold as he held onto me. "I'm not ready for more," he admitted against my neck.

"It's okay," I said. "Whatever you want."

"I want to hold you."

I nodded because I couldn't find the words to go with the emotion that clogged my throat. Cain released me long enough to lead me to one of the two beds in the room. He worked the covers back and then toed his shoes off after removing a gun and holster from his ankle. I took my own shoes off and waited.

"Your shirt," he said softly.

Although I wasn't thrilled for him to see me with all the bruises that still covered my body, I didn't hesitate to remove my shirt. He took my hand and urged me into bed. I lay down so I was facing away from him. I didn't move when I felt him slide against my back, his skin brushing mine. His arm curled around my waist and he worked the other beneath my head. I took a risk and pulled the hand he had at my waist higher across my chest and covered it with mine. I used my other hand to reach up and twine my fingers with the fingers near my head.

Cain didn't speak, nor did he try to move away from my touch at all.

We just lay there like that for what seemed like hours before I felt his breath on the back of my neck even out and I knew he was asleep.

But I couldn't relax enough to let my eyes close. Not when I could feel so many ridges of marred skin against my back. So I wept silently for Cain and I held on as tight as I could to the parts of him he would let me touch.

~

It was dark outside when I woke up and I knew instantly that Cain was no longer at my back. An unreasonable fear went through me that he'd left me, but as soon as I sat up, I saw him sitting at the small table by the window. Like in my brother's guest room, his eyes were on me.

"What time is it?" I asked.

"Almost nine," he said. "I ordered us some food. It's not safe for us to go out to eat somewhere."

I nodded. He'd closed the outer curtains so the room was dark except for the light just above where he was sitting. I reached for the light next to the bed and turned it on. I felt weird without my shirt considering Cain was once again fully dressed. I swung my feet over the edge of the bed and searched the floor, but my shirt was gone.

"On the bed," Cain said softly. I glanced to the foot of the bed and saw my shirt neatly laying across it. I tugged it on. The air was awkward between us and as much as I wanted to talk about what had happened between us this afternoon, I couldn't make myself speak the words.

Not when Cain was looking so relaxed and...disconnected.

I let my thoughts drift to the events at the bank. "He must have had a warrant to get into my box, huh?" I asked.

"That or the BOLO was enough to convince the bank to give him access...I'm not sure what the law is when it comes to stuff like that. Daisy never found any warrants on you so if he used one, it wasn't legit."

"But that lady called the cops when she recognized my name, right?"

Cain nodded. "He probably convinced her to put a note on your account to call the cops."

"He got everything," I said softly as I shook my head. "If Lucy's phone can't be fixed-"

"Even if it can't be fixed, Ethan, Eric is never getting to you or her again. I promise you that."

I knew what he was talking about and while the doctor in me rebelled, the man in me knew it was the only way to stop Eric from hurting someone else. If it had just been me he'd hurt, I could've lived with that, even if it meant running for the rest of my life. But Lucy's life was at risk and I couldn't subject her to that future.

"What if I turn myself in?" I asked, though the idea filled me with dread. I wasn't sure what scared me more, the idea of prison or the idea of ending up in Eric's control again. With prison, I had a chance of maybe someday getting out…with Eric, I had no chance of anything.

I looked up when I heard the chair creak and I watched as Cain walked over to me. He hovered above me, his big body towering over mine. He put his leg between my knees and slowly forced my legs open until he was standing with one leg between mine, the other on the outside of my left leg.

"That's. Not. An. Option," he said slowly and then he was leaning over me, his mouth seeking mine. I groaned as his tongue dueled with mine and then he was pushing me back onto the bed, his weight following me down. I tentatively held onto his waist as he kissed me and when he didn't tense up, I let my fingers press into his sides so I'd have something to hold onto. I was quickly losing control of my reaction to him, but was saved from embarrassing myself by begging him to fuck me when there was a knock at the door. I jolted at the sound and tried to scramble free of him.

"It's the food," Cain said softly against my lips before kissing me gently. He lifted off me and went to answer the door. My eyes instantly fell to his ass as he reached into his back pocket for his wallet.

Jesus, what was wrong with me? It had taken weeks for me to let Eric kiss me for the first time, months till we slept together, but with Cain I would have done anything to feel him inside me.

I'd never been particularly fond of sex with Eric because he'd always been on the rough side and hadn't cared about my pleasure, but with Cain I knew it wouldn't be like that. I didn't know how I knew, I just did. The problem wasn't with the physical aspect of any relationship I pursued with Cain. It was my heart that was in jeopardy.

I'd thought myself in love with Eric, but I realized now that what I'd had with him hadn't even been in the same universe as love. I'd been indebted to him…grateful that he'd wanted me. *That* was what I'd loved about him. I could have interchanged him with just about any man who'd shown me even an ounce of kindness or interest and I'd have said the same. But looking at Cain, feeling him wrapped around me in that shower, hearing his whispered words in my ear… his belief that I was perfectly fine the way I was…it was already piecing back together my damaged heart. From the moment I'd told him I didn't believe in hope anymore, that was all he'd been giving me.

I couldn't fall in love with this man…I just couldn't. I'd survived Eric because of his brutality. I couldn't survive losing the many things Cain had been giving me.

"Scoot over," Cain said as he stopped at the edge of the bed, two pizza boxes in hand. I crawled backwards on the bed until I was sitting on the far side of it, my body angled towards Cain. He put the boxes down on the end of the bed and sat down with his back against the headboard. "I got different kinds," he said.

"What?" I asked dumbly as I let my eyes roam over his face. He was so beautiful with his golden boy looks.

"The pizza," he said as he opened both boxes. I managed to snap out of my trance long enough to look at the different options. Each pizza had different toppings on each half. I grabbed a slice of one with just some sausage and pepperoni on it. Cain did the same.

"I would have pegged you for a supreme kind of guy," I said.

He shook his head. "No, I like things simple," he said. "What about you?"

I glanced at the pizza. "Pre-Eric, I liked a lot of comfort food and stuff that was convenient just to grab and go. With Eric, it was all salads and protein shakes…lots of organic, healthy stuff."

"And now?" Cain asked.

"Now, it's whatever's available," I murmured. "But the future? The future's wide open."

He smiled at that and the sight had my insides fluttering.

"Potato chips?" he asked.

"Definitely potato chips," I said with a smile.

We ate in silence for a while. I had to give myself a pep talk when I went to reach for a second slice of pizza, but fortunately I managed to not make it a big thing and Cain didn't call me on it. I watched Cain pack away a total of four slices before he closed the box and reached for a napkin to wipe at his hands and face.

"You missed a spot," I said as I pointed to a fleck of sauce at the corner of his mouth. I wanted so badly just to reach out and wipe it away myself, but I held back.

Instead of reaching for a napkin, Cain sat up and shifted until he was just inches from me. "Will you get it for me?" he asked softly, his voice heavy with desire.

Yep, this man was going to be the death of me.

I reached out with my hand, but all I did was gently grab him by the chin. Then I was leaning forward and pressing my lips to the side of his mouth. I heard him suck in a breath when my tongue flicked over the little bit of sauce. His lips were on mine a moment later. The kiss grew heated quickly, but when Cain pulled away from me, I let him go.

"I don't understand this," he whispered.

"It's okay," I said even as the disappointment flowed through me. "It's the stress, the close quarters. I know you're not really attracted to me-"

His lips on mine shut me up, as did the feel of his cock beneath my fingers when he grabbed my hand and placed it on his groin. "You want to tell me again that I'm not attracted to you?" he growled.

I shook my head. When he released my hand, I slowly pulled it away from his lap, though it practically killed me to do it.

"What is it that you don't understand?" I asked as my eyes met his.

"This...this need I have for you," he murmured as he reached up to trail his thumb over my bottom lip. "Sex has always been this thing I occasionally wanted, but never needed," he said softly.

"Have you ever been with a man before? Or been attracted to one?"

He shook his head. "But I honestly can't say I've been particularly attracted to women, either," he admitted.

"But surely the women you've been with-"

"They were escorts," he interjected. I was momentarily rendered speechless.

"Why?" I finally said dumbly. "You're so gorgeous, you could have anyone you wanted."

He dropped his eyes and I instantly felt bad. "I'm sorry, I didn't mean to judge."

"You weren't," he said. "It's a valid question." He lifted his eyes and said, "I knew any woman I dated would want to touch me, kiss me. I couldn't let anyone close enough to do that. And I didn't want to explain why not. Escorts didn't care...not what position I fucked them in, which was always from behind, and not that they weren't allowed to touch me. I tried to be with a girl the normal way after...after what happened, but when she put her arms around me, I panicked and pushed her away. She fell to the floor..."

Cain shook his head. "I apologized, but I'd scared her. She never spoke to me again."

"How old were you?" I asked.

"Sixteen. I couldn't explain myself or tell her about the attack."

"Will you tell me about it?" I asked as I reached up to brush my fingers against his temple. He leaned into the touch. Instead of answering me, he reached down and grabbed the pizza boxes and put them on the floor next to the bed. Afterwards, he leaned back against the headboard.

"Can I hold you while I tell you?" he asked.

I was tempted to tell him he never had to ask my permission to hold me, but I held my tongue and instead said, "Where do you want me?"

CHAPTER 13

CAIN

I was worried the nerves would come back when Ethan settled his head on my chest and wrapped his arm around my waist, but thankfully my stomach didn't rebel at the contact. When I'd asked him to touch me earlier after I'd kissed him for the second time, I hadn't been sure I'd be able to go through with it. But watching his hands as they'd skimmed over my body with infinite gentleness had been mesmerizing. Yes, there'd been a twinge of fear there, but the need to feel his touch had been greater.

I let my hand settle on Ethan's back while I closed the other over the one he had resting over my heart. I loved the feel of his weight on me. I would have thought the sensation of being held down, even by someone as slight as Ethan, would have been too much, but it was oddly comforting.

And kissing Ethan…well, there was just no equal to that. I hadn't lied when I'd told him that my need for him confused me. I'd already accepted that his gender wasn't the issue…it was that one person could hold such power over me. Maybe I should have been more freaked out about being attracted to a man, but I suspected my past had a lot to do with that. When everything had gone to hell for me, I'd just started exploring my sexuality. It was true that I hadn't been attracted to any boys in my class, but there really hadn't been that many girls either. My fucked-up childhood even before the attack had given me a perception on love and relationships that wasn't really all that healthy and that I hadn't wanted to emulate. The attack had just sealed the deal.

"I grew up in a small town about a hundred miles from Lexington in Kentucky. My mom was a bank manager and my dad was a CPA. They met in college and got married after graduation. I came along a few years later. I don't really remember things getting bad until my sister, Hailey, was born. I was six. I only remember bits and pieces... fighting, my mom with bruises, my dad bringing her flowers. By the time Daniel came along, things were clearer."

"He was nine years younger than you, right?"

"Yeah," I said, not surprised that Ethan remembered my siblings' ages. "My dad was really possessive of my mom and her time. As she started working her way up the corporate ladder at work, he seemed to grow more and more resentful. I never saw him actually hit her until I was ten. I tried to stop it, but my father told me to stay out of it. My mother told me to take my brother and sister to my room. It never made sense to me," I said softly.

"What didn't?" Ethan prodded when I got too lost in the past.

"How they could yell and scream at each other like that and then the next day they couldn't keep their hands off each other. Even with my mother covered in bruises, she'd just *melt* into him. Like she was the happiest woman in the world. And things would be fine again until it all started over again."

I felt Ethan start to rub small circles into my chest and I wished I'd had the sense to take my shirt off before lying down with him.

"I noticed as I got older that my dad seemed more and more resentful of us kids. But he never took his anger out on any of us. Even if we did something wrong, like if we broke a dish or something. Somehow it was my mother's fault. It was like he was doing his best to pretend we didn't exist. I once asked him why he'd even had us if he didn't want us around."

"What did he say?" Ethan asked.

"He didn't answer me. Just told me to ask my mother. I stopped trying to stop him from going after her when she yelled at me one day to mind my own business...that I couldn't understand how much my father loved her. Something...something changed for me after that. Instead of trying to stay home to referee fights with them and to protect my brothers and sisters from them, I escaped...found any excuse I could not to come home. I felt so guilty for it, but I couldn't just watch him do that to her...and watch her take it," I said softly.

I let my hand begin to roam up and down Ethan's back as the memories cascaded over me. The weight of his hand as he continued to caress me helped keep me grounded.

"A few months after I turned fifteen, my parents had this really bad fight...bad enough that someone called the cops. My dad wasn't arrested, but the cops made him leave. I knew he wouldn't be gone for long, but I tried to talk my mom into leaving him. I thought maybe she'd see the truth if he wasn't around to beg her forgiveness. She looked at me like I was crazy for even suggesting it. My dad came back about a week later, but he was different...really different," I said.

"How?"

"There was no more yelling, no fights if dinner wasn't on the table on time, no cursing if a dish got broken or milk got spilled. He started paying attention to me and my brothers and sisters. I was suspicious at first."

"You thought it was too good to be true," Ethan offered.

"Yeah. Weeks went by and I waited for him to explode, to go back to his old ways. But he didn't. He and my mom were happier than I'd ever seen them."

"What about you and him?"

"He seemed to make more of an effort to get to know me. I...I started to hope that maybe the worst of it was over. That we were going to be a real family."

I fell silent as a ripple of shameful heat went through me.

"What happened, Cain?" Ethan asked, his voice gentle.

"He picked me up from school early one day to take me to a baseball game – it was just a minor-league team but I was so excited. We talked about everything on the way there and back. He told me how proud he was that I was so good at sports. It was one of the best moments in my life. By the time we got home, I was on cloud nine. When we got inside, he asked me what I wanted for dinner since my mom was working late. My brothers and sisters weren't around so I figured they were staying with the lady across the street who used to babysit sometimes."

I felt Ethan stiffen in my hold, but he never let up on touching me with gentle presses of his fingers.

"I was standing there in the kitchen looking through the refrigerator for something for dinner when he said my name. The look in his eyes…I'll never forget it. He looked both happy and sad at the same time and it didn't make sense because we'd had a great day. He…he was still wearing his jacket."

A chill swept through me as I was once again in that kitchen, watching my father walking towards me, that melancholy look in his eyes.

"Cain, look at me."

The sharp order had me snapping my eyes open.

When had I closed them?

"Take deep breaths," Ethan said softly. I noticed he wasn't touching me anymore.

"Did I hurt you?" I immediately asked since I couldn't remember him sitting up.

"No," he said gently. "Take a few deep breaths for me, okay?"

I nodded and did as he said. I felt some of the tension leech out of me and it wasn't until I looked down that I saw that my hands were fisted.

"Ethan, did I hurt you?" I asked again when I felt a little more clear-headed. I sat up so I was eye level with him and I scanned his body for any injuries.

"No, you didn't," he said. "I swear it. You just…you got really tense and quiet."

"I'm sorry," I whispered. "I didn't mean to scare you."

I was surprised when he grabbed the back of my neck. "Cain, look at me," he ordered, though he kept his voice quiet. "You didn't scare me. I was trying not to scare you, okay? That's why I moved."

I saw the truth in his eyes and nodded.

"Do you want to finish your story?" he asked.

I nodded again. But I didn't lie back down as I said, "I was standing there and he was walking to me, his arms open. I was...I was actually excited that he wanted to hug me. He never really had when I was a kid. It took everything in me not to cry when he put his arms around me and told me everything would be better now." I shook my head. "I didn't even feel it at first...there was just this pressure in my stomach and then this weird tugging feeling. And then everything got really hot and then really cold all at the same time."

I felt Ethan's fingers on my cheek, but I couldn't look at him. I was staring at my stomach, watching the long blade being pulled out of my body. "Twelve times," I murmured. "He stabbed me twelve times as I was lying on the kitchen floor before I managed to turn over so I could try to crawl away. I thought he'd just let me go because there was no way I was going to make it very far." I shook my head. "But no, he had to make it fifteen."

"Cain," I heard Ethan whisper brokenly.

"He kept telling me he was sorry, but that it was better this way. That he couldn't share her anymore...he loved her too much." I lifted my eyes to see tears streaming down Ethan's face. "I let him too close to me...I trusted him, even though I knew deep down that something was off."

"You couldn't have known," Ethan said.

I nodded because he was right. I hadn't known that kind of evil existed, and certainly not within the man who'd given me life.

"I woke up in the hospital a month later. The blood loss led to a coma. I was partially paralyzed from the knife hitting some nerves near my spine."

"Your brothers and sisters?"

"After I'd left for school, he'd kept the other kids home. They found Hailey in the bathroom...it looked like she'd tried to lock herself in there. Daniel was on the floor in his room. Justin was next to him. Amanda was still in her crib."

Ethan let out a muffled sob and then he was pushing into my arms. He felt so good there that I ignored the reflexive need to check his hands and just held onto him. "Your mom?" he asked.

"She was the one who found us. The others had been gone a while...long before he even came and got me from school. No one knows how I managed to hang on after having lost so much blood. I was in the hospital for three months. Physical therapy helped with the paralysis. I went to live with my grandmother in Indiana when they discharged me."

Ethan pulled back from me and wiped at his face. He wiped at mine too which made me wonder if I'd been crying. I hadn't felt any tears, but then again, I was so numb I wasn't sure what I was feeling anymore.

"What about your mom?"

I shook my head. "When she refused to accept that my father had been the one who'd done it, my grandmother sued for custody of me."

Ethan shook his head in disbelief. "She didn't believe you?"

"No. Even after I woke up from the coma and told her what had happened, she insisted I was confused. That it was a stranger who'd done it."

"What happened to your father?"

"He was arrested, but they couldn't hold him on anything until I woke up and told them who'd attacked me When I did, he took off. My mother helped him escape."

"But they caught him, right?"

I shook my head. "He's still out there somewhere."

"And...and your mother?"

"She still lives in the same house...waiting for him, maybe. I don't know."

"Jesus, I'm so sorry, Cain," he whispered and then he was hugging me again. "Is this okay?" he asked.

I nodded and pulled back so I could brush my lips over his. "It's good," I reassured him.

Really good, but I kept that fact to myself.

～

"Do you think we should try to go to the hospital I went to after..."

When Ethan's voice dropped off, I shifted so I could press a kiss to his temple. We were lying in bed much like we'd done the day before when I'd asked him to let me hold him. His back was to my front and his fingers were roaming over the ones I had resting on his chest. We'd slept in the position all night long, though I hadn't slept much because I'd been struggling with the implications of what was happening to me.

After telling Ethan my story the night before, we'd lain there in silence for a while before I'd had to get up and check in with Ronan. Ethan had used the time to shower. Ronan and I hadn't really discussed strategy since, in truth, we didn't have one beyond trying to get Lucy's phone fixed so we could pull the video off it. Ronan was making arrangements for Ethan and I to meet a guy who had the skills needed to repair the damaged phone, but until he tracked him down, Ethan and I were rudderless.

Which was fine by me because I had no problem spending some down time with him. We'd have to find a different hotel today if I didn't hear back from Ronan, but otherwise it would just be me and Ethan laying low.

After Ethan had finished his shower, I'd gone to take one myself. I'd given Ethan my phone so he could talk to Lucy and by the time I'd come back out, Ethan had been in bed.

In the wrong bed.

Instead of making him get up and join me in the bed we'd been using earlier, I'd merely crawled into his bed. I'd been about to ask him if it was okay when he'd snuggled back against me with a soft sigh before I'd even gotten completely settled. He'd left his shirt off to sleep, as had I, so I'd gotten to spend the entire night reveling in the feel of his skin against mine. He'd had one nightmare in which he'd begged someone to stop, though it took no thought to know who that someone was. A few whispered words in his ear had settled him and he'd slept through the rest of the night.

I'd used the time to try to understand what was happening to me. It was like I'd told Ethan. For whatever reason, my body didn't care that he was a man…I'd never been more attracted to someone in my entire life. And while the idea of trying to navigate the physical aspects of being with a man instead of a woman was a little daunting because of the newness of it all, I knew I would love every moment of it because I couldn't get enough of him and we'd barely even done anything. My brain was another matter, though. I'd never been in a relationship before, so I had no idea what that meant. The idea that whatever this thing between us was could someday morph into something twisted and ugly like what my parents had had, scared the hell out of me. They'd claimed to love each other so deeply that nothing else existed for them…not even their kids. I could see myself having the same depth of feeling for the man in my arms, but what if it turned into something like what my parents had had? No, I would never hurt Ethan, but what if I became obsessed…what if I lost myself in the process and I ended up hurting him in other ways?

I'd tried to remind myself that my parents' relationship wasn't normal and that I should look to the many pairings and threesomes within my own social circle as guides. But my mind always went back to my parents.

And I hated that.

I was also making a pretty big presumption. Maybe Ethan didn't even want to see if there was something between us. We'd known each other for a little over two weeks and he had been and still was under an immense amount of stress.

"I can practically hear it," Ethan said softly.

"What?" I asked.

"You thinking about things."

He turned in my arms, but he was careful not to touch me. He tucked his hand under his head so he could watch me.

"Sorry," I said. I remembered his question about the hospital. I knew he meant trying to get his medical records that had evidence of the aftermath of Eric's brutal beating and rape. "He will have notified them to contact the police if you show up to get a copy of your medical records."

Ethan sighed and fell silent. He reached out to brush his thumb over my cheek. Early morning light was filtering into the room through the curtains. It wasn't much, but I could make out his face.

"Morning," he said softly.

"Morning," I responded with a smile. He looked so rumpled and relaxed that I couldn't help but feel at ease.

"What has you thinking so hard?" he asked.

"You," I admitted. "This," I said as I motioned between us with my chin.

"Is that good or bad?" he asked.

"Good for me," I murmured as I reached out to cup his cheek. I leaned in to kiss him lightly.

"But you think it's bad for me?" he asked, his brow furrowing just a bit.

"I think you're under a lot of pressure right now and things will look very different when all this is over."

"What things?" he asked.

When I didn't say anything, he softly said, "You?" His thumb trailed over my chin. "Do you think I'll see *you* differently when things are settled?"

I nodded. "I'm not an easy man, Ethan."

"I'm not looking for easy, Cain." He fell silent for a moment before saying, "I'm not seeing you as some knight in shining armor. Yes, you make me feel safe, but it's so much more than that. I'm...I'm hoping that when things calm down, you might want to get to know me better. Like I want to know you."

"What do you want to know?" I automatically asked because I had no interest in waiting for shit to calm down.

Ethan smiled. "Um, okay, what's your favorite color?"

"Black."

He chuckled. "I guess I should have known that because of your truck, huh?"

"What's yours?"

"Blue," he said softly as his gaze held mine. "Soft, pale blue that looks almost silver." His thumb skimmed the skin next to my eye and I instantly knew why he was looking into them so intently. I shifted my weight until I was leaning over him.

"I want to change my answer," I murmured as I looked into his bright green eyes right before I leaned down and kissed him. Ethan laughed against my mouth, but it didn't last long. As soon as my tongue stroked over his, he was moaning and kissing me back. His arms went around my neck and I was glad he was too far gone to ask me if I was okay with it.

I didn't want him to be afraid to touch me anymore. Even though I knew there were some things I just wasn't ready for yet, I wanted that responsibility to be on me to tell him rather than him obsessing over what was or wasn't okay when it came to physical contact between us.

I would have kept kissing him if his stomach hadn't chosen to let out a loud growl at that point.

"Oh my God," Ethan whispered just before he covered his face in embarrassment. I laughed and kissed his nose between his fingers.

"I guess my man is hungry," I said with a chuckle.

Ethan stilled and dropped his hand. He watched me for the longest time before saying, "Yes, he is."

The moment was heavy between us and I knew why. But I couldn't regret calling him mine because it felt like he was. And even that tiny confirmation from him…

I levered up on my elbow so I could look down at him. "We need to switch hotels so we can grab something on the way."

"Are we going back to Seattle?"

"Not yet. We're going to meet a guy who will hopefully be able to fix Lucy's phone. Ronan's tracking him down to see where he is."

"He works for Ronan?" Ethan asked.

"Yes and no…he's sort of a free agent."

"What if he can't fix it?"

I knew what Ethan was asking me. He already knew what the plan was in terms of Eric if we ended up with no evidence against the man. Secretly, a part of me wanted that to happen, but I also knew what it meant for Ethan and I couldn't actually hope for it. Even if we took Eric out, Ethan wouldn't be a free man. He'd never be able to go back to his old life. He'd always be on the run. Yes, Ronan could set him up with a new identity, a new life...probably even as a doctor somewhere, but he wouldn't be able to see his family again nor could he keep Lucy with him unless he was willing to subject her to a life of hiding as well.

And I knew he wouldn't do that.

"We'll cross that bridge when we come to it," I hedged.

"You promised never to lie to me, Cain," Ethan said softly. "And while that wasn't exactly a lie, it wasn't the truth either."

I sighed and said, "If our only choice is to eliminate Eric, your name will never be cleared."

"I'll have to disappear," he whispered. "Hide for the rest of my life." His eyes shifted away from me. "But Lucy would be safe, right?"

"She'd be safe. The state would likely try to find a relative to take her in. If they can't, she'd have to go into foster care."

"They wouldn't let my family have her, would they?"

"No," I admitted. "Probably not."

Ethan rolled onto his side, away from me. "She'd be safe, though," he murmured.

"Whatever happens, Ethan," I said as I rolled him back on to his back. "You'll both be safe and you can still have a life. You can still practice medicine. Ronan can make that happen for you."

"But I won't get to be me anymore," he said.

"No, you won't."

He nodded, but his expression was solemn.

"Talk to me, Ethan," I said softly as I saw him checking out mentally.

He shook his head. "I...I'll sound so ungrateful," he said quietly. "And I'm not, I'm really not."

"I know that. It's okay, you can tell me."

He closed his eyes for a moment before saying, "I was just thinking that he'll still win. Even if he no longer walks this earth, I'm still his prisoner…it'll be like I never escaped. I'll still lose everything I was trying to get back."

I leaned down and brushed my mouth over his. "The phone's going to work, Ethan. I know it." He started to open his mouth to speak, but I cut him off with another kiss. "That's not a lie. I know it in here," I said as I used my hand to tap my chest. "It's going to work and you're going to be able to go home again."

Ethan studied me for a long time before nodding, and then his arms were around my neck as he pulled me down into his embrace. I wrapped my arms around him and just held him until the tension eased out of him and he said, "Feed me or I'm going to fight you for the leftover pizza."

I laughed and said, "Okay, but you're going to have to let me go first."

Ethan didn't loosen his hold on me. Instead he said, "Never mind."

I chuckled at that and gave him exactly what he wanted…no, what he needed.

CHAPTER 14

ETHAN

I wasn't someone who typically resorted to stereotypes to define people, but admittedly, when Cain had told me we were going to meet the man Ronan had tasked with fixing Lucy's phone, I'd imagined a tall, young, thin, geeky guy with glasses and an eager beaver personality.

I got the tall part right, but that was as far as it went in describing Vincent St. James.

First off, the man was in his late forties and there was nothing geeky about him. With his short black and silver hair and a body that rivaled any man's half his age, he was the epitome of a silver fox. He was taller than Cain which probably put him near the 6'5 mark and he had huge biceps and a broad chest. If I hadn't already been in complete and utter lust with the man at my side, I definitely would have looked twice at Vincent and several times after that, too.

There was nothing eager beaver about Vincent either. He was cold and aloof as Cain introduced us and he made no effort to shake either of our hands, which for Cain's sake, I was glad for.

The man had ended up meeting us at a house deep in the George Washington and Jefferson National Forest in West Virginia. He hadn't said if the house was his or not and we hadn't asked as he'd let us inside. Nor had he offered us any kind of food or beverage as he'd led us to the kitchen and accepted the envelope containing Lucy's phone

"Do you have the passcode for it?" Vincent asked without looking up from the phone. His eyes were examining the cracked screen.

"Yes," I said.

He slid a pen and small pad of paper across the island to me and I quickly jotted down the code.

"Did it power on at all after it was dropped?" he asked.

"No," I responded. "We tried plugging it in but it seemed like it wasn't charging."

Vincent nodded and then looked up at us. "I'll need a few days with it...if I need to order parts, might be longer. If you're staying in the area, there's a hotel about ten miles from here. It's open during the off season." His gaze shifted to Cain. "It'll be pretty quiet."

Cain nodded. "You have my cell?" he asked.

Vincent gave him a nod, though his eyes were back on the phone.

Neither man exchanged any additional words as Cain took my hand in his and led me from the kitchen. It was the second time he'd grabbed onto my hand, the first being just outside the bank right before the cops had shown up. But unlike that time, this time I was actually able to enjoy the sensation of his callused skin against mine. Not to mention that he was holding my hand on purpose, not just as part of some act.

"What now?" I asked.

"It's not worth flying back to Seattle to wait so we'll check out the hotel. You okay with that?"

As much as I missed Lucy, the idea of getting to spend a few more days with Cain in complete and utter privacy was a welcome relief and for the first time since we'd left the hotel that morning, I felt my spirits lift. Admittedly, I hadn't done well after Cain had voiced what I'd already known – that my life was not going to be what I wanted it to be if that phone couldn't be fixed. I'd felt guilty for coming off as an ungrateful jerk, especially considering how much harder things would have been without Ronan and Cain, but knowing I'd be losing my family all over again, along with the freedom to be the real me, had been devastating.

After we'd checked out of the hotel and gotten some food, Cain had returned the rental car and we'd taken a cab to a different agency and gotten a new rental. They were steps I wouldn't have even considered taking if I'd been on my own. The drive to West Virginia hadn't taken long and we'd spent much of it talking about our childhoods. Cain's had been tough to listen to because there'd been so little joy in his life compared to my more stable upbringing, even after he'd gone to live with his grandmother after getting out of the hospital. He'd admitted that his life with her had been good and that she'd been kind to him, but he'd been unable to connect with her like he would have been able to had the circumstances been different. His aversion to being touched had started even before he'd left the hospital and his grandmother had not been an exception to that. Like the girl who'd tried to kiss him, when his grandmother had gone to hug him for the first time, he'd lashed out at her. While he hadn't hurt her, he'd known she was afraid of him after that and she'd never again tried to have any kind of physical contact with him.

He'd been sent to a shrink after his stay at the hospital, but his trust issues had made him practically unreachable at that point. Being around other people hadn't worked either and he'd dropped out of school by the time he was sixteen. He'd gone on to get his GED a year later, but hadn't had any interest in college so he'd stayed in Indianapolis to be near his grandmother, despite their strained relationship. He'd worked odd jobs over the years, mostly ones where he hadn't had to interact with a lot of other people. When his grandmother had died just after his twenty-first birthday, he'd left Indiana. He hadn't told me what he'd done after that, though I did wonder if it was at that point that he'd met Ronan and started working for him.

When we hadn't been talking on the drive to West Virginia, I'd been thinking about my conversation with him that morning. He'd been so certain that my interest in him was tied to the fact that he was protecting me and helping me finally get away from Eric once and for all. Like I'd told him, feeling safe was just a sliver of what had my feelings for him growing stronger and stronger the more time I spent in his company. I was scared of how quickly I was losing parts of myself to him. It had been a little over two weeks since he'd tackled me in the snow and put a gun to my head, but yet, everything was different.

He was different.

I was too.

But maybe it wasn't that I was necessarily different…he was just making it okay for me to be the real me. The me I'd wanted to be with Eric, but hadn't been good enough to be. I kept trying to remind myself to take it slow with Cain because I needed to make sure I really knew him, but then I'd go back to how slow I'd taken things with Eric. I'd spent months getting to know Eric before I'd slept with him and before I'd told him I'd loved him, yet I'd known nothing about him… nothing that was real anyway.

With Cain, I knew in my gut that every time he spoke to me, every time he touched me, it was him. Really him. Time wouldn't change that. The man I was already starting to fall for was the man I'd be completely in love with next week, next month, next year. I'd never been more certain of anything in my life.

But as badly as I wanted to give myself permission to feel that for him, I knew I couldn't. Because if I felt it, I'd tell him. And I knew he was in no position to hear it. The psychological damage his father's brutal attack had done to him stood between us like a brick wall. I could reach Cain through the tiny cracks, but it would take much, much longer to knock the whole thing down.

Was I up to the task?

Absolutely.

If he would let me.

"I'll stop in here and grab us some snacks," I heard Cain say and I jerked myself from my thoughts enough to see him pointing at a small grocery store.

"Okay," I said as he parked the car.

"I'll be able to see the car from the windows," he said as he nodded at the building. "Lock the doors. If you see anything suspicious, you take the keys and go," he ordered softly. "Drive back to Vincent's and I'll meet you there."

I nodded. I knew he'd rather have me with him, but it was too dangerous. Someone could recognize my face. "I'll be fine," I said when he hesitated.

He nodded crisply and then he leaned over and kissed me, not caring who saw us. "Lock this," he reminded me and as soon as he closed the door, I locked the car.

The man was a complete and total enigma.

He'd been betrayed in the cruelest of ways and by the two people he should have been able to trust above all others, yet he'd still managed to come out on the side where he was giving to others what had been denied to him.

I shook my head and laughed, though there was nothing funny about the situation. I was kidding myself to think I wasn't already in love with the man. My heart didn't give a shit that my brain was saying there was no way it was possible, that I hadn't known him long enough…that I didn't know enough about him to harbor such intense feelings. But I was tired of trying to pretend to feel something I didn't. I'd spent too many months, years even, doing that very same thing with Eric. Trying to convince myself I'd loved the man, even though in my heart I'd known I hadn't.

But with Cain it was the real deal. It was what my mother had said being in love was like when I'd asked her about it when I was fourteen and had developed my first crush on a boy in my class.

It's like someone handing you the final piece of a puzzle you've been trying to finish for years. The picture still makes sense without that last piece, but you still know something's missing. And then you get that final, perfect piece and you realize 'making sense' never would have been enough.

Cain was my last puzzle piece. I'd thought I'd be able to just jam some guy in there who might fit "close enough," but no, all that had done was damage the entire puzzle.

I forced myself to focus on my surroundings, but more so because thinking about all this was just making me more tense. Cain would need to be the one to set the pace. He'd already hinted that he wasn't ready for more physical contact between us and I would respect that. Since I now knew his reservations probably had nothing to do with exploring his sexuality and everything to do with the trust that would be required to be with me in that way, I was more than willing to wait for as long as it took for him to be comfortable exploring that side of our relationship.

If that was even what we had.

Hell, if he decided he'd never be ready to give me that much of himself, I'd find a way to live with that. He was worth it.

Problem was, I wasn't sure I was. Not with my entire future up in the air.

At Cain's approach, I disengaged the locks on the car. He had just one plastic bag with him and he handed it to me when he got in the car. I glanced inside to see a few pieces of fruit, some bottles of water and soda and several snack-sized bags of potato chips.

I smiled at that and cast him a glance. He winked at me.

Actually winked.

And it was the sexiest thing I'd ever seen.

"Trying to fatten me up, are you?" I asked as I pushed the chips aside to see what was at the bottom of the bag.

He didn't respond and I realized a moment later why he hadn't.

Because he'd been waiting for me to reach the bottom of the bag.

Where there was a box of condoms and a bottle of lube.

Heat flooded my cheeks as I turned to look at him. He brushed his mouth over mine and said, "I was hoping we could try some stuff out over the next few days and if it goes well, when you're healed, maybe we can...if you're ready, I mean..."

His voice dropped off as his mouth fitted over mine. I was breathing heavy by the time he pulled back.

"Is that okay?" he asked, his voice carrying a hint of worry.

I nodded because I was still too surprised to do much else. "It's more than okay," I said. The idea of making love to Cain didn't frighten me in the least because to be frightened, I'd have had to compare him to Eric and that wasn't even remotely possible. I'd been lucky enough to test negative for everything after Ronan had run my blood and urine samples under his own name at his hospital, so that was one less thing to worry about. And I knew the damage Eric had caused during the rape had healed as well. I knew there was a possibility I could panic at some point during the actual act, but I knew Cain would work through it with me, just like I would work through any residual trauma he might face with me.

"Good," he said softly and then he kissed me again before he got the car moving.

"And, Cain," I said just before he pulled onto the main road.

"Yeah?"

"I'm all healed…and I'm very, very ready."

For someone as big and strong as Cain, it was hard to watch him struggle like he was.

We'd arrived at the hotel several hours earlier. It was a really nice place and just as Vincent had suspected, it was pretty much deserted. Cain still hadn't been willing to risk having someone recognize me, but that hadn't meant we couldn't have room service delivered in place of eating at the hotel restaurant. We'd ended up ordering an early dinner and watching a movie on one of the premium channels, though I'd fallen asleep about halfway through it. Not because the movie had been boring, but because I just couldn't have gotten any more relaxed than I'd been…with my head resting on Cain's chest as his fingers had trailed up and down my spine, causing little shivers of delight to spread throughout my entire body. He'd woken me up with little kisses and asked if I wanted to order any more food from room service before going to bed, but I'd declined.

I'd suggested a shower together before going to sleep in the single, very large, king-sized bed covered in thick pillows and luxurious bedding. Cain had agreed, but as I'd watched him pause as he'd started to remove his shirt, I'd fallen silent to see what he would do.

He'd been sitting on the edge of the bed for several minutes now, his back to me. I'd leaned back against the headboard when I'd realized he was struggling, but now I moved forward so I was sitting off to his side. I made sure not to touch him as I said, "What's wrong?"

"I don't want to mess this up," he admitted.

"How do you think you're going to mess this up?" I asked.

He just shook his head.

"We don't have to do anything you don't want to," I offered.

"I want to," he said quickly. "I just don't want to do to you what I did to the others."

"You mean the girl when you were sixteen?" I asked, thinking he was referring to the girl who'd tried to kiss him.

"That...but the escorts too," he said softly, the shame in his voice clear as day. "I know they weren't expecting me to act like I was their boyfriend or something, but the way I treated them...like they were just bodies."

My heart hurt for him, but as badly as I wanted to touch him, I didn't. I moved so I was sitting next to him rather than off to his side.

"I know you didn't see them that way."

When he didn't respond, I finally took a chance and touched him, just enough so I could turn his face to look at me. "And I know you don't see me that way either...you're just not wired that way. I really just want to be with you, Cain. Even if that means I can't touch you with my hands...I'll find other ways to touch you...to show you how much you mean to me."

I risked taking his hand in mine. "Come take that shower with me," I urged.

His fingers gripped mine hard as he nodded and then he was following me into the bathroom. I got the water in the shower going and then turned to face him. I slowly removed my shirt and then waited for him to do the same. My socks were next. He mirrored my every move, never taking his eyes off mine. I didn't even scan his body like I wanted to because I didn't want to risk losing the tenuous connection I had with him. I took his hand in mine and led him into the shower stall so that I was facing the spray of the shower and he was at my back. Since I couldn't see him anymore with him behind me, I watched our reflection in the mirror which I could see through the glass shower door.

I could see Cain's eyes traveling the length of my back. He was no more than an inch or two behind me, not close enough to touch, but close enough that I could feel the heat coming off his body. I was glad to see in the reflection that he was hard...it was one less hurdle to have to worry about.

I grabbed the body wash from the shelf in the corner of the shower and squirted some into my hand before giving it to him. I began washing my body, but paused when I felt his hands skim over my shoulders. His touch had goose bumps covering my arms and it was all I could do not to reach for my aching cock. He took his time exploring me after that. My back, my ass, my thighs. Occasionally his cock would nudge my ass, but he kept the contact to a minimum. He seemed content just to get his fill of touching me.

"You're so beautiful, Ethan," he murmured in my ear before placing soft kisses along the column of my neck.

I would have told him I thought he was the most beautiful man I'd ever met...the most beautiful person, actually, but he kissed me before I could. His hands moved to my chest and soon he was worshipping the front of my body just like he had the back. The only place he didn't touch was the one place on my body that needed it above all others.

"Oh God, Cain, I'm sorry, I'm not going to last," I admitted as I reached for my dick and began stroking it. Humiliation tore through me that I couldn't even give him this moment, but his touch had been just too incendiary.

"I want to watch you," he murmured and then I felt his cock nudging the crack of my ass as his hips began to match the pace I'd set on my dick.

I began pushing back against him and let out a sigh of relief when his shaft slid between the globes of my ass.

"Look at us, Ethan," I heard Cain whisper as he continued to glide his fingers all over my chest.

I looked at the mirror which was quickly steaming up, but I could still make out our bodies. His larger one bracketing mine, his tanned flesh golden against my paler skin. I barely even noticed the bruises because my gaze was on his ass as he flexed every time he slid his cock through my crease. My own dick was flushed red and at some point, I'd grabbed one of Cain's hands with my free one. Our faces met in the reflection and I saw the same longing in his eyes that was in mine. He needed this as badly as I did.

Electricity fired up my spine as the ending drew near.

"Show me how to please you," Cain whispered right before he closed his hand over mine on my dick. The move startled me and I paused for a moment before quickly fisting my dick again and jerking it with desperate tugs. Cain's hand held mine for a few drags before he pushed my hand away and then took over.

"Oh fuck, yes," I cried as his rough skin scraped over my oversensitized flesh. I held there, surrounded by him as he worked my dick in his hand and his dick in the cradle of my ass. I'd had plenty of orgasms by my own hand and a few even with Eric, but none of them had been anything like this. I felt so out of control and yet so completely safe as Cain's touches sent me higher and higher. In that moment, I forgot how broken we both were and just felt.

His scars didn't exist.

Neither did mine.

We were just two people finding in each other what we couldn't find in ourselves.

I came without warning. One moment I was standing on the edge, the next I was flying right over it. Cain's mouth searched out mine over my shoulder as I let out a cry of relief. I tried to kiss him back, but the blissful agony that was shooting through every cell of my body made it impossible. I was barely aware of Cain's rough shout against my lips as his body jerked behind me and white-hot heat pulsed over my hole and slid down my crease, easing the way for his dick to jerk against me. I had enough sense to look at the mirror one last time right before the steam completely obliterated us from view.

What I saw matched what I felt as Cain wrapped his arms around me from behind, his hold wonderfully tight.

He fit perfectly against me.

He *was* the missing piece of my puzzle.

I just hoped I was his.

CHAPTER 15

CAIN

"Hello?" Guilt went through me at the sound of Ronan's voice. I'd definitely woken him up. Even with the three-hour time difference, the man had clearly been in bed despite it only being just after midnight in Seattle.

"Cain?" Ronan said quietly. I could hear rustling and suspected he was getting out of bed so he wouldn't wake his husband up. "Everything okay?"

"Yeah," I said, though it wasn't the whole truth. Yes, things were fine in that Ethan was still safe which was what Ronan had been asking. But no, things were not even close to fine otherwise.

Why had I done this? Why had I made this call? Why hadn't I just stayed in bed with Ethan wrapped in my arms and told myself I was overthinking things as usual? Sleep would have claimed me eventually. But instead I was sitting on the closed toilet in the bathroom on the phone with a man who needed to be able to count on me to be a ruthless killer, not a simpering, agitated mess of a man who'd just had one of the most incredible…and confusing encounters of his entire life.

"What's going on, Cain?" Ronan asked, his voice gentle…and knowing.

"You knew," I said. "You said he'd touch me in other ways." I hated that my voice almost sounded accusatory.

Ronan let out a soft sigh and then I heard what sounded like a chair scraping along the floor.

"I'd tell you not to fight it, but my guess is you will anyway."

"I have nothing to offer him, Ronan. I'm so fucked up in the head…"

"That's not true and you know it," he countered. "You've been protecting yourself for a lot of years, Cain. It's normal not to be able to let someone else in…to be able to trust them to keep you safe."

"It's not that," I admitted. "I trust him. I…I know I can get past this shit with him. But what happens after that?"

"What do you mean?"

"He's got a big family…one he wants to be close to again when this is all over. He should have someone who fits into something like that. He's going to be an uncle soon, for Christ's sake. Can you really see me in a room full of people with a kid on my lap?"

"Did you ever think you'd see me with a husband and three kids, Cain?" he responded. "Things change…people change."

"What if I can't?" I whispered, giving voice to the crux of my fear.

"You need to ask him that. I already know the answer, but it won't mean jack shit coming from me and we both know that."

I nodded even though the man couldn't see me. "Ronan, if he has to go into hiding, I'm going with him."

"I suspected as much," the man said. "I spoke to Vincent. He's not sure about the phone. He's got a few things he needs to try, but he needed to order some parts. Let's not make any decisions until he knows for sure it's DOA."

"Yeah," I said. "How's Lucy?" I asked.

"She's doing as well as can be expected. She helps Seth with Jamie during the day and hangs out with Willow the rest of the time doing whatever it is girls their age do," he said with a chuckle.

"Good," I said. "I should let you go back to sleep," I murmured.

"Talk to Ethan, Cain. Make decisions together instead of making them for him. Don't learn the hard way that not letting him have his say will just hurt him more."

"Okay," I said, though I wasn't sure it was something I could do. "Night, Ronan."

"Night."

I hung up and flicked off the bathroom light. Ethan was still in the same position I'd left him in, but as soon as I crawled into bed with him, he rolled over and plastered himself against my front. I was glad that I no longer felt the need to check his hands or pull away from him in any way. I had no doubt I could get to a point where physical contact with him wasn't even a question mark anymore – tonight in the shower had proven that. Even with him in the same position I'd often been in with the escorts I'd hired in the past, the experience had been nothing like those encounters. The mirror had been nice, but I hadn't needed it to know that Ethan had taken as much pleasure from the act as I had. And I'd loved how he'd clung to me at the end as he'd come in my hand, his body's release coating my skin for the briefest of moments before being washed away by the water. My own orgasm had been more powerful than I'd ever had with anyone else and I hadn't even been buried inside Ethan's amazing body. I'd thought I'd need to take things slow so I wouldn't inadvertently hurt Ethan by pushing him away, but I knew that wouldn't happen. Tonight had been proof that he just wanted to be with me, no matter how passive a participant he might have to be. But he hadn't been passive.

Not even close.

No, he hadn't touched me much, not physically anyway.

But he'd done so much more.

Every word he'd spoken, every whimper that had fallen from his lips...even the fact that he'd trusted me so completely despite what his piece of shit ex had done to him just two weeks ago was proof enough that what Ronan had predicted had happened.

Ethan was touching me even when he didn't lay a finger on me.

And I'd never felt more at peace in my life.

But the future was a big sticking point for me. I'd meant what I'd told Ronan…if Ethan were forced to continue to hide, even after we eliminated Eric as a threat, I would go with him no matter what. But as much as I wanted to be with Ethan, I couldn't wish a life of running on him, even if it meant a future with him was more certain. No, he deserved to be with the family he loved and who loved him back. Even if I couldn't share that life with him.

"You okay?" I heard Ethan ask as his hand settled over my heart. It seemed to be a favorite position for him. Or maybe it was because I'd limited him to so little of my body.

"Yeah," I said. I thought back to what Ronan had said about letting Ethan decide what was best for him. I reached for the light next to the bed and turned it on. Ethan buried his face in my chest while he let his eyes adjust. "Sorry," I said as I dropped a kiss to the top of his head. "But I need to ask you something."

"S'Okay," he murmured sleepily.

I waited until he was able to look at me before pressing him onto his back. "Hi," he said with a happy smile.

He'd been doing that a lot lately. I hoped I was the cause.

"Hi," I whispered before settling my mouth on his. I felt his fingers thread through my hair and shivered at how good it felt. I was so ready to see how good it would feel having him touch me everywhere. But I needed to make sure he and I were on the same page before this went any further.

I forced myself to release his mouth and said, "When things go back to normal, I need to know if you still want this…me." I put my finger over his lips when I saw that he was going to answer me right away. "I need to know if you still want me even if I can't change…if I can't be that guy."

"What guy?" Ethan asked softly.

"The one in your letter…that damn goodbye letter," I growled as even the thought of him having had to write that letter pissed me off all over again. "The guy who loves your family as much as you do. I'm not saying I couldn't love them or that I'd ever make you choose between us because I wouldn't," I said hastily. "But I may never be that guy who watches football with your dad at Thanksgiving time or goes fishing with your brothers or dances with your mother at our wedding-"

"Our wedding?" Ethan interjected, his pretty green eyes going wide and his lips spreading into a big smile. "You think about stuff like that?"

"Focus, Ethan," I said with a smile. "And yes, I think about stuff like that because you're it for me."

He grinned and then dragged me down for a kiss. I let him take control of it before pulling back and shaking my head.

"Right, focusing," he said quickly as he tried to pull his face into a mask of seriousness. "Is it my turn to talk yet?"

"Not yet," I said, though I was the one having trouble focusing now because that happy look was back and more prominent than ever. But reality forced me to sober. "I promise to try all that stuff, but I need to know if I can't be that man, that you still want this…me. Truth, Ethan," I reminded him.

He scowled at me at that, but it didn't last long. "Okay, is it my turn now?"

"Yes," I said with a sigh because I knew he hadn't really thought about it.

"Don't do that," he ordered and then he was pushing me onto my back. I didn't even feel the slightest bit of anxiety as he settled his weight on me. "Just because I already know the answer to your question doesn't mean I didn't think about it, Cain. It just means I don't need to think about it because I'd already come to that decision on my own. First, my dad hates football, but my brothers love it. Dad's the fisherman so just swap the two and your examples work. And you shouldn't dance with my mother because she's a terrible dancer. But more importantly, I don't need you to change because I love *you*. Not some version of you that you think is better because there is no such thing. I want the version of you who thinks this version of me is just perfect and doesn't care if I gain ten pounds or fifty or that I like nerdy things or that I get too emotional sometimes."

I barely had time to register what he was saying because I was still stuck on his declaration which had been delivered with no hesitation whatsoever.

He loved me.

"I want the you who brings me potato chips, but doesn't care if I eat one or one hundred. I want the you who will spend the rest of his life reminding me that he has me and knows I have him too. You're it for me too, Cain Jensen. I'll help you figure out how to trust again, but only if you want that. I don't care if it takes a month, a year, a hundred years and I don't care if it never happens. What we have right here, right now…what we had in that shower…that's what I want. That's the version of you I want."

He kissed me before I could even respond, which was a good thing, because I didn't know what to say. I hadn't known what to expect, but it sure as hell hadn't been that.

I quickly rolled him onto his back and covered him with the weight of my body. I groaned when I felt his legs shift so that I could lie between them. Our cocks brushed against each other and I cursed the fabric separating us.

"I need to feel you," I whispered roughly against his mouth as I skimmed my hand down his body. I managed to shove the boxers he was wearing down enough to reach his cock. Unlike in the shower, there was no hesitation this time and I eagerly wrapped my hand around it and began stroking. Ethan let out a harsh groan and then he was bucking up against me, thrusting into my hand. I felt his hands sliding down my back, his fingers gripping me hard. But just before he reached my ass, he stopped.

"Don't stop," I immediately said. "Touch me like you want to, Ethan. You'll know if I need you to stop."

His emerald gaze held mine for the longest time before I felt his hands move again. "I love you," he whispered.

I wanted to say the words back, but they got stuck in my throat.

I was frozen in place as Ethan's warm hands slid beneath the athletic shorts I'd worn to bed. I closed my eyes as he caressed my ass and then gave me a gentle squeeze.

"Fuck," I whispered and then I was grinding my cock against his.

His hands urged me on, gripping my ass hard as he pulled me forward onto his leaking cock. I managed to free my own cock and Ethan cried out as our flesh came into contact. I took us both in hand and began pumping frantically, but I knew it wasn't enough.

It wasn't what I needed.

"I need to be inside you," I said to Ethan between the light kisses I was placing on his lips.

He managed a nod, but nothing else. His skin was deliciously flushed and his eyes had gone dark with lust.

I slid up his body enough so I could reach past him to get to the nightstand where I'd stashed the lube and condoms. The position had my chest hovering just above his lips and he took complete advantage and ran his tongue over one of my nipples. The sensation had me dropping the lube back in the drawer just as I closed my fingers around it, but I didn't care because it felt so damn good that I wanted him to do it again.

He did.

Over and over.

And then his teeth gently bit down on me. His hands were still gripping my ass causing me to grind against his stomach.

"Jesus," I muttered as I snatched the lube and a strip of condoms and practically yanked the drawer off its rollers as I pulled my hand free. I surged up to a sitting position so I could tear one of the condoms open. My fingers were shaking so bad that I had to stop what I was doing so I could try to get ahold of myself.

Ethan sat up and took the condom from me. "Let me," he whispered before kissing me gently.

I nodded because the embarrassment was just too keen to allow me to speak.

Ethan's fingers carefully rolled the latex down my shaft. He kept brushing gentle kisses over my mouth as he did it. "Don't," he murmured softly.

I knew that he knew what was happening to me. "It's never been like this," I admitted.

"I'm glad," Ethan responded. "For me either."

"I need to get you ready, right?"

Ethan nodded as he searched out the bottle of lube. "Or you can watch me get myself ready," he suggested softly.

I'd already been burning with lust, but his words took me to a whole other level. "Yes," I croaked as I sat back on my heels so he could move his body more freely. Ethan smiled a soft, sexy smile that had just a hint of shyness as he squirted some lube onto his fingers. He handed me the bottle, but before I could get some lube to slick over my cock, Ethan was lying back on the bed and shifting his legs wide. The sight of his pink hole fluttering in anticipation had me swallowing my tongue.

I'd seen similar images on the internet when I'd watched some gay porn after realizing my attraction to Ethan was just that and not some weird, one-time thing. But the guys on those sites had nothing on Ethan.

Nothing.

I watched in rapt fascination as Ethan rubbed a finger over his hole several times before breaching his body. I managed to look up at him long enough to see his hungry eyes on me. "Touch yourself," he encouraged as his eyes fell to my cock. I managed to get some lube on my hand and then I was stroking myself as Ethan's middle finger disappeared completely inside his body. A small groan left his lips as his ass flexed. Just the thought of how tight his body was gripping that finger had me pumping desperately into my hand. I moved closer to him so I could rest my free hand on his thigh as he pleasured himself. Instinct had me lifting his leg onto my shoulder and pressing forward so it was bent back on himself. The move opened him up even farther. He whimpered as he pressed a second finger into his body and I watched in a near daze as he twisted his wrist back and forth before sliding his fingers in and out of his depths in slow, smooth glides.

His cock was jerking against his abdomen and glistening streaks of pre-cum covered his skin. I had no idea what possessed me to do it, but I leaned down and ran my tongue over his belly and was rewarded with a harsh curse and a new, sweet flavor flooding my taste buds. More liquid seeped from the head of his dick and before I could give it much thought, I licked over his crown and then closed my mouth around the tip so I could suck up more of his delicious flavor.

"Oh God, stop or I'll come," Ethan shouted and I felt his hand on my shoulder, pushing me back. When my eyes met his, he said, "Now, Cain. Fuck me now."

I looked down to see he'd removed his fingers and his hole was slightly open and waiting. I grabbed my cock and moved it into position and slowly slid forward. Ethan threw his head back and gasped as I breached him. Instinct had me going slow, but it was hard to get a read on Ethan with the sounds that were falling from his lips.

Was I hurting him?

"Ethan," I said as I stilled. "Talk to me." I hated that I needed his guidance on this, but my embarrassment was secondary to my need not to hurt him.

"It's good," he murmured as his eyes popped open. "Don't stop."

I released his leg and shifted over him as I pushed into him a little more. I kissed him softly and said, "Tell me what it feels like."

Sweat was dotting Ethan's brow. His muscles were so tight around me that I had to wonder how he wasn't crying out in pain. Even though just my crown was inside of him, the heat and pressure had me wishing I could just plow into him. And I knew once I was there, I'd never want to leave

"Burns," he whispered. "But in a good way. It…it's spreading out to the rest of my body."

I slid farther into him and was rewarded with another strangled moan. "Feels so good," he managed to say. "I need you all the way inside of me. Please!"

I obliged him and pushed in slowly until there was no place left for me to go. My dick was sheathed in the hottest, tightest grip I'd ever known. "I knew it," I groaned.

"Knew what?" Ethan asked. At some point he'd slid his arms beneath my armpits so he could wrap his hands over my shoulders.

"That we'd fit perfectly together," I said. I looked down to where we were joined. There was no space between us, just my balls pressed against him.

Ethan's mouth sought out mine for a deep kiss before he whispered, "I knew it too." I had no doubt that he was talking about more than just our bodies being a perfect fit.

I slowly pulled out of Ethan just a little before sliding back in, wanting to make sure the move wouldn't hurt him. When a strangled cry of pleasure left his throat, I knew he was okay and I dragged my dick out of him until just the head was holding him open, then I surged into him in one smooth glide.

"Yes," he called out as his legs came up to wrap around my lower body. My body tensed for the briefest of moments at the sensation of being caged in, but I ignored it and thrust into him again. His cries of pleasure spurred me on as my own body was screaming at me, demanding relief. When I'd been with the escorts, it had often taken me a long time to get off. With Ethan, I was there within a handful of strokes. It was exhilarating and humiliating at the same time.

But the embarrassment didn't linger because Ethan kissed me hard and said, "Harder! I'm so close."

His lack of shyness drove me on and I began slamming into him. My abdomen was grinding against his dick, but since I wasn't sure if it was enough stimulation to get him off, I released one of the arms I had wrapped around his shoulders so I could reach between us. But Ethan's voice stopped me.

"No," he murmured. "Keep your arms around me!" I obeyed the demand and wrapped myself around him as completely as I could and then sought out his mouth as I began ramming into him with jerky, unpracticed movements. I shifted my hips just a little and was stunned when he let out a keening wail.

"Yes, right there!" he cried out.

I suspected I'd managed to hit his prostate so I kept my hips in the same position and lunged forward, reveling in the way his eyes slid shut and his head fell back. I latched my mouth onto his neck and sucked hard as I pounded into him. I felt electricity shoot up my spine as my balls drew up tight against my body and my cock began to surge in anticipation. I was slinging into Ethan so hard that if I hadn't had ahold of him, he would have hit the headboard. The bed shook as

I fucked him over and over again and just as I felt my release start to wash over me, Ethan cried out my name. Liquid heat drenched my abdomen as he came and I moaned as his fingers bit into my shoulders. My orgasm threatened my vision as the pleasure took over every part of my body. Tears of relief stung my eyes as I emptied myself inside of Ethan, the condom preventing me from marking him the way I wanted. The climax continued for what seemed like hours and all I could do was lay there as my body jerked and my hips kept sending my cick deeper and deeper into Ethan's warm body. His inner muscles massaged me through the aftershocks that followed, but I wasn't aware that he was kissing my shoulder and neck until my body finally relaxed and collapsed completely on top of him.

I was too spent for words and there wasn't enough energy in my sated body to even consider climbing off him. All I managed was to turn my head so I could reach his lips. Even then, Ethan was the one who had to do all the work as his mouth made love to mine. I loved how one of his hands was gripping my ass to keep me inside him.

I didn't bother to tell him I had no plans on going anywhere for a while.

And if I had my way, I'd spend the rest of my life just like this.

Lost in him.

CHAPTER 16

ETHAN

My body ached in the best way as I shifted just enough to straighten one of my legs. Unlike the past couple of mornings, I'd awoken a few minutes earlier to find Cain wrapped around the front of my body, rather than the back. It was actually the position he'd fallen asleep in after he'd moved off me enough the night before to pull free of my body and dispose of the condom. He'd fallen asleep before me so I'd gotten to lie there beneath his deliciously heavy body and enjoy the feel of his skin against mine. I'd let my fingers explore his back and even though he'd been asleep, he'd let out more than one breathy sigh as I'd caressed him.

I hadn't planned to tell him that I loved him, but when he'd started talking about our wedding and me being it for him, I'd been a goner and nothing on this planet would have kept me from telling him how I really felt. I knew his wedding talk had just been a hypothetical he'd come up with, but I clung to the hope that it was something that would be in our future.

It wasn't lost on me that he hadn't told me he loved me back, but it didn't bother me as much as I thought it would. Maybe because I'd felt the things he hadn't said through his every touch as he'd made love to me. I'd felt bad for him that he'd been so uncertain about the logistics of being with me in that way, but once he'd realized he wasn't hurting me, he'd given me all of himself.

I had no doubt about that.

With Eric, sex had always been another way for him to show me how much power he had over me. He most certainly hadn't been okay with me ever taking the initiative, like I had with Cain when I'd seen him struggling to get the condom on. On its best day, sex had become a chore with Eric…no different than cooking for him or answering the endless questions about where I'd been all day and what I'd done. At worst, it had been used as a weapon against me…a brutal punishment meant to hurt and humiliate. Sex with Cain wasn't even sex. It was us telling each other things that we couldn't find words for. The way he'd clung to me, the words he'd whispered into my ear after he'd collapsed on top of me, his length still buried deep inside my pulsing body, his hot breath fanning my face as he'd pumped into me, his arms holding me so tight against him that there'd been no room for anything to come between us…all those things were proof that he hadn't just fucked me to get off.

The best part, even better than my mind-blowing orgasm, was that he'd let me touch him.

Everywhere.

I'd only felt him tense up briefly once and that was when I'd instinctively wrapped my legs around him to keep him close. But his tension hadn't lasted so I'd held on to him like that the entire time. And the fact that he'd changed our sleeping positions so that it was *my* arms around *him*, holding *him*, was very telling.

Maybe I'd managed to punch some holes in that brick wall of his after all.

Cain shifted on my chest and I smiled when he nuzzled my nipple. He shifted his hips so that his morning erection was pressed against my hard dick instead of my thigh where it had been while he'd slept.

"Nu-uh," I said as I bent down to press a kiss to his head. "You need to feed me first." I gently threaded my fingers through his hair and tilted his head up so I could kiss him for real.

"Morning," he murmured against my mouth.

"Morning," I said softly and then I was kissing him deeply. I didn't care in the least when he levered off me so he could lie flat on top of me. But when he began to place kisses down my neck and chest, I reminded him, "I need to shower first. I didn't clean up after last night." I'd barely noticed the cum I'd spewed all over my belly and chest the night before, but I was more than aware of it now, and I knew he was covered in my spunk too since he'd been pressed tight against me when I'd come.

Without the need to even touch myself.

Another first.

"I like the way you taste," he said softly as he continued to lick at my chest.

And just like that, my dick went from hard to painful and I squirmed against him. "Not fair," I moaned as he sucked on my neck before soothing the spot with his tongue. "I didn't get to taste you."

"We'll need to do something about that," Cain murmured against my skin.

"Now," I blurted out. "We should remedy that now."

Cain paused and lifted so he could look me in the eye.

"Can I?" I asked.

He nodded. "You'll be the first," he said softly.

What?

"You've...you've never?" I stammered. "But the escorts?" I said and then instantly regretted it since I didn't want that time in his life to darken what had happened between us...or what I thought was about to happen.

He shook his head. "Too personal," he murmured. His hand came up to stroke my face. "I like having all these firsts with you."

"Me too," I said.

"I've been tested," he said. "I tested negative after my last time with one of the women a couple years ago. I haven't been with anyone since. I have the results in my email if you want to see."

I shook my head because it hadn't been something I'd ever worried about. "I trust you, Cain. I know you'd never put me at risk. I tested negative too."

He nodded. "Where do you want me?" he asked, his eyes going dark with need.

"Shower?" I suggested.

He chuckled...a sound I was quickly growing to love and hoped I'd hear a lot in the days and years to come. "This will already be our third shower together," he said with a smile.

My thoughts drifted back to that first one. It seemed like a lifetime ago. "I felt it even then." I said softly. "That first time in the shower," I clarified.

"Felt what?"

"That you were going to change everything for me."

"I did too,' he admitted. "Though I didn't want to face it. I'd convinced myself it was some fluke, the attraction I had for you. I...I went outside that night and jerked off. I tried to think of a woman I'd been with while I was doing it, but all that kept coming to mind was you. Your eyes, the feel of your skin, how good you tasted when I kissed your shoulder."

"I thought I'd imagined that part," I said as I lay there, completely shocked that he'd felt some of the same things I'd felt in that shower. The image of him jerking off to thoughts of me was increasing my lust tenfold. "Shower," I said as I pushed at his shoulders to get him to move off me. I didn't care in the least that I was totally naked as I grabbed his hand and dragged him to the bathroom. This time, I pushed him into the stall first once I had the water running. I maneuvered him so his back was to the wall and kissed him hard before working my way down his body. I was careful to keep glancing up at him to make sure he was okay as I neared his lower half. I sank to my knees and let my eyes connect with his. His blue eyes were full of hunger as he nodded. I could tell he was a little nervous, but not enough that had me worried he wasn't ready for this.

I didn't rush anything, despite how hard we both were. I let my eyes roam over Cain's thick shaft. He was beautifully built and thicker than I'd realized, though that shouldn't have surprised me considering how full I'd felt the night before when he'd slid into me. He was bigger than Eric, but despite that and the fact that he'd never been with a man before, he'd still been gentler with me than Eric had ever been, even when he'd taken my virginity.

I pushed thoughts of my ex out of my head and focused on the amazing man before me. I nuzzled his cock before tentatively licking the length of the entire shaft. I'd performed oral sex on Eric countless times and he'd been an exacting teacher, so I knew how to bring Cain pleasure, but I still couldn't help but be nervous. I shifted my eyes up to make sure Cain was still good and saw that he had his head pressed back against the wall and his eyes were closed. I licked him a few more times and then teased his balls with gentle licks and kisses. It wasn't until he groaned my name that I shifted enough to be able to suck his crown into my mouth. His hips immediately punched forward and I automatically grabbed his base with my hand so he wouldn't instinctively shove his cock down my throat since that was what I was used to. But unlike Eric, I knew Cain wouldn't take pleasure in watching me gag on his flesh as he used my mouth.

I cursed myself for letting Eric get into my head again. I took more of Cain's stiffness into my mouth and sucked gently. I felt Cain's hand settle on my head, but he didn't try to control me or hold me in place so he could jam his cock down my throat. I was disappointed in myself that I'd even thought such a thing was a possibility, but I figured, like Cain, I had to knock some holes in my own walls before they'd completely fall.

It took just a couple of minutes to relax my gag reflex enough to deep throat Cain's cock and I languished in the sensation of him filling me so completely, but in such a different way. I loved that he was letting me control the pace, though I knew there'd be a day where I would revel in him fucking my mouth however he wanted.

"Fuck, so good, Ethan," I heard Cain say and I lifted my eyes so I could look at him. His face was drawn tight with lust and I marveled at the way he watched me. His finger came up to stroke my cheek gently as he began thrusting in and out of my mouth in soft, short glides. I rolled his balls in my hand as I increased the suction. Cain's eyes closed again and then both his hands were in my hair. He fucked my mouth harder, but never gave me more than I could handle. He was just as aware of me as I was of him.

I used my free hand to stroke my own cock as I worked Cain over. His pulsing flesh was proof of how close he was. He was panting heavily now and the sound had my own orgasm nipping at the edge of my sanity. I wanted Cain to come before me, so I released my dick and reached up to grab his ass like I had the night before. I forced him forward as deep as he could go, ignoring the stinging in my eyes as my gag reflex started to kick in. I risked letting my fingers slide through his crease and when he didn't jerk away from my touch, I pressed one of my fingers over his hole. Cain let out a rough curse and then he took over, surging into my mouth and then back against my finger. He came within a matter of seconds. As the first ropes of cum trickled down my throat, I grabbed my dick and jerked hard and fast. He was still spewing in my mouth as my own release hit me. I cried out around his dick and then tore my mouth away as the orgasm consumed me. I felt cum hitting my mouth and chin, but didn't care because I was too blinded by my own climax to do anything but glide my hand up and down my wet shaft so I could ride out every second of the blissful pleasure I was being dragged to my feet moments later and then a heavy mouth was crashing down on mine.

I was stunned when Cain licked up the remnants of his cum. It was something Eric had hated with a passion. But that wasn't enough for Cain because then he was grabbing my hand and licking my fingers clean before the water could wash away what was left of my own juices. Then Cain's mouth was back on mine and I could taste our mixed flavors as he kissed me.

When the pleasantness of the orgasms began to fade, we washed each other off, facing each other this time. Cain didn't seem to have any problem with my hands anywhere on him, including his backside.

"How hungry are you?" Cain asked once we were done washing each other and he pulled me into his arms and began brushing light kisses on my lips.

"I could eat," I said. "Or not," I added when I felt his dick stirring against me.

Cain turned us so that my back was to the wall of the shower. He began kissing me hungrily and my ass flexed in excitement. "Let me go get the lube and a condom," I murmured, though I was very tempted to go without the condom. But despite testing negative, I'd need to be tested again in a couple of months to make sure I was one hundred percent safe, so I knew that wasn't an option yet.

"Don't need them," Cain murmured against my lip.

I was about to protest, but shut my mouth when Cain suddenly sank to his knees in front of me. "Cain, you don't have to," I said when he studied my dick for several long seconds. Yes, I wanted like hell for him to take me into his mouth, especially since it would be a first for me just like it had been for him, but I didn't want him doing something he wasn't ready for.

But he ignored me and gave me a long lick that had my toes curling. He had my dick completely hard again with just a few touches of his silky tongue and then he was sucking me into his mouth.

I didn't argue again after that because as he pulled me deeper and deeper into his mouth and went to town with the suction factor, I knew the answer to my question.

He was very, very ready.

~

"*E*than, wake up."

The urgency in Cain's voice got through to me like nothing else could. My limbs felt heavy and sluggish as I jerked awake. My ass was deliciously sore as I sat up, but I ignored the sensation as I searched out Cain who was sitting on the edge of the bed, jerking his pants on.

"What? What is it?" I asked as I automatically threw the blanket off me and climbed out of the opposite side of the bed. I ignored my nudity as I began searching out my own clothes.

"We need to go."

"Did something happen?" I asked as I found my clothes sitting neatly on the dresser. I hadn't remembered putting them there after Cain had plucked them off me the night before. He must have folded them himself at some point after I'd fallen asleep after we'd made love. After our lovefest in the shower the previous day, we'd gotten cleaned up and gone to get some breakfast from the drive through of a fast food restaurant. We'd taken the meal to a secluded nature area near the hotel and had sat at one of the picnic tables to eat. The air had been cool around us so there'd been no other people in the park which meant there'd been no worry that I might be recognized. After eating, we'd even gone for a walk during which Cain had held my hand the entire time. Once we'd arrived back at the hotel, we'd spent the day and night in bed, wrapped around each other until I didn't know where I ended and Cain began. We'd stopped feasting on each other's bodies only long enough to order room service. I'd lost count of how many times Cain had fucked me, but it hadn't been enough.

It would never be enough.

"No," Cain said quickly. "But I need to go. Get dressed, I'm taking you to Vincent's."

I stilled at that. He was leaving me?

"What? Why?" I asked, hating that I sounded like a whiny child.

"It's not safe for you to come with me,' he said as he pulled his shirt on.

I'd never seen him so agitated before. Yes, he was in a rush, but there was something else happening too. 'Cain, talk to me," I said. "Please," I added when he didn't slow his actions down.

He finally stopped and I was glad when he came to me and took my hand in his before leading me to the bed. I'd managed to get my pants on, but nothing else.

"Ronan's tech girl, Daisy, just called me. She's got some information for me that suggests my father might be back in the town I grew up in."

"What kind of information?" I asked as I began pulling on the shirt I'd been holding in my hands.

"The attack on me and my brothers and sisters made national

headlines. People all over the country started donating money to my mom to help pay my medical bills and to also pay for my brothers' and sisters' funerals. It ended up being a lot of money. Even after all my hospital bills were paid, there was over fifty thousand dollars left in the account."

"Okay," I said, not understanding where he was going with this.

"My grandmother sued for the money...not for herself, but for me. So I could use it to go to college or start a business or whatever I wanted when I turned twenty-one and got control of the trust the money was in." Cain got up long enough to get my shoes and socks for me.

"After my grandmother died, I went to see my mother. I was so pissed that she hadn't believed me...that she'd defended my father even after I'd told her the truth about what had happened. Knowing she helped him escape..."

I nodded in understanding. "I get it," I said softly.

"She told me I'd never understand and tried to convince me I was confused about that day. That my father loved me, that he still loved me despite everything I'd said. She said that one day I'd see and we'd be a family again. I knew..." His voice dropped off for a moment. "I knew at that point that she was still in touch with him. Don't ask me how, I just did. She was so...certain about how things would play out."

"What did you do?" I asked.

"I started following her in the hope she would lead me to him. But she never left town, didn't sell the house. I started to think maybe I was wrong, but then I met someone who told me I wasn't."

"Ronan," I said softly.

"Guys like my dad are exactly why Ronan started his group. On the five-year anniversary of the murders, my mother did an interview with a national news organization. She spent the entire time defending my father despite all the evidence to prove he'd been the attacker. My father was tried in absentia," Cain said.

I nodded in understanding. "That means they have a trial whether the defendant is there or not, right?"

"Right," he said quietly. "He was convicted so if they ever find him, he goes right to jail. No second trial. My mother was charged with aiding and abetting, but the prosecutor ended up dropping the charges when he decided he didn't have enough evidence."

"So how did Ronan get involved?"

"He saw the interview my mother did and then started looking into the case. When he saw me trailing my mother looking for proof she knew where my father was, he reached out to me and made me an offer."

"A job in exchange for helping find your father?" I guessed.

"Not quite. I asked for the job when he explained who he was and what his team could do. He resisted at first, but then he took me on and taught me what I needed to know. He told me that he'd found evidence of my mom emptying out her 401k account a few weeks before I'd confronted her after my grandmother died. But the money trail stopped as soon as she took the money out of the account. No wire transfers, no spending it on something for the house or herself. It was just…gone."

"She gave it to your father," I murmured.

"That's what Ronan suspected. Either she went to him or he came to her. That's why Ronan was trailing her. Ronan suggested I give her access to the account that had the fifty-thousand in it. That way would we could monitor it and if she touched it, we'd know."

"So she took money out?" I asked. "Is that why Daisy called you?"

"Yes. She took all of the money out. First time in almost four years she's touched it."

I understood and quickly climbed to my feet. "She's giving it to your father or going to join him," I said. I grabbed my bag and began jamming my few belongings into it. "Let's go," I said.

"It should only take me a couple of days to deal with this and then I'll come get you at Vincent's. Hopefully we'll know more about the phone by then."

"I'm not going to Vincent's," I said calmly. "I'm going with you."

"No, you aren't."

I'd already braced myself for the argument that I knew was coming. "Let's fight it out in the car, Cain," I said as I headed for the door. "But I'm telling you this," I said as I snatched the car keys off the table. "You aren't winning this one." I didn't even give him time to respond before I left the room.

CHAPTER 17

CAIN

I didn't like giving or receiving the silent treatment when it came to the man next to me, but I was too wired to apologize to him like I should have. I'd ignored what he'd said about winning the argument until we were within a couple miles of Vincent's house and he'd made a random comment about how he hoped Vincent had a couple of certain over-the-counter medications at his house, because mixing them would have interesting effects, even on such a big guy. I'd suspected he'd been bluffing, but knowing he was adamant about coming with me had made me realize he could easily do something to Vincent that would piss the man off. And while I didn't exactly *not* trust Vincent, I couldn't say I trusted him not to do something like lock Ethan in a room or something similar in a twisted attempt to keep Ethan from getting away and following me. In truth, I couldn't even be sure Vincent could be bothered to care about keeping Ethan from coming after me since the man had barely even agreed to let Ethan stay at the house with him.

So I'd reluctantly, and angrily, turned the car around and gotten us on the highway that would lead us west. That had been twenty minutes ago and neither of us had spoken since.

It was a far cry from the last couple of days where all we'd done was talk.

And make love.

I had no clue how many times I'd lost myself in Ethan's beautiful body...or how many times he'd told me he loved me as he'd hung on to me. It didn't matter if I fucked him hard and fast or slow and long, the end was always the same. Explosive orgasms that had left me shaking and wanting more at the same time. And Ethan's words of love whispered in my ear.

If I'd had any doubt about wanting a future with Ethan, it had died a quick death after the past couple days. And any reservations I'd had about someday having the love I felt for him turn into something obsessive and wrong had been obliterated after he'd told me he loved me for the first time and said his feelings wouldn't change even if I couldn't change. I'd known then that I could and would change. Not just for him, but for me. I'd used things like talk of our wedding as examples of how fucked up I was, but I'd ended up planting seeds that had grown in the silence of my mind whenever I held Ethan in my arms as he slept. The idea of watching Ethan come to life as he was welcomed back into his family was exciting to me.

I didn't even feel a shard of possessiveness at the thought of sharing him with the people who loved him. And I knew he'd make sure to give me what I needed by helping me navigate the waters with his family as I explained to them that it would take me time to let them in to the place where only Ethan currently existed. I'd also been giving lots of thought to Lucy. Ethan had mentioned that the girl had no one else. The idea that she'd be a permanent part of our lives didn't bother me in the least. I'd probably be a lousy father figure for her, but I could learn from Ethan's example. And if all I could ever be was an overprotective, brotherly type to her, that was just fine by me. I'd be damn good at scaring off the boys who thought she was just any old girl they could mess with.

As the car ate up the miles and miles of road that were taking me back to the house where my life had ended in more ways than one, I tried to focus on what I might find there. Ronan had called shortly after Daisy had, but I'd ignored the call since I'd known what he wanted.

He wanted me to wait for back-up.

When he'd approached me years ago about helping me find my father, he'd told me it would be my decision whether or not my father would face the punishment the courts had decided upon or whether I would be his judge, jury and executioner.

It was a decision I still hadn't made.

I would have thought it would come to me as I got closer and closer to the possibility of finally putting my past to rest, but I found myself too preoccupied with other thoughts. And none of them had to do with the man who'd slid a butcher knife into my gut as easily as he'd carved our Thanksgiving Day turkey with it.

No, my thoughts were one place and one place only.

I reached across the console separating us and took one of Ethan's loosely fisted hands in mine. As soon as I laced our fingers, he tightened his grip and I heard a whoosh of air escape his lungs. He pulled my hand to his mouth and brushed a kiss over my knuckles before settling our joined hands in his lap. He held onto it for the rest of the drive, only letting go when I made the final turn of our journey and pointed out the place I'd never wanted to see again in my life.

Home.

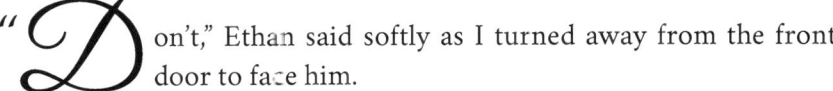

"Don't," Ethan said softly as I turned away from the front door to face him.

I sighed, not surprised that he knew I was going to ask him one more time to wait in the car. We'd spent several long minutes having the same argument in the car and I'd finally given up when I'd realized he'd just follow me if I tried to force him.

Resigned, I turned my attention to the door and tried the knob. The house I'd grown up in sat on a quiet street with just a few houses that sat on larger lots. I didn't see any people around nor were there any cars parked on the street. It was just after lunch time so I figured most people were at work or school. The house across the street that had belonged to the older woman who'd babysat for my parents on occasion looked abandoned because the grass and bushes were horrendously overgrown.

My mother's car wasn't in the driveway, but that didn't mean anything since she just as easily could have parked it in the garage. Daisy had said the withdrawal from the account had gone through just after eight this morning. I'd asked her to call the bank where my mother worked to see if she was still there but she'd gotten her voicemail and when she'd spoken to another employee, she'd been told my mother had gone home sick.

It was a promising sign, but since it had taken a couple of hours to get here, I also knew I could already be too late.

I wasn't surprised to find the door locked when I tested the knob so I pulled out the tools I needed to pick it. It took less than a minute and then I was tucking the tools in my pocket and pulling out my gun after making sure there was no one around to see us. I used the edge of my T-shirt to wipe the knob before turning it.

To Ethan I said, "Don't touch anything inside and stay behind me."

I still had no idea what the plan was in terms of what I would do if and when I saw my father, but little of it would have to do with my mother. Even if I decided to pull the trigger instead of calling the cops, my mother's presence would have nothing to do with it. Yes, she'd point the finger at me if she was ballsy enough to contact the cops and admit she'd been harboring a fugitive, but Ronan would have a rock solid alibi in place for me before I even left Kentucky.

I carefully pushed open the door and scanned the entryway before giving Ethan permission to enter. He used the sleeve of his shirt to quietly close the door behind us. The house was dark since all the curtains were drawn and I didn't hear any voices. Ethan stayed close behind me as we worked our way through the lower level of the house. A quick glance in the garage showed that my mother's car was indeed in the garage.

That fact had my adrenaline spiking higher.

Silence followed us as we made our way back towards the front door. I'd just stepped on the very first step of the staircase when I heard my mother scream, "No!"

The fear in her voice was reminiscent of all those days when I'd had to stand by helplessly and watch as fist after fist fell on her frail body. I darted up the stairs, hoping like hell Ethan would keep up.

"Please don't! Stop!" she cried out.

Even though I didn't hear the tell-tale signs of flesh hitting flesh, it didn't matter because I knew he could be doing to her what Ethan's ex had done to him. As much as I hated my mother for what she'd done, she was still my mother.

The door to her room was slightly ajar. I heard her let out another hoarse cry just before I kicked open the door and stormed into the room, gun drawn. I found her instantly, but nothing about the situation made sense. Instead of seeing her on the floor or bed with my father's body on top of hers, she was standing in the corner of the room...alone. There were no tears streaking down her face, no red marks on her skin or blood seeping from fresh injuries. The only thing off about her was how flushed her face looked.

Like she'd just run a marathon.

But then I saw it...the same thing I'd seen so many times when I'd begged her to believe me over my father.

I spun around, but was too late. Standing behind me just inside the door was Ethan with the barrel of a gun pressed against his temple and my father standing right behind him, using Ethan's body as a shield.

My mother had set me up and I'd fallen for it, hook, line and sinker.

CHAPTER 18

ETHAN

The pain in Cain's eyes as he came to the conclusion I'd reached the second I'd felt the gun pressed against my head was hard to see, but it was compounded by the fact that I'd made things worse for him. With his father using me as a shield, Cain's chances of getting out of this unharmed were greatly diminished. But since he'd run into the room intent on saving his mother, it was just as likely that he'd be lying dead on the floor right now with a bullet in his back.

"Put it down, son," I heard the man behind me say. I could tell he was a little taller than me, but I wasn't sure if it gave Cain enough room to maybe shoot him in the head. I doubted he'd do it anyway since the man could end up reflexively shooting me in the process, but part of me still wanted him to do it. If he didn't, the likelihood he'd get out of here alive was slim to none.

"Don't," I said to Cain, hoping he'd get the message, but he ignored me and dropped the gun to the floor.

"Moira, get the gun," the man said. I watched in disbelief as Cain's mother hurried to do the man's bidding. Her eyes met her son's, but she didn't speak to him.

As soon as she reached us, the man released me and shoved me forward. Cain put me behind his back and kept his arms out to prevent me from trying to go around him.

"Ain't that sweet, honey?" the man said as his dark eyes scanned his son. "Our little boy's gone and got himself a boyfriend. Told you he was a pansy," he said as he glanced at his wife. He took Cain's gun and tucked it in his pants at his waist.

"Let's just go, Jimmy," Moira said as she settled her hand on her husband's arm.

I saw a large suitcase sitting on the floor near the door and another smaller bag next to it.

Jimmy was a big guy, but not as heavily built as Cain. His hair was dark, but it looked like a bad dye job. He was wearing dirty jeans and a stained, button-up shirt. A long black trench coat hung off his narrow shoulders. I wondered if he'd worn a similar coat when he'd attacked his son ten years earlier…it would have been easy to hide a knife in the folds of a coat like that.

Jimmy studied his son for a moment and then said, "Nah, Moira." He shook his head slightly. "Look at him," he said as he waved the gun in Cain's direction. "Seen that look in his eyes before," he murmured. "Boy thinks he can come between us like he did when he was a kid."

"No, Jimmy," Moira said quickly as her eyes flicked to Cain. "If we just tie 'em up like you said-"

"Shut the fuck up, Moira!" he shouted. "You so stupid you can't see it?" he added. To Cain he said, "That's right, ain't it, boy…you're gonna keep huntin us."

I wasn't surprised when Cain didn't answer.

"See, Moira," Jimmy said knowingly.

As he raised his arm, Cain's mother shook her head and then she was stepping in front of the gun. "No, baby, he won't. He'll listen to me."

"Like he listened to you when he was a kid? Always gettin between us!" His eyes jerked back to Cain. "You ain't gonna stop, are ya?"

"No," Cain said without hesitation.

"Honey, don't say that," Cain's mother said, her voice high and desperate. She turned to face Cain and I was stunned to see her close the distance between her and her son by more than half. "Tell your father you know he didn't do those things you accused him of…tell him you were confused."

"I wasn't confused about who stuck that butcher knife into my body fifteen fucking times, Mom!" Cain said coldly. "Just like Hailey wasn't confused about who she was trying to hide from in that bathroom or whose eyes were the last ones Daniel and Justin saw as they begged for their lives or who little Amanda was looking up at just before a fucking knife went clean through her body, the mattress and the bottom of her fucking crib!"

"No," his mother began to shake her head. I was surprised when Cain ignored his father and stepped forward enough to grab his mother by the arms.

"It was him, Mom!" he whispered, his voice heavy with sorrow. "You know it! I know you do!"

She shook her head violently, but I didn't miss the tears streaming down her cheeks.

"That's how he loves you," Cain ground out. "By killing your kids! That's what he called them, too, did you know that?" Cain bit out. "Yours, not yours and his! He never wanted us. He told me that the day he buried that knife in my body over and over and over again. He said he gave you kids because *you* wanted them and he'd do anything for you!" Cain released his mother and pushed her away from him. "If that's love to you, you're as sick as he is."

Moira's sobs increased as she buried her face in her hands.

"Moira, sweetheart, you know that's not true. Everything I've done, I've done for you. I came back for you, didn't I?" Jimmy kept his gun on Cain while he moved closer to his wife. "I was a free man, but I risked everything to come back to get you. So we can be together."

Moira half-heartedly nodded as she wiped at her eyes. But she didn't move forward towards her husband. "Maybe…maybe we can tell the judge how stressed you were back then…that you didn't know what you were doing."

I saw Cain stiffen at his mother's words and I knew it was the first time she'd admitted the truth out loud.

Jimmy's face fell and I saw his gun drop just a little. I knew Cain had a gun in his ankle holster, but I doubted he'd manage to reach it in time if Jimmy chose to fire.

"I know you didn't mean to do it," Moira quickly said and then she was striding up to Jimmy. She put her hands on his forearms as she looked at him imploringly. "I know you loved them, but you were under so much pressure with your work and me not being home as much."

Jimmy nodded. "I just wanted to be with you."

The despair in his voice sounded off and there was something about his words that weren't quite right.

"I know," Moira said softly. "It's my fault," she whispered. "I should have taken better care of you."

I wanted to vomit as the woman twisted things so she could take the blame for the man's cold-blooded actions that had stolen four lives and destroyed a fifth.

"I just wanted us to be together forever...like you promised."

"Mom," I heard Cain say even as his mother wrapped her arms around her husband and leaned her head against his chest.

"I'll convince the judge, Jimmy. I'll make him see and they'll put you in the hospital for a little while. And I'll come see you every day and then when you're better, I'll be waiting. Just like I've been waiting all these years."

"I love you, Moira. Only you," Jimmy whispered as he brought his arms in to wrap around his wife.

But I knew even before Cain shouted a strangled, "No!" that he wasn't going to hug her.

The gunshot reverberated throughout the room and I watched in stunned silence as both Jimmy and Moira fell to the floor in a heap.

"No!" Cain cried out and then he was on his knees next to his mother. I reached his side just as he rolled her onto her back. The bullet had gone clean through her back and chest and I glanced up long enough to see it had pierced Jimmy's chest as well.

But whereas Cain's mother's lifeless eyes were staring back at us, Jimmy's were full of determination as he lifted the gun that was still in his hand to his head. I looked away as he pulled the trigger. I saw Cain stare in disbelief at the blood and brain matter splattered against the clean, white walls of his parents' bedroom.

"Mom," Cain called out as he cradled his mother's body in his arms. I put my finger against her pulse, though I didn't really need to.

"Ethan, please, you have to help her," Cain whispered as his haunted eyes met mine.

"I'm sorry, Cain," I said softly as I removed my finger from the woman's neck. "It's too late."

"No," he said with a shake of his head.

"I'm sorry," I repeated as I put my arm around his shoulder. He rocked her back and forth in his arms as he whispered something I couldn't understand and then he was gingerly putting her body back on the floor.

"I'll call 911," I said as I reached into his pocket for his phone.

"No," he said, closing his hand over mine. His voice sounded like he'd swallowed broken glass.

"We need to call the police," I reasoned.

"No," he repeated. "We can't risk them finding out who you are. We need to go."

"Cain, no," I said.

He ignored me and pulled me to my feet as he stood. He wiped at his face with his arm. His hand was covered in blood from where he'd been holding onto his mother, but that was it since most of her blood had been and still was seeping into the carpet.

Cain held onto my hand as he wiped the bloody one on his jeans. He tugged his shirt off and led me around Jimmy's body after grabbing his gun from the dead man's waistband. "Don't step in the blood," he said. I did as he said and followed him from the room. He used his shirt to wipe at the doorknob. "Did you touch anything on your way in here?"

"No, nothing," I said.

As we made our way back downstairs, he wiped the bannister down. At the front door, he used the shirt to open it, peered outside and then quickly wiped the knob behind us as he locked the door and pulled it shut.

He was too calm for my liking, but I knew he was focused on getting us out of there. "Get in," he ordered as we reached the car. He went to the trunk where he dumped his shirt and grabbed another one from his bag. By the time he got in the driver's seat, he was wearing it.

"Cain, we need to call someone," I said as he got the car started.

"Someone probably heard the shots," he said roughly. "I'll have Daisy monitor the police scanners and if they don't get a call, I'll have her place an anonymous one."

"I'm sorry about your mom-"

"I need to focus, Ethan." The comment stung, but I knew where it was coming from. He was in shock at the turn of events. He might have hated what his mother had done, but he hadn't hated *her*.

I remained silent for the rest of the drive and only half-listened as he called Ronan and told him what had happened. I couldn't hear Ronan's side of the conversation, but based on Cain's clipped one-word answers I doubted anything the other man had said got through. Cain hung up after telling Ronan to have Daisy monitor things to make sure the cops were notified, but he still refused to talk to me or even look at me. It took a couple of hours to get back to the hotel in West Virginia. Even though we ended up in a different room, the layout was the same as the one we'd been in.

Cain disappeared into the bathroom as soon as we got inside. I heard the water in the shower come on. Disappointment flared that he hadn't wanted me to join him, even just to be with him to provide comfort, but I pushed the useless emotion away. I cleaned up the little bit of blood that had sprayed on me using the sink outside the bathroom and then changed into a clean shirt and a pair of sweats. It was close to dinner time, but I wasn't hungry and I doubted Cain was either so I didn't order any room service. I sat down on the edge of the bed and waited, but it was a good twenty minutes before I finally heard the bathroom door open.

If I'd thought Cain would be calmer, I was both right and wrong. To someone who didn't know him, he appeared outwardly calm. But I'd been around him enough to see the telltale signs that he was agitated. The way his hands fisted, the tiny tick in his jaw, the way he swallowed hard over and over. He ignored me as he started to rifle through his bag.

"Cain, talk to me," I said softly, but he didn't respond.

When I went to stand next to him, he jerked away as soon as I touched his hand to stop him from yanking stuff out of his bag.

"Don't," he snapped. "I'm not…I'm not a good person to be around right now," he said angrily.

Ignoring his statement, I said, "It wasn't your fault. You know that, right?"

"No, I don't know that!" he shouted. "What I know is that my mother is dead. She wouldn't be if I hadn't gone there!"

"Yes, she would," I countered. "You and I both know he would have killed her the second she refused to give him what he wanted – when she finally stood up to him. Today, tomorrow, six months from now! You said it yourself, he was sick! What they had wasn't love. It was obsession. It was ownership. It was him needing her to make him feel powerful and in control."

Cain let out a hoarse shout just before he swiped his hand at the bag on the table, knocking it and its contents to the floor. His anger should have frightened me, but it didn't. I knew it wasn't directed at me and even if it had been, he wouldn't have hurt me.

"God, she was such a fucking fool!" he snarled. His anger was like a living thing, but I heard the subtle crack in his voice.

"She couldn't see him the way the rest of the world did," I said softly as I reached out to stroke his back. I was glad when he didn't lash out at me for the touch. I knew he was okay with physical contact between us when he was calm and relaxed, but I hadn't tested the theory when he was agitated.

Until now

"I kept telling myself I didn't care what happened to her…"

"I know you did," I murmured as I urged him forward into my arms. "She knew it too. She cared about you too or she wouldn't have tried to protect you back there."

Cain's arms wrapped around me. His body was still shaking and I had no doubt it was a mix of the adrenaline wearing off and the emotion that came with realizing his mother was really gone.

"I need you," he murmured against my neck.

"I know," I said softly and then I was searching out his lips.

The first touch of our mouths coming together set him off. He tore at my clothes as his mouth fiercely consumed mine. My shirt was yanked unceremoniously from my body and then his hands were shoving my sweats down so he could grip my ass.

He was already shirtless so the only thing keeping me from feeling all of him was the athletic shorts he'd put on after his shower. But I quickly changed that by shoving the shorts down. He moaned in my mouth as my fingers closed around his cock. As I massaged his dick, he played with my hole. He pulled his mouth free of mine long enough to get his finger wet and then he was swallowing down my moan of approval as his finger sank deep inside of me. Within a minute, I was grinding back against his finger. "Fuck me now, Cain," I demanded.

He obliged me by spinning me and bending me face down over the table. The position should have bothered me since I knew he'd only ever fucked the escorts from behind, but I knew this was what he needed. Not because he didn't want me to touch him or to avoid the connection, but because he wanted it hard and fast and he wanted to be in complete control.

I lay there, the cool wood absorbing some of the heat coming off my skin. I watched as Cain quickly searched out the lube and condoms. He suited up and then he was at my back, pressing a lubed finger deep inside of me. More lube was worked into my body with a second finger, but Cain didn't linger. His cock pressed between my cheeks a moment later and he didn't let up until his balls were brushing my ass. I forced my body to relax as he pulled out and slammed back into me. The burn was amazing, but there were no words to describe the pleasure that followed and shimmied along every nerve ending. As Cain began rocking into me, I grabbed the edge of the table to keep myself from sliding too far forward. At the same time, Cain grabbed my hips and held on with brutal force as he pounded into me, his heavy balls slapping against my skin.

I felt Cain drape himself over my back as he closed his hands around my shoulders. He slowed his pace so that he was sliding into me deep and hanging there for several beats, drawing out the amazing bursts of electricity firing up my spine and spreading out through my limbs.

"Cain," I whispered as sweat began to break out all over my body. I needed to come so badly, but the rhythm was only keeping me on the edge, not sending me over. "Please, I need to come."

"Not yet," Cain murmured in my ear before he kissed a spot just behind it. I wanted to cry as he lavished attention on the tiny scar there. It was the same place Eric had hit me with his gun during the beating and rape that had sent me to the hospital a year earlier. The fact that Cain would be so focused on me even after everything that had happened made it impossible to keep the emotions at bay.

"I love you so much, Cain," I said softly as I turned my head so I could see him. My position didn't allow for much movement, but it didn't matter because Cain's lips closed over mine as he continued to roll his hips against mine. When the kiss ended, Cain levered off me and I let out a cry of protest when he pulled free of my body. But before I could beg him to get back inside of me, he pulled me upright and then turned me around and eased me down on my back on the table. He dragged my ass to the edge and then thrust into me in one smooth motion. His mouth was back on mine as he began pounding into me. I wrapped my legs around him as he clasped my hands with his and held them above my head.

"I love you, Ethan," he murmured against my mouth. "I can't lose you," he added between kisses. "Ever."

"You won't," I promised. My orgasm was crawling up my spine, but I wanted to stop it because I didn't want this moment to ever end.

But Cain was ruthless as he drove me higher. I expected him to come with me, but I could tell he was going to send me over first. I cried out as he shifted his hips and began hitting my prostate. It took just three thrusts to push me over. I screamed as the violent release crashed through me. I was barely aware of Cain watching me as my body bucked and thrashed on the table. He fucked me through the orgasm as ropes of cum splattered my chest and even my chin. His mouth was right there to lick away the small spot and then he was kissing me hard as he began slinging in and out of me. The aftershocks became mini orgasms as he continued to pound me and when he finally exploded deep inside of me, more cum jerked from my dick and hit my belly and his. Cain released my hands and clasped my face as his mouth opened over mine in a throaty shout that sounded a lot like my name. He held me tight as his dick pulsed inside of me. I could feel the heat of his release through the condom.

I struggled to catch my breath as I clung to Cain. He wasn't faring much better than me as his hips continued to push against mine. Quakes of pleasure caused his body to shiver in my hold. I managed to reach down to rest my hands on his ass. I wanted to make sure he stayed inside of me for as long as possible. Not just because I needed his thickness filling me, but because I needed that connection to him.

He loved me.

I'd known it from his touch, but the words still made everything right in my world. No matter what happened over the next few days and weeks, in this moment, my world was perfect. And it would be that way as long as I had this man with me.

I knew that without a shadow of a doubt.

I kissed Cain's temple as I said, "You know what's next, right?"

Cain chuckled against me. "Shower," he said tiredly.

I made a move to get up as I said, "I can always take it by myself." As predicted, he shook his head and kissed me hard.

"Not on your life," he muttered. And then to my surprise, he was lifting me by the backs of the thighs. I instinctively locked my legs around his waist.

"I'm too heavy," I insisted, but he just kissed me again which took talent since he'd started walking us both towards the bathroom.

"Never," was all he said and then I shut up because I had a lot more important things to do to my man then argue with him.

CHAPTER 19

CAIN

"No Eric, don't, please. I'm sorry." Ethan's whispered words while he slept had me tightening my arms around him. "Shhh, baby, you're safe," I murmured to him as I dropped a kiss to his head. He snuggled against my chest and sighed. The sleep-laden sound of my name falling from his lips should have made me smile.

It didn't.

I couldn't smile. Couldn't eat. Couldn't think.

Because I was still stuck in that room watching my mother pledge herself to the man who'd finally managed to take everything from me.

The whole thing seemed to have happened in slow motion, but I still hadn't seen it coming. No, I hadn't been foolish enough to think my mother would somehow miraculously convince my father to give himself up, but I hadn't seen what was coming until it had been too late.

Until I'd heard the finality of my father's tone.

Ethan had known. He'd had his hand on my back through the entire ordeal and I'd felt him dig his fingers into me at the exact moment my father had told my mother he'd just wanted to be with her.

Right before she'd taken the blame for everything on herself.

Yeah, Ethan had known.

Because he'd lived that life.

I remembered his declaration in the cabin that Eric would kill him. He'd had no doubt about it, had accepted it even. But unlike my mother, he'd fought back anyway. He hadn't waited until it was too late to take a stand.

But it didn't change the facts.

I knew now that Ethan had been right that night when he'd told me Eric would end his life. I hadn't understood that at the time.

But I got it now.

My phone vibrating on the nightstand caught my attention. I reached for it and scanned the text that had popped up.

Phone's fixed.

My insides tightened, but before I could respond to Vincent, another text appeared along with an attachment.

Lucy's video.

I carefully eased Ethan onto his back. He eventually released me and rolled onto his side away from me, but he still had ahold of my hand. I let him hold onto it for a minute until he relaxed his grip enough to let me slide it free. I went to the bathroom and shut the door and left the light off as I woke my phone up and opened the video. I turned the sound down low enough so I could still hear, but that it wouldn't carry.

I hit play and waited. The video started and while the image was jerky at first, the sound was clear enough.

"You think I don't know about your dirty little secret, Eric?" a woman's shrill voice yelled.

The image stilled and I could see a woman wearing an expensive-looking dressing robe standing just in front of a railing in what looked like an ornate hallway.

"I don't know what you're talking about Patricia!" Eric snapped.

The guy was huge. My height and built like a brick wall. Definitely someone who spent a lot of time at the gym. I focused in on his meaty fists.

Ethan wouldn't have stood a chance against him.

"I hired a PI!" she screamed. "He saw you with some guy from your gym, Eric. In your car! You going to tell me he just fell asleep with his head in your lap?" the woman sneered.

"Watch yourself, Patricia," Eric warned, his face going dark as he eyed the woman.

"Get your shit and get out! And if you know what's good for you, don't contest the divorce or I'll make sure everyone knows the truth about their hero!" The last word was said with pure venom. I didn't miss the fact that the woman's words were slurred or that she looked unsteady on her feet.

"Listen to me you little cunt," Eric snarled as he grabbed her by the throat and yanked her to him. "I'm done putting up with your shit. You think you're so much better than me?" he asked. "You think you can hide behind your daddy's money? You think that gives you the right to treat me like I'm nothing?"

"You are nothing!" she returned as her fingers wrapped around the wrist holding on to her. "No one gives a shit about you anymore, Eric! They've forgotten all about you! But they'll have a field day when they find out you're a fucking queer who's been lying to them all this time!"

"Fuck you, Patricia," Eric said, his voice deadly. And with one hard shove, the woman flew backwards over the railing. The video jerked as her scream was abruptly cut off after a second or two. I heard what sounded like a muffled cry and assumed it was Lucy. The video cut off at that point.

I sent the video to Ronan and then sent him a message telling him to have Daisy find the PI Patricia had mentioned. If we were lucky, the man knew about Ethan. If we were really lucky, he'd have witnessed Ethan's bruises. It wasn't a guarantee that it would clear Ethan's name, but it would go a long way to proving he hadn't been stalking Eric or that he'd abducted Lucy because he was obsessed with the man.

I sat there in the dark for a while as I considered the turn of events. Having the video was good news, but I knew it wasn't enough.

I dialed Vincent's number.

"Yeah," was all he said.

"I need a favor," I said quietly. I didn't wait for Vincent to answer. I just sent Ethan a silent apology and then told Vincent what I needed.

CHAPTER 20

ETHAN

You're mine, Ethan. Do you hear me?

I jolted awake as if the words had just been whispered into my ear instead of two weeks earlier, just before Eric had shoved his dick into me.

"No, I'm not," I said out loud. I hadn't been able to say those words back then, but I could now. Even with Eric still hunting me, I was free.

I looked behind me to see if I'd woken Cain, but he wasn't beside me. I saw a figure sitting at the table in the corner, but there wasn't enough light from the laptop he was looking at to see his face.

But I knew it wasn't Cain. Panic tore through me, but before I could do anything, the man said, "Easy." I recognized the gruff voice instantly and managed to suck a deep breath into my lungs.

Vincent.

"What are you doing here? Where's Cain?" I asked. Since I was naked beneath the blanket, I couldn't get out of bed.

"He had some stuff he needed to do."

I flicked on the light next to the bed. "What stuff?" I asked. I saw my clothes sitting on the end of the bed. Not caring if Vincent was watching or not, I grabbed them and began tugging them on. A glance at the clock showed it was just after one in the morning.

"Don't know, don't care," the man said.

"You're lying," I said as realization began to dawn. There was only one reason Cain would have left me without saying anything.

My accusation had Vincent sitting back in the chair. His hard eyes swept over me and his jaw tightened. But I didn't give a shit that he was trying to intimidate me. When he didn't respond, I went around the bed and reached for the room phone.

"He left his phone here for you," Vincent cut in. "Said you'd need it to call the girl."

I followed Vincent's gaze and sure enough, Cain's phone was sitting on the dresser.

"He said you knew the passcode."

I went to the phone and entered the code. Cain had changed it a few days earlier…to the day we'd met.

I scanned his text messages and felt my heart lurch when I saw the most recent one that Cain had sent to Ronan.

"You fixed Lucy's phone," I murmured. I was tempted to watch the video, but I had more important things to deal with.

Vincent didn't answer. I turned to look at him. "Where is he?" I asked.

"I think you know the answer to that."

Fear spread through my chest as I lowered myself to the bed. "He went after Eric." I shook my head. "Why?" I whispered. "We have the proof."

Confusion went through me as I tried to make sense of Cain's actions. He'd been so adamant that the phone would be fixed and I'd finally be free. So why had he left to go after Eric?

Things became clear as I thought back to the day before. I shook my head in disbelief. "We have to find him," I said as I stood up and searched out my shoes. "Cain's going to kill him."

"Seems to me the fucker needs killing," Vincent drawled.

His lack of concern pissed me off. "Eric won't be alone, you asshole!" I shouted.

"Your man seems pretty capable of handling himself."

"Fuck you, Vincent!" I yelled as the panic began to consume me. I snatched Cain's phone off the dresser. If the asshole wouldn't help me, I'd find someone who would.

Vincent was on me before I reached the door. He shoved me against it when I tried to push past him. "Relax," he said, his voice still irritatingly calm.

"Don't tell me to relax," I bit out. "He saved my fucking life, Vincent! In more ways than one! I'm not going to just sit here..." My voice cracked as I struggled to keep the tears in check. "I'm not going to just sit here and do nothing. I'm not...I'm not going to lose him now. Not after it took so long to find him."

Vincent took the phone from me and then pointed to the bed. "Sit," he said, his voice hard and cold.

"No!" I yelled.

"Sit the fuck down, Ethan!" the man demanded, finally letting some of his temper loose. "I can't track the girl's phone if I have to worry about you taking off."

I fell silent at that. Was he really going to help me?

"Lucy's phone?" I asked. "He took it with him?"

He nodded and pointed to the bed. I went and sat down and watched him return to his computer.

"What if I call him on it?" I asked. "Maybe he'll listen to me and stop all this."

"I saw the man's expression when he left here. He was on a mission."

I felt helpless as I watched Vincent work. Helpless and pissed. I knew why Cain had done it, but it still hurt to know he'd made that decision without talking to me. And just as soon as I knew he was safe, I'd let him know that that shit wouldn't fly in the future.

We had a future.

I had to believe that.

"Here," Vincent said as he turned the laptop towards me. I got up and went to look at it. I didn't recognize the name of the town, but based on the fact that there weren't many neighboring towns, it looked like it was in the middle of nowhere.

"Virginia?" I asked. "Eric lives in Maryland and works in D.C."

"I'm thinking your man wanted to get him on more neutral turf." Vincent clicked some keys on the screen. The view changed to an aerial of the location. "Looks like an old farmhouse," he murmured. "Abandoned probably."

"We have to go," I said.

Vincent was silent for a moment, his jaw ticking. He finally got up and handed me the laptop. I watched him shrug on a long jacket and then he was grabbing a huge gun from the chair next to his.

"You do everything I tell you when we get there, you got it?" he said.

I nodded. I would have said or done anything at that point to get him moving.

I followed him out of the hotel to a vintage-looking muscle car. As soon as I was settled in the passenger seat, I grabbed Cain's phone from the cup holder where Vincent had put it and used the maps feature to figure out how far away we were.

"An hour to get there," I whispered. In an hour, everything could be over.

Vincent turned the engine on. The whole car vibrated from the powerful idle. "Half an hour," was all Vincent said just before he put the car in gear and hit the gas.

~

It was pitch black when we reached the road that led up to the farmhouse a mere 28 minutes later. The phone's position hadn't changed which had me both worried and hopeful at the same time. If Eric had gotten ahold of the phone, he would have either destroyed it or at least taken it with him when he'd left the house. But the same could be said of Cain. He clearly was still at the house. Maybe Eric hadn't even arrived.

Vincent pulled the car off the driveway and into a small grove of trees. "What are you doing?" I asked. I was shaking badly.

What if we were too late?

"We can't risk anyone hearing the car," Vincent murmured. I got out of the car and watched as he pulled several guns from the trunk of his car along with a knife. "Can you keep up?" the man asked as he quietly closed the trunk.

I nodded. The worst of my injuries had healed and while I knew it would be a challenge to keep up with the much fitter man, I'd kill myself trying. I suspected my spiking adrenaline would help.

"Here, take this," he said as he handed me a gun.

I began to shake my head, but then thought better of it.

Vincent used a small flashlight to show me the safety on the gun and explained that I needed to leave it on until we were closer. I swallowed hard and nodded. I was programmed to heal, but I'd kill in a heartbeat to keep myself and Cain safe.

I hurried after Vincent as he began jogging up the driveway. The pace wasn't as fast as I'd thought it would be, but I realized that was because the man was scanning our surroundings as we went so I didn't argue. But all that changed when I heard gunshots ring out.

No!

I managed to keep the protest to myself, but panic had me running as fast as I could. Vincent took off ahead of me, but I managed to keep up enough that I never lost sight of him...that or he went slow enough so he'd have eyes on me the entire time. I wasn't sure and it didn't matter.

I was breathing hard by the time we reached a small shed just beyond the house. Vincent motioned to me and I followed his line of sight to see Cain's rental car in front of the house. There were two more cars right next to it.

So Eric *had* brought help and he hadn't bothered trying to hide it.

Another gunshot sounded. I felt around the gun I was holding and flicked the safety switch to the off position.

"Stay behind me," Vincent ordered.

I nodded, but wasn't sure if he saw the acknowledgement because he was jogging across the yard. My lungs were burning from the stress and exertion and I kept expecting someone to jump out at us, gun drawn. More shots were volleyed and I looked up at the house long enough to see the muzzle flashes through the second-floor windows.

I sent up a silent thank you because I had to believe that every shot fired meant Cain was likely still alive.

But as we reached the front door, the shots stopped. I wanted to rush past Vincent and get into the house to find Cain, but I managed to stay in control. I would be no good to Cain dead.

My eyes had adjusted pretty well to the dark so I was able to see Vincent's hand gestures as he silently communicated with me. I stayed behind him as we entered the house. I nearly jumped when a flash of light appeared in front of us, but I realized it was coming from Vincent's flashlight. The light showed that the front door opened into a living room. There was furniture, but it looked old. The house smelled of mold and there was a layer of dust on everything. It was like the place had been forgotten in time.

Vincent's light fell on a body lying on the living room floor. I could see blood on the guy's head where he'd been struck with something and more blood was coming from both knees. I swallowed hard as I realized he'd been shot in both of them. To my amazement, I saw the man's chest rise and fall. Vincent stooped to grab the guy's gun which was more than a foot away from the man's empty hand. He tucked it into his waistband and then continued moving forward. We swept the entire first floor quickly, encountering another body in the kitchen. He too was still alive and had exactly the same injuries as the first man.

As we made our way to the second floor, I could hear what sounded like flesh striking flesh.

Relief flooded my system. I wanted to rush past Vincent to get to Cain, but the man in front of me was methodical about checking our surroundings before moving forward. By the time we reached the room where the fighting seemed to be happening, we'd encountered three more bodies, each still alive and sporting the same wounds as the men downstairs. Vincent had eventually given up on collecting all their guns and merely kicked them far enough away that the men wouldn't be able to easily reach them if they woke up.

"Do it!" I heard Eric shout as we reached the last room on the second floor. "Because that's the only way he'll ever be safe from me!"

"Cain, we're coming in," Vincent said before he pushed the door open. He flipped the light switch on. I was shocked there was even power, but my surprise was short-lived when I saw the sight that greeted me.

Cain was standing over Eric who was sprawled on the floor. His gun was pointed at Eric and I could see he had a small flashlight attached to the gun, presumably so he could see in the dark.

I wondered how Eric had even managed to speak because his face looked like hamburger. There was blood coming from his mouth as well as several cuts. If I hadn't heard his voice, I wouldn't have known it was him.

Cain sported a few cuts himself, but they were minor. His knuckles were covered in blood.

"You shouldn't have come, Ethan," I heard him say softly, though his eyes stayed on Eric.

"You shouldn't have walked out on me," I murmured. I slowly made my way to Cain until I was standing just a couple feet from him. "Why are you doing this?" I asked. "We have the video."

The brittleness in Cain's eyes made me nervous. Not that he would hurt me, but that I might not be able to reach him.

"He'll never stop," Cain responded quietly. "He'll get off or he'll get out or he'll find someone to do his dirty work for him." Cain's eyes shifted to me for the briefest of moments. "You were right, Ethan. It was never a matter of 'if.' It was and always will be 'when.'"

"I didn't have you when I said that, Cain. I didn't have a lot of things."

Cain shook his head. "I can't be with you 24/7 for the rest of your life. This is the only way."

I took a few more steps closer until I was standing next to Cain. He was so rigid it looked like his entire body would snap in two if someone touched him. But I wasn't someone.

I put my hand on his arm. "Please don't do this."

"He'll never stop, Ethan," Cain repeated, his voice softening, desperate now. "He's like *him*."

I knew who *him* was. And Cain was right. Eric was as sick as Cain's father had been.

"But I'm not like your mother. I'm not pretending that his feelings for me are anything other than hatred. And I'm not scared of him anymore."

I glanced at Eric and realized it was true. The hate in his eyes didn't spark fear in my belly. The promise of vengeance didn't have me wanting to run.

I turned my focus back on Cain. "I want to fight back, Cain. I want to tell the world what he did to me. I want to watch them put him behind bars where he'll finally know what it feels like to have no power, no control…to have his every move dictated. To wake up every day knowing that that's his life. I want him to have to live with knowing who put him there. Please don't take that from me," I said gently. "I love you for wanting to keep me safe, but I need this to end on my terms."

"You think anyone will believe you?" Eric said with a laugh. He coughed and spit up some blood. "You and that little bitch have nothing on me! I'm a fucking hero! I saved more lives in one day than you'll save in a lifetime, you pathetic piece of shit."

I felt Cain's arm tighten in response.

"You're mine, Ethan!" Eric snarled. "I don't care how many times you let him fuck your fat ass, you're still mine and you know it! I'm so deep inside of you that you'll never be free of me!"

"Don't," I said sharply as I saw Cain start to pull the trigger. I stepped in front of the gun and Cain immediately lowered it.

"Ethan," he said, his voice pained.

"He can't touch me ever again, Cain. You're not going to lose me. I promise."

Cain nodded and then he was pulling me forward into his embrace. My whole body started shaking as the relief crashed over me. I heard Eric spewing vile words at me, but I didn't care what they were. I was only interested in the man holding onto me.

Until a gunshot rang out.

I jumped in Cain's hold and spun around, terrified that Eric had somehow managed to pull a gun on us. But it took just seconds to realize the shot hadn't come from him...it had been aimed at him.

Eric let out a shriek as a bullet pierced the ground dangerously close to his head. I saw a bullet hole in the wood floor next to the other side of his head. I watched in mute fascination as Vincent continued to fire at Eric, narrowly missing his body with each shot.

Missing on purpose.

"Okay, okay!" Eric screamed as he pulled himself into a ball in a desperate attempt to protect himself.

Vincent strode right up to Eric and straddled him. "Turn over you fucking little coward," Vincent said, his voice as deadly calm as it had been when I'd argued with him in the hotel room.

"Vincent," I began, but Cain wrapped his arm around me from behind, his message clear.

I fell silent as I watched Eric slowly roll to his back, his eyes wide with fear. But it was short-lived because his face twisted into an ugly sneer. "Do you have any idea who I am?" he shouted. "I'm a fucking cop, asshole. You're all going to prison for this!"

"The question you should be asking yourself is, do you know who I am?" Vincent drawled.

"Yeah, I know who you are, old man! You're the fucker who's going to spend the rest of his life behind bars. I have more friends than God! All I have to do is snap my fingers and you're fucked."

"Is that so?" Vincent asked.

"Yeah, that's so," Eric bit out. "Secret Service, FBI, the fucking White House! Take your pick! I've got people in all of them."

I had a good enough view of the scene playing out before me to see Vincent smile. But it was a dangerous smile. I watched as he pulled out his phone. "Let's give one of your people a call, shall we?"

Eric was caught off guard by the comment, but he rallied quickly, so sure of himself. "John Fordham," he said easily. "Director of the FBI," he added with a cocky smile. "His direct number is in my phone-"

Eric's voice dropped off suddenly when Vincent hit a button on his own phone. The man kept eye contact with Eric as he said, "Yeah, it's me." He was silent for a brief moment before saying, "I've got a friend of yours with me," he said. "I'm afraid your friend is threatening one of my friends." Vincent's voice was relaxed, but ice cold. I actually felt a shiver run down my spine.

"Eric Palmer," Vincent murmured. "Said you're one of his people."

Vincent listened for a moment. "Maybe you should talk to him," he said. "Oh, and he doesn't know who I am...maybe you want to clue him in?" I watched in disbelief as Vincent handed the phone to Eric.

Eric hung there for a moment, clearly surprised by the turn of events. Then he grabbed the phone and put it to his ear. "John, you need to help me. 372 Old County Line Road in Helenville-"

His voice dropped off suddenly as he listened to the other person talk. Even with his battered face, I could see the transformation happening. Shock, then disbelief, then stark fear. It was at least two minutes before Eric spoke again, his words desperate this time. "No, wait John, you can't just leave me here!"

Eric went silent, refusing to let his eyes meet Vincent's. Vincent took the phone from him and pocketed it. "Cavalry on the way?" he asked knowingly. I didn't miss the amusement in his voice.

"People...people will figure it out," Eric stammered. "They'll be looking for me and they'll know Ethan was behind it all," he whispered. I felt Cain stiffen behind me, but before he could say anything, Vincent got up into Eric's face.

"He told you who I am, right?" Vincent asked.

Eric nodded jerkily.

"Did he tell you what I do to people who threaten my friends?"

Eric shook his head.

"That's because no one's that stupid," Vincent murmured. "You that stupid, Eric?"

To his credit, Eric was smart enough to keep his mouth shut.

"Now here's how this is going to go," Vincent said easily. "You *are* going to walk out of here because my new friend, Ethan, wants it that way. But just remember that when you're in that tiny little cell that he's" – Vincent looked over his shoulder at me – "going to put you in, I can reach you there. I can reach you, your family, your friends, your fellow cops who might be inclined to help you send Ethan a message…from this moment on, I own your ass. Not the courts, not the prison guards who are going to put you in that little hole that no one will even remember you're in. Ethan gets even a hangnail and I'll take it out on your ass."

Vincent shifted off Eric long enough to put his gun to Eric's groin. "One word from me and you won't even have the benefit of solitary confinement to keep you safe from the men you put behind bars. And Eric," he added softly. "They're going to love having a little bitch like you to play with."

And just like that, he pulled the trigger.

Eric screamed in agony and put his hands over his groin as he folded in on himself. Vincent straightened and turned away from him. When his eyes fell on me he said, "What? He'll live…probably."

I started stripping off my jacket, but Cain grabbed my arm. "You are not helping him," he said.

"Yes, I am," I returned. "I want his ass alive so he can rot in jail."

"Don't worry, Doc. Ambulance will be here any second." It didn't surprise me in the least that Vincent knew I was a doctor.

"How do you know?" I asked.

"Because John knows me too well," Vincent said with a slight smile.

And sure enough, a few moments later I heard the sound of a siren off in the distance.

"We should go," Vincent said. "It'll take John a while to sort all this out with the local cops."

"Are we going to be arrested?" I asked. I knew, despite Vincent's threat, that Eric would tell anyone who'd listen what had happened here.

But Vincent didn't answer me. As Cain's warm fingers closed over mine, I didn't even spare Eric one last look before following Cain from the room.

EPILOGUE

CAIN

Six Months Later

"I swear, it's like that thing with cats," I grumbled as I carefully shifted the baby in my arms. I held my breath to see if she would wake up, but fortunately, she didn't.

"What thing?" Ethan asked. His mouth was pulled into a wide smile as he settled down on the couch next to me. He held out the bottle of beer he'd brought me, but with my arms full of sleeping kid, I didn't want to risk waking her.

Ethan chuckled and held the bottle up to my lips so I could take a drink.

"You know how cats always gravitate to visitors who don't like them? That's what this is," I said as I motioned to the baby.

"Probably don't let my sister hear you referring to her daughter as a cat," he said as he shifted so he could lean against my side. His eyes fell on his niece. I never got tired of seeing the love in his gaze when he watched her doing something even as simple as sleeping.

"You want this, don't you?" I asked.

Ethan straightened enough so he could look me in the eye. "Do you?" he asked, carefully.

I glanced at the baby. Yes, it had scared the hell out of me early on when I'd held the baby for the first time, but I was getting used to her gentle weight and squirming little body. And the way she looked at me with her big blue eyes…it was indescribable.

I'd never lied to Ethan and I wasn't about to start. "It scares me," I admitted. "This," – I motioned to the baby – "I kind of like," I said. "But it's different when it's your kid. I don't want to mess that up."

Ethan reached up to stroke my face. He did that a lot these days. And of course I loved it when he did.

"I know you'll make an amazing father, Cain. I've seen the proof. But we can wait as long as you need for you to see that too. And if all you ever want to be is the favorite uncle who's the only one who can get the babies to sleep, then I'm good with that too."

I leaned over to kiss him softly and said, "I'll get there, Ethan."

"I know you will," he whispered against my lips.

I smiled and pulled back. "You nervous about tomorrow?"

He nodded. "But ready, too."

That didn't surprise me. Ethan wasn't the kind of guy who should be sitting around doing nothing. He needed to work…he needed to save lives and heal people.

Things hadn't been easy after we'd left Eric on the floor of that farmhouse. Not that night and not in the weeks and months that had followed. To say Ethan had been mad at me for going after Eric like I had, was an understatement. He hadn't spoken to me at all on the drive back to the hotel, nor as we'd packed up our stuff and headed to the airport so we could fly back to Seattle. He'd let loose on the plane though, and I'd let him because I'd realized his anger had stemmed more from fear than anything else.

I'd also loved the fact that he hadn't been afraid to stand up to me and say what was on his mind.

I couldn't regret going after Eric that night, despite what I'd put Ethan through. My fear of losing him had just been too great to ignore. After I'd called Vincent to ask him to stay with Ethan, I'd used the time to scope out where I wanted to bring Eric and the cronies I knew he'd be bringing with him for our little get together. It had been easy to search for properties nearby that had been foreclosed on and the farmhouse in Helenville had fit the bill. Once I'd gotten there, I'd turned Lucy's phone on, called her piece of shit stepfather and told him that if he ever came near Ethan again, I'd rip his fucking throat out. Then I'd just waited for the man to track the phone and predictably, within a couple of hours, Eric and his flunkies had pulled up, not even trying to hide their arrival.

I'd waited outside until the men had gone inside. After that, it had just been a matter of taking them out one by one, the silencer on my gun making it easy to get the drop on them. I hadn't killed any of them since I couldn't have been sure why they were there. Eric was a master manipulator. He could have just as easily convinced some of his cop buddies that he was going to rescue his abducted stepdaughter and needed help.

So I'd hobbled each man instead of eliminating them and then I'd gone in search of Eric. I'd found him in the room where I'd left Lucy's phone. He'd been armed, of course, but it had taken next to nothing to disarm him. Then I'd tossed my gun on the single piece of furniture in the room, a worn out looking bed, and I'd shown him the same exact amount of mercy he'd shown Ethan.

None.

Eric had gotten a few punches in, but my guess that his bulk had been the result of weights at the gym and nothing more had been right because the guy hadn't been able to fight for shit. Sure, he'd been able to throw a punch at someone like Ethan who hadn't known how to block it or fight back, but the first time I'd slammed my fist into his nose, breaking it, he'd screamed and covered his face, forgetting to block his body from the next punch. I'd let him experience the pain for the amount of time it had taken him to take another swing at me, then I'd slammed my fist into his gut, knocking the wind from him. I'd played with him for a lot longer than I should have, but it hadn't been until he'd stayed down and started spewing filth about how I'd just made things worse for Ethan that I'd grabbed my gun off the bed and pointed it at his head.

I'd struggled to give Ethan what he wanted when he'd asked me not to end Eric's life. But his need to get justice had outweighed my need to eliminate the threat against him all together. I'd already made the decision to have someone else take Eric out if there was even a hint that he was going to follow through on his threat not to let Ethan go, but that wasn't something I'd shared with Ethan.

But surprisingly, Vincent's threat seemed to have done the trick. No, Eric hadn't gone completely silent, but he had been careful about what he'd said about Ethan when things went public a few days after the encounter in the farmhouse. Once we'd reached Seattle, Ronan had worked with a team of lawyers to determine how Ethan and I would turn ourselves in. There'd been no way either of us were going to let Ethan be taken back to D.C. since that would have put him in contact with the cops who worked with Eric. We'd been talking about going to the Feds when they'd ended up coming to us after Vincent had called Ronan to tell him he'd sent them our way.

But there'd been no arrests.

There had been some questions, but very few about the night I'd gone after Eric. Most had been about Ethan and his relationship with Eric. Ethan had told them everything...every ugly detail. He'd shared what he'd known about the death of Eric's partner in the home invasion as well. The PI Patricia Palmer had hired hadn't panned out in terms of connecting Eric to Ethan, but we'd caught a break when Daisy had found the original files Ethan had transferred from the digital recorder to CDs using the computers at his work. While he'd deleted the files from the computers after transferring them each time, he hadn't realized the files went into a different folder to await final deletion. Daisy had made copies for us and then left the files there so the Feds could find them for themselves. Between the video of Patricia Palmer's death and the evidence of the torture Ethan had endured, the Feds had promised that Eric wouldn't be walking away from any of it. He'd been arrested while in the hospital recovering from Vincent's gunshot to the groin, an injury that had resulted in permanent damage that meant the man would have a close relationship with a catheter for the rest of his life. I'd fully expected Vincent to be arrested at some point, but we'd heard neither hide nor hair from the man since that night and the Feds had been tight-lipped about his whereabouts and had only shared that "Mr. St. James isn't currently a suspect or person of interest in any crime."

Eric had ended up pleading no contest to his wife's murder after the video had surfaced. He'd agreed to the plea after the prosecutor had offered him a reduced sentence. While neither Ethan or I had been thrilled at the lighter sentence, it had gone a long way in re-establishing Ethan's reputation. More importantly, it had meant Lucy hadn't had to testify. But it had also spurred Ethan on to pursue justice for the crimes he'd suffered. Eric hadn't agreed to a plea deal in the multiple counts of assault and rape that had been brought against him, but he hadn't testified in court either. Not after Ethan had held his ground when he'd been cross-examined and most definitely not after the damning recordings had been played in court.

It hadn't been easy for Ethan to have parts of his past go public like that, but he'd stayed strong as he'd fought for justice for himself. Eric had been found guilty less than a month ago and just in the past week he'd been sentenced to another thirty years in prison, which was on top of the twenty he'd gotten for his wife's death. With parole, there was a chance he'd get out early, but that was a ways off. And the likelihood was high that he'd be brought up on charges for his partner's death soon since the Feds had found proof Eric's car had been in the neighborhood the night of the murders.

All in all, it would be a long time before Eric saw the outside of prison walls. And that was assuming he even survived prison long enough to convince a parole board that he was a changed man.

While Ethan had been completely vindicated, it had been a rough journey as he'd had to relive the past and have every part of his private life exposed for the entire world to see, but luckily, he'd recognized early on that both he and Lucy would need to seek psychological help to deal with the trauma they'd both faced. I was still on the fence about talking to a professional about my own past, but I hadn't completely dismissed the idea and Ethan hadn't pressed me one way or the other.

With the multiple trips to D.C. for the trials and sentencings, we hadn't had much time to settle into a life together. I myself had struggled with letting Ethan out of my sight for something even as simple as him running to the grocery store because I'd been convinced Eric would send someone after him. Ethan had accommodated my need to be with him at all times in the beginning, but it had just been this past week that he'd finally put his foot down. He'd reminded me as he'd headed out the door to go fill out his paperwork at the hospital he'd gotten a job at, that he might not know for sure if I'd followed him, but that he'd be asking me if I had when he got home and since I refused to lie to him, he'd know the truth either in my answer or in my silence.

It had been the longest hour of my life and I'd spent all of it checking the app on my phone that would show me the location of Ethan's phone. It was a concession he'd been more than happy to grant me.

As we'd navigated our way through the process of getting justice for Ethan, we'd had to make some decisions about our future together. Lucy had been a glaring sticking point because Ethan had been certain I'd object to the girl living with us permanently. And while I'd quickly divested him of that notion, it had taken a little more effort to smooth things over with Lucy. While she'd been relieved to learn that Ethan had started the process of becoming her foster parent with the goal of adopting her eventually, she'd been less sure about me. Although I'd managed to make amends with her just before leaving with Ethan for D.C., she hadn't completely trusted me. I'd had no doubt some of that had been because of the struggles I'd still faced being around her once we'd returned to Seattle. I'd finally taken her aside and explained what had happened to me as a child and promised her that I'd get to a point where I trusted her just as much as I trusted Ethan. My honesty had gone a long way with Lucy and while she and I occasionally butted heads, mostly due to my overprotectiveness, we'd somehow managed to make our little group of three into a family.

Once things had been ironed out with Lucy, Ethan and I had needed to make some other decisions, namely where we would make our home. He'd been more than willing to stay in Seattle, but it had never even been a question in my mind. Ethan had needed to go home and home was San Francisco. He'd cried when I'd told him that, as had several members of his family when we'd video chatted with them later that night. It hadn't taken more than a few days for me to get my stuff together since I'd pretty much been living out of hotels in the four years since I'd left Indiana. It had been Ethan who'd suggested I donate my grandmother's house in Indiana to a charity for victims of domestic abuse since it was completely paid for and we didn't need the money, so I'd done just that. Ethan had gone with me to Indiana long enough to get the only things I'd really wanted…the pictures of my brothers and sisters that my grandmother had put into frames and hung in our kitchen so it would feel like they were with us every time we'd eaten a meal in there.

I hadn't done anything with my parents' house after the police had contacted me to notify me of their deaths. Nor had I claimed their bodies. I'd simply told the police to treat them as they would any unidentified persons because that was what they'd become to me. A lawyer had contacted me a couple of months later, but I'd refused to accept the meager inheritance I'd been left as the only next of kin. I'd told him to give everything away, including the fifty thousand dollars my mother had taken from my trust to fund her escape with my father.

I was about to tell Ethan he'd do great at his first day on the job the following day when his sister, Eden, came into the living room. She did a little happy dance when she saw that her daughter was asleep.

"You're a miracle worker," she whispered to me as she reached down and took the baby so she could put her down in her crib.

I'd gotten along better with Ethan's family over the months since we'd moved to San Francisco. It had taken me a long time to adjust to the sheer volume of people I was around on a regular basis, but they'd all been understanding once I'd explained my past to them. None of them ever pushed me to interact with them more than I was comfortable with and they never looked down on me like I should have just been able to get over my weird fear and move on. I'd gotten to a point that I could comfortably sit around a table with them for a meal or join Ethan's brothers in the living room as they fanatically cheered on whatever favorite local sports team was playing. Ethan and I had even gone to a baseball game with the family a month ago. I'd been tense, but Ethan had worked it out so his family was sitting on both sides and directly behind us. I'd still spent an inordinate amount of time watching for threats, but I'd been able to relax enough by the end of the game to enjoy it. Ethan had been worried that a baseball game would trigger memories of the day of my attack for me, but it hadn't. Maybe it was just easy for me to compartmentalize, but I'd put that day behind me…it had died along with my parents. Yes, the aftereffects still lingered, but I knew that with Ethan's and his family's support, they too would be a thing of the past soon enough.

"You're going to do great, tomorrow," I said to Ethan once his sister had taken the baby upstairs. "That hospital is lucky to have you."

"They're not going to be happy about the press that comes along with me," Ethan sighed as he leaned against me. I draped my arm over his shoulders and kissed his temple.

"They'll lose interest soon," I said softly. The reporters had been relentless in the six months since the truth about Eric had come out. The hope had been that the chaos would die down as soon as Eric was sentenced, but word had gotten out that Eric would likely be facing charges for the death of his partner and the man's wife. It would be yet another trial Ethan would have to testify in. The good news was that the crime had occurred in Virginia where the man and his wife had lived. Which meant the prosecutor there could seek the death penalty against Eric. Chances were high the case would never get that far since Eric would likely agree to any plea that would save his neck. But the flip side was that the plea would likely be life in prison with no chance of parole instead of the death penalty. Either way, the likelihood that Eric would ever see the light of day was growing slimmer and slimmer.

"Hope so," he said with a sigh. "Ready for things to get back to normal," he said. He chuckled and said, "Well, as normal as things can get for us anyway."

I smiled at that.

"Did you talk to Ronan yet?"

I shook my head.

"Cain," Ethan said with a sigh.

"I know, I know, I will," I said. "I just need a little more time."

Ethan sat up and then turned to face me. "I'm safe, Cain. Eric wouldn't dream of touching me at this point. He can't," he added. "He's got no friends left to convince that he's getting a raw deal, not after the cops started looking into him for his partner's death. And he hasn't got even a penny to his name to hire someone to come after me. I'm more in danger of getting a papercut at work than I am from him."

"I know," I said with a nod. This wasn't the first time we'd had the conversation, but that was because my fear continued to rule my actions. I'd been telling Ethan for weeks now that I would let Ronan and Memphis know to put me back in the rotation, but I hadn't actually made the call because the thought of being away from Ethan even for just a night scared the hell out of me. I'd expected Ethan to have an issue with me continuing to work for Ronan, but he'd quickly disabused me of that notion one night when he'd told me to get my ass into gear and go save people who needed saving. I supposed even if the experience with Eric hadn't made him realize what kind of evil existed in the world, knowing what had happened to me and my brothers and sisters would have.

"I'll call him tonight when we get home. Promise." Ethan gave me one of his happy smiles and then leaned in to kiss me.

"Thank you," he whispered.

"For what?" I asked.

"For being you. For letting me be me."

I sighed against his mouth and then kissed him long and deep.

"Yeah, they're at it again," I heard Lucy say as she walked through the front door. Ethan smiled against my mouth, but he went on kissing me. When we separated, we saw Lucy sitting in the oversized plush chair next to the couch, her eyes on her phone. Ethan's mom was standing behind the chair, her expression one of pure happiness.

"You two are just so cute together," she said with a sigh and then she was coming around to give Ethan a kiss on the cheek.

"Hi, Mom," he said with a laugh. "Where's Dad?"

She harrumphed and said, "Out talking boobers with Mr. Delvaney from across the street."

"Boobers?" Ethan asked.

"She means bobbers," Lucy clarified without looking up from her phone.

"Boobers, bobbers, whatever," the older woman said with an impatient wave. She grabbed Ethan's chin and just looked at him for a while before leaning down to kiss him again. "I'm making your favorite tonight," she said. "Chicken Parmesan." She looked at me and said, "Yours is next weekend."

I smiled because no matter how many times Ethan and I insisted that she didn't have to keep making our favorite dishes every time we came over, especially since the rest of the family rarely got a say in the matter, she kept doing it anyway.

"Thanks, June," I said softly. I wasn't surprised when she reached out to briefly cup my face. Of all the family members, Ethan's mom struggled with my aversion the most since she was such a tactile person. But I'd started to accept, even welcome, her little touches before she remembered herself. I had no doubt I'd soon be the recipient of her giant, no-holds-barred hugs.

And I was okay with that.

"You are so going to have to dance with her at our wedding," Ethan said once his mom had wandered off to the kitchen.

I laughed and said, "Is that you asking me to marry you?"

"No," Ethan said. His fingers brushed at the hair above my ear. "When I ask you, it's going to be much more memorable than that."

"So, *you're* going to ask *me*?" I said. "Does that mean I can't ask you?"

Ethan smiled. "No, it doesn't mean that at all."

A loud sigh came from Lucy's vicinity. Ethan and I chuckled. The girl had definitely settled into her new role as our kid just fine. "What's up, Lucy?" Ethan asked.

She finally put down her phone and swung her hair over her shoulder. She'd started to let her natural hair color return so it was an odd mix of mostly black and a brownish-reddish color at the roots. I'd heard her in deep conversations with Ethan's sister about the pitfalls of coloring versus not coloring her hair to match her real color, but I'd wisely made myself scarce for that conversation.

"Can I go to the movies with some friends tonight?"

"It's a school night," Ethan reminded her. Although Lucy had started school only a week earlier, she'd managed to amass a slew of new friends.

"I'll be home by ten," she offered. She quickly glanced at me and said, "And no, there won't be any boys there."

I smiled at that because I'd already threatened to run a background check on any boy she brought home. She'd been outraged of course, but she'd hugged me five minutes later when I'd backed off my threat after she'd promised to let me show her some self-defense moves.

"What do you think?" Ethan asked me.

"I think her eye-gouging is good, but she needs to work on the neck jabs and she's nowhere near ready to break someone's nose." Ethan shoved me hard and shook his head. Lucy was smiling wide.

"Fine, you can go. But nine, not ten. And if you're late, he," – Ethan pointed to me – "will be driving you and your friends to and from school for a month."

"Ew, no," Lucy said. "All my friends keep telling me how hot they think he is!"

"Your friends have good taste," Ethan said with a smile. "Nine o'clock, Lucy, and not a minute later."

"Fine," she harrumphed and then she was getting up, her eyes back on her phone as she began texting as she walked towards the kitchen. I wasn't surprised when she stopped behind the couch we were sitting on so she could wrap her arms around Ethan's neck and give him a kiss on the cheek. There was no hesitation on her part or tension on mine when she did the same to me. As soon as she was done, her eyes were once again glued to her phone as she left the room.

"Her friends think I'm hot," I said to Ethan with a wink.

He laughed and kissed me. "Shut up," he whispered. The kiss grew heated and I was about to roll him beneath me on the couch, his family be damned, when the front door opened and Ethan's father and oldest brother strolled in.

"Son," Ethan's dad said knowingly as he took in his son's flushed cheeks.

"Dad," Ethan practically squeaked. The man ambled into the kitchen, but no such luck with Devon who plopped down in the chair Lucy had been sitting in and reached for the TV remote.

"You know what you need to do, right?" I said to Ethan as I settled my hand on his thigh.

"No, it's your turn."

I shook my head. "I did it last time."

"No, you didn't."

"Yes, I did," I said firmly.

"It's your turn, little brother," Devon said without looking away from the TV as he searched through the sports channels. "Cain did it last time."

"How do you even know what we're talking about?" Ethan asked.

"Because you have the same conversation every time you have the house to yourselves for a little while. And since I heard Lucy telling Mom earlier that she was going to ask you about going to the movies tonight..."

Devon's eyes finally shifted to us. "Your turn to fake the headache so you guys can get out of here tonight, Ethan."

"So, does everyone know when we're faking it?" Ethan asked.

"Pretty much."

"Why didn't you say anything?"

"Like what?" Devon asked.

"I don't know, something!" Ethan said in exasperation.

Devon thought on it for a moment and then suddenly yelled, "Mom, Dad, Ethan and Cain are leaving early tonight!"

"Devon!" Ethan shouted.

"Which one has the headache this time? It's Ethan's turn, right?" I heard Ethan's dad call just before Ethan's face went bright red and he buried it against my chest. I laughed and kissed the top of his head.

"Told you it was your turn."

"Oh God, right there," Ethan groaned as his hands closed over my ass to urge me on. We hadn't managed to make it to our bed after locking the bedroom door. Hell, with the way Ethan had been playing with me on the drive home from his parents' house, we were lucky we'd even made it out of the car. I'd only managed to get us to the bedroom because I hadn't wanted to risk Lucy walking in on us if she happened to end her night early...or we lost track of time, which had happened before.

I'd ended up fucking Ethan up against the door at first, but like so many times we came together, I always felt an undeniable need to see his eyes when he came, so I'd pulled out of him long enough to maneuver him onto his back on the floor. He'd groaned in delight as I'd slid back into him, my bare cock nailing his prostate on the first glide. But I hadn't let him come like he'd wanted. No, I had to take full advantage of the fact that Lucy was out of the house.

Which meant making my lover scream as loud and as often as possible.

So I'd spent the better part of an hour taking him right up to the edge, but refusing to send him over. And now he was clinging to me like nothing else existed in his world but me.

That was always the way of things when we made love. The world continued on around us, but in those moments it was just me and him in our perfect little bubble.

"Love you," I whispered against his lips as I slowly fucked in and out of him. He was trembling in my arms as the orgasm began to build in intensity once again. Sweat covered his skin. Mine too, for that matter.

It had taken the better part of a month for all of Ethan's bruises to completely heal. I'd already known him to be beautiful, but finally seeing his body without the proof of everything he'd been through had been freeing for me in more ways than it probably had been for him. But the best part was the transformation that had happened after the bruises faded.

Because that was when his inner wounds had begun to heal.

He'd started to put on weight in recent months, despite the stress he'd been under with the trials. More importantly, he hadn't obsessed over his weight or any of the things that had set Eric off in the past. Ethan turned out to be a little bit of a slob when it came to leaving his clothes on the floor. He'd panicked the first time he'd found me cleaning up his clothes off the bathroom floor, but I'd quickly and easily dissuaded him of the notion that it bothered me by treating him to one of our infamous shower trysts. And nothing pleased me more then to find my man sitting on the couch eating potato chips. No, he didn't go crazy and eat the whole bag. He ate to his heart's content and that was it. Sometimes he ate healthy, other times not so much. He often joined me for my morning run, but if he had something else to do, he didn't stress about it and he no longer worried that I would accuse him of slacking off.

My Ethan had finally gotten free and I was loving watching every moment of him rediscovering himself.

Sex with Ethan was something I couldn't even describe with words. To say it got better and better seemed an impossible thing, but somehow it did. He was both giving in bed and demanding too. He took just as he gave…with everything he was. And he'd never pressured me for more than I was ready for. Even when I'd broached the subject of him fucking me for the first time, he'd told me it was something I needed to choose for myself and he would be there either way. While I'd trusted Ethan implicitly, it had taken me longer than I would have liked to accept giving up that much control. It wasn't that I didn't want to, I just didn't know how. But it had finally happened a few months ago and while the experience had been incredible, my favorite times with Ethan were the ones where I got to watch him come apart in my arms. Where I got to drive him to that place where he was completely free and untouched. It was something only I could give him and that made it all the more meaningful to me.

"You need to come, baby?" I asked as I sipped at his lips.

Ethan only managed a nod. His breaths were coming in heavy pants as he clung to me, moving his hands to wrap them around the backs of my arms. His legs locked around my lower back as he lifted his ass to force me deeper inside of him.

"I love you, Cain," he managed to get out between kisses.

"Enough to marry me?" I asked softly.

Ethan stilled at that, his eyes going wide. Then a small smile spread across his mouth. "Is that you asking me?" he whispered.

"Yeah," I murmured as I brushed my mouth over his.

"You realize we'll have to come up with a different story to tell my family about how you proposed, right?"

I chuckled. "Is that you saying yes?"

"You know it is," he said softly. "I've been ready to marry you from the moment you first mentioned our wedding, Cain Jensen."

I smiled at that and pushed into him, hitting that spot inside him that had a loud moan spilling from his lips.

"I've been ready to ask for just as long, Ethan Rhodes."

I kissed him deeply then, as I increased my thrusts. Ethan became louder the closer he got and I drank in every sound, especially as he began saying my name and telling me he loved me. When he flew apart in my arms, I fucked him through the orgasm so I could watch every emotion pass through his bright green eyes. My own control was shattered when Ethan's fingers brushed over one of the scars on my back. It was something he did often and it never failed to remind me that he was the only reason *my* wounds on the inside had healed as completely as the ones on the outside.

"Fuck," I shouted as I began to shoot deep inside of him. "Love you so much, Ethan," I growled as I pressed my mouth against his as my orgasm snapped the coil that had been building and building to a near painful end. The release cascaded over me in perfect waves of pleasure, one right after the other until I couldn't do anything but rest all of my weight on Ethan. I knew he loved it though, because he wrapped his arms around my back to hold me close as my dick continued to pulse inside of him.

I came back to myself to find him kissing my neck.

"What will this make?" I asked as I forced myself to separate from him just the tiniest bit. "Our third shower of the day?"

Ethan smiled. "I can go take one by myself," he offered.

"Shut up," I growled before kissing him long and deep.

Because he and I both knew that was one offer I'd never take him up on.

The End

Scroll to the next page to check out a sneak peek of Phoenix and Levi's story

SNEAK PEEK

REDEMPTION (THE PROTECTORS, BOOK 8) (M/M)

PROLOGUE

PHOENIX

"Hello, my girl," I said while simultaneously signing the words as soon as the door opened. The little girl beamed up at me as she stood in the open doorway. Her little fingers began moving lightning fast. So fast that I had to interrupt her with a reminder to slow down. Her sheepish grin was almost too much for me.

"*Phoenix, Daddy Seth is taking me to see Ace. Uncle Magnus says I can ride him.*"

I smiled at that and bent down to her level since she had to crane her neck to see me otherwise. I'd never met the horse Magnus DuCane owned and had recently brought with him to Seattle after leaving Texas, but I'd heard, or seen rather, Nicole asking her fathers if she could go see the big animal often enough. I suspected the men had a horse-crazy daughter on their hands.

"That's exciting," I said as I slowly signed out the right words.

"Phoenix, hi, come on in," I heard Seth call as he made his way down the hall towards us. I wasn't surprised to see his and Ronan's youngest child, Jamie, in tow, the boy's cherished Spiderman doll clutched between his chubby fingers.

It had been nearly five months since Ronan and Seth had taken the three orphans in as foster children and from everything I'd seen, they'd managed the impossible and made themselves into a family. I knew they were eager to adopt the children and had already started the process of making the situation permanent. While the kids had initially been reserved around both men, they'd warmed up pretty quickly once they'd realized they were finally safe and in a home that would give them the love and security they'd lost after their parents had died in a car accident.

I'd been surprised by Nicole's attachment to me, especially considering both the fact that she was deaf and shy around strangers and that I wasn't what someone would consider a non-threatening guy. With my dark skin tone, heavy build and tattoos, I wasn't the kind of man a kid like Nicole would have necessarily interacted with on a regular basis. But for some reason, she'd been intrigued by me from the get-go and I'd been more than happy to return her affection.

Even if being around her was both joyous and painful for me at the same time.

"Hey, Seth," I said as I rose and moved into the house. "Heard you have a big afternoon planned."

The young man had his hands full with a couple of jackets, a large tote bag slung over his shoulder and a smaller bag that looked packed full of snacks, sippy cups and several carrots.

And I'd never seen him looking happier.

I'd known Seth for less than a year, and while I hadn't met him before he'd become involved with my boss, Ronan Grisham, it hadn't taken a genius to know how difficult the young man's life had been and how much he'd suffered. At the tender age of fourteen, he'd lost both his parents in a brutal home invasion which had also left him severely injured and traumatized. A few months later, his older brother had been stolen away from him when he'd been murdered by a group of homophobic fellow soldiers. Ronan, who'd been in a relationship with Seth's brother at the time, had been badly injured in the same attack. I didn't know all the details, but I knew enough that both men hadn't really started living again until they'd found each other.

And now they had it all and deservedly so. It was clear as day in

Seth's eyes every time he looked at his children or his husband. The same could be said of Ronan.

I was happy for them, though their joy was a near constant reminder of my own loss.

"Yeah," Seth said with a sigh as he looked at all the stuff in his arms as if trying to make sure he wasn't missing anything. He looked up at me with a big smile. I liked how he signed even as he spoke so that Nicole could follow the conversation. It was a habit I was trying to remember since I never wanted the little girl to feel left out. "Ronan's in the study-"

"I'm here," I heard Ronan interject as he walked towards us. While his eyes were on his husband, I didn't miss the tension in his frame. I couldn't help but wonder if his obvious agitation had anything to do with why I was here. I couldn't tell if Seth had noticed or not, because by the time Ronan reached us, he'd relaxed both his stance and his expression.

"Have fun," Ronan said as he leaned down to talk to Nicole. "Daddy Seth is going to take lots of pictures for me and I'll come next time, okay?"

I had no trouble understanding Nicole's response.

"Promise?"

"Promise," Ronan whispered as he signed. Then he was tugging the girl into his arms. Jamie was next, but Ronan stood up with him as the boy clung to him. He leaned in to kiss Seth. "Text me when you get there?"

I was envious of the intimacy between the two men. Every look and every touch they shared spoke volumes. Becoming fathers hadn't changed any of that.

"I will," Seth said softly.

To Jamie, Ronan said, "You have fun with Matty and Leo. Clothes stay on, right?" he said

Jamie considered him for a moment before saying, "Leo says I can run faster without them."

I stifled a chuckle. I'd seen Magnus's young grandson, Matty, and his best friend Leo take Jamie under their wing at Matty's fathers' wedding at Christmas. Between the superhero shoes Jamie was wearing and his insistence that nudity was a precursor to enhanced abilities, Ronan and Seth were out of luck. They'd already lost their youngest to his hero worship of the two slightly older boys.

Ronan shook his head, but there was no mistaking the grin on his face. "Do what Uncle Dante says, okay?"

Jamie nodded eagerly and then his arms went around Ronan's neck. "Bye, Daddy Ronan," he said softly.

"Bye, Son. See you soon, okay?"

Jamie nodded. Ronan put him down so the little boy could put his free hand on the neck of Bullet, the large German Shepherd that was always wherever the kids were.

"Dante's babysitting?" I asked.

Seth laughed. "He is. He's called me three times in a panic about what snacks to give the kids and to ask if I thought he and Aleks were enough to handle the three boys or if he needed to bring in backup."

I smiled. Leave it to Dante Thorne, Magnus's soon-to-be-husband, to turn babysitting three boys under the age of six into a mission.

"Okay, we should go," Seth said as he gave Ronan one last lingering kiss. "See you later."

Ronan nodded and then he was helping Seth get the kids out the door. I wasn't surprised that the dog was going with them.

The second the door closed, Ronan's mask of contentment slipped away. It was startling to see the level of anger in his eyes. He didn't say anything as he turned on his heel and began striding towards the study. I wisely kept my mouth shut because I knew his fury had nothing to do with me.

Though it was undoubtedly why I was here.

"I need you to look into something for me," Ronan said as he went to his desk and sat down. He punched some keys on the keyboard of his computer while I sat down in one of the guest chairs on the opposite side of the desk. The printer began spitting out pages and as soon as it was done, Ronan snatched them up and slapped them down on the desk in front of me.

The first thing I saw was a mug shot of a young man with spiky blond hair and light green eyes. I guessed him to be no more than nineteen or so and a quick glance at the arrest record showed my guess was right.

Levi Deming, eighteen.

The arrest report was several years old, putting the guy's current age at 24.

"Drug possession?" I asked as I read the charge. Ronan's group rarely went after people for drugs unless their crimes hurt other people. There was nothing on the report to indicate the kid had committed any other crimes besides being caught with a minimal amount of heroin, not even enough to warrant an additional charge of intent to distribute.

Ronan didn't say anything as he turned his screen so I could see it. The image looking back at me was a still shot of a suburban street. The image was grainy and had been taken at night, but there was enough light coming from the street lamps to make out a couple of houses and a car parked in front of one of them. I glanced at the date stamp on the image. It had been taken a week ago.

Before I could ask Ronan why he was showing me the image, he punched a key on the keyboard. The image changed to one that was nearly identical. The same car was parked in nearly the exact same spot, but the date was different. It was one day after the date on the first image.

Ronan continued moving forward through the images, four in all. Same car in the same spot four nights in a row.

"These are from a security camera from this house here," Ronan said as he pointed to a spot on the screen that was across from the house the car was sitting in front of.

"Okay," I said, still confused as to why he was showing me the images. A car sitting in front of a house was nothing. More than nothing, actually.

But one look at Ronan and I knew it wasn't nothing. He was practically seething. As a trauma surgeon, the man typically oozed calm and collected, but right now, he was anything but.

"The car," – Ronan pointed at the single car on the screen – "is registered to Curtis Deming, Levi Deming's father."

I didn't respond since the man clearly wasn't done.

"That house," – he jabbed his finger at the house the car was parked in front of – "used to belong to Seth's parents."

Tension crept into my bones as I started to suspect where the conversation was headed.

"I've been having Daisy monitor Levi Deming's movements for the past year. When he used his debit card to buy gas at a gas station on Mercer Island where the house is located, she hacked into the security system of the house across the street from Seth's old house and found this." He motioned to the image on the screen.

"You sold that house, right?"

He nodded. "Last fall before we got married."

"That's the house his parents were killed in, wasn't it?" I asked. "And Seth was attacked."

"Stabbed," Ronan said, the fury in his voice barely leashed. "His mother was raped and stabbed to death in an upstairs bedroom while Seth and his father were being held downstairs. Seth was…" Ronan's voice dropped off and I watched him swallow hard. "Seth was tortured to get his father to talk – to reveal the location of a safe that didn't exist. When the men didn't get what they wanted, they slit his father's throat and stabbed Seth and left him for dead." Ronan paused long enough to get ahold of his emotions. I'd seen the man deal with the most brutal of killers and never once had he lost his cool. But now, he barely seemed to be holding it together.

"Three men," he bit out. "One was the stepson of Seth's father's business partner."

"And the other two?" I asked.

"Ricky Deming," Ronan said quietly, though with no less danger in his voice. His finger dropped to the picture on the desk in front of me. "And his younger brother, Levi."

I felt my insides drop out as my eyes fell back to the picture. The guy looked like nothing more than a scared kid who'd gotten in over his head. He was scrawny and pale and slight enough that a stiff wind would likely blow him over, so the idea of him wielding a knife and torturing innocent people before brutally murdering them seemed too far-fetched to believe.

"The stepson is gone – he helped his stepfather kidnap Seth last summer."

I nodded. I'd heard about that. One of Ronan's first recruits into the group, Mace Calhoun and one of Mace's lovers, had helped Ronan find Seth. Both abductors had been killed in the process.

"And the other two?" Clearly Levi was still alive or I wouldn't be sitting in Ronan's office watching the man trying to keep himself from imploding with rage.

"I had Ricky terminated. He murdered his ex-girlfriend, but got off with a sweetheart plea deal. Served less than three years. Before that, he'd been charged in two different rape cases but prosecutors couldn't make the charges stick."

I nodded. "You think he's the one who killed Seth's mother."

Ronan jerked his head in a brief nod.

"And Levi?"

"Served three and a half years for drug possession. Had been keeping his nose clean." Ronan's gaze returned to the computer screen. "Until now," he said ominously.

I had to admit, it didn't look good. It was unlikely the guy knew Seth and Ronan had sold the house. Which meant there was only one reason he was returning to the scene of the crime.

He wanted a second bite at the apple.

Since he'd already know his way around the place, it would make it that much easier for him to make a second attempt to get what he and his brother had missed out on the first time around.

"So no charges were ever brought against any of them for what happened to Seth and his parents?"

Ronan shook his head. "We decided to give Levi a chance to clean up his act."

I nodded. The fact that the guy had been caught with heroin on him was a clear sign of a possible motive for why he'd go after Seth again. Addicts did stupid things to get their next fix. In the man's muddled mind, Seth would be an easy target, despite the fact that he was no longer a child. Not to mention that Seth was an extremely wealthy young man – something that was public knowledge. It wouldn't be hard to locate Seth either through the shipping company he still owned or the house he and Ronan had recently bought just north of Seattle.

I almost felt sorry for the guy. A second chance from someone like Ronan, especially after such a brutal attack on the man who was his entire world, was like winning the fucking lottery. The kid had squandered that…big time.

"I want you to monitor him," Ronan said. "And if he so much as even jaywalks, I want you to terminate him."

Ronan's ruthlessness didn't surprise me, but his level of certainty at how this would all play out unnerved me just a little bit. Not to mention the stakes. If I fucked this up and Levi got another chance at Seth…

I couldn't even consider the possibility.

I wouldn't fuck up, no matter what. I owed Ronan everything. If this kid gave me even one sign that he'd returned to his old ways, I'd take him out with much more mercy than he and his brother had shown Seth and his family.

"You have someone watching Seth and the kids?" I asked.

Ronan nodded. "Seth doesn't know. And I want to keep it that way."

I'd suspected as much. Seth had been struggling with anxiety ever since the attack. It had made him borderline agoraphobic before Ronan had come along. Ronan and Seth had the perfect life now and Ronan wouldn't let anything threaten that, especially not a foolish addict who didn't even have the brains to seek out a new target.

"Consider it done," I said as I stood, snagging the stack of papers off the desk.

Ronan nodded, but didn't stand to walk me out. He looked… defeated. I suspected that came from the fear he was feeling, not to mention the fact that he was having to keep such a secret from his husband.

"I'll send the rest of the information to you," Ronan said. "Last known address, financials, that kind of thing."

I gave him a quick nod and turned to go, but then thought better of it. "Ronan," I said quietly and waited until he looked up at me. "Nothing will happen to him."

A soft sigh escaped Ronan's lips, but he didn't say anything. He merely nodded.

I left the study and headed towards the front door. I couldn't say I was particularly excited about potentially ending the life of young Levi Deming, but Seth and Ronan were family now.

And I always protected my family.

ABOUT THE AUTHOR

Dear Reader,

I hope you enjoyed Cain and Ethan's story. Up next is Phoenix's story.

As an independent author, I am always grateful for feedback so if you have the time and desire, please leave a review, good or bad, so I can continue to find out what my readers like and don't like. You can also send me feedback via email at sloane@sloanekennedy.com

Join my Facebook Fan Group: Sloane's Secret Sinners

Connect with me:
www.sloanekennedy.com
sloane@sloanekennedy.com

ALSO BY SLOANE KENNEDY

(Note: Not all titles will be available on all retail sites)

The Escort Series
Gabriel's Rule (M/F)
Shane's Fall (M/F)
Logan's Need (M/M)

Barretti Security Series
Loving Vin (M/F)
Redeeming Rafe (M/M)
Saving Ren (M/M/M)
Freeing Zane (M/M)

Finding Series
Finding Home (M/M/M)
Finding Trust (M/M)
Finding Peace (M/M)
Finding Forgiveness (M/M)
Finding Hope (M/M/M)

The Protectors
Absolution (M/M/M)

Salvation (M/M)

Retribution (M/M)

Forsaken (M/M)

Vengeance (M/M/M)

A Protectors Family Christmas

Atonement (M/M)

Revelation (M/M)

Redemption (M/M)

Non-Series

Letting Go (M/F)

Printed in Great Britain
by Amazon